Witchcraft

Emma Mills

Witchcraft

Copyright © 2012 Emma Mills

All Rights Reserved

License Notes

This book is a work of fiction. The names, characters, places and incidents are products of the writer's imagination or have been used fictitiously and are not to be construed as real. Any resemblance to persons, living or dead, actual events, locales or organisations is entirely coincidental.

Witchcraft

Copyright © 2012 Emma Mills

www.witchbloodthenovel.com

www.twitter.com/EmmaMwriter

Cover Image : Laura Zalenga

www.laurazalenga.de

ISBN-10: 1479311251

ISBN-13: 978-1479311255

For Tom

CHAPTER ONE

I guess it's easy to say in retrospect, but I probably shouldn't have answered the door. Nevertheless, the incessant banging was rudely interrupting my daydreaming.

The hammering on the door paused, and my eyes flicked over to an old, leather bound book sitting on the dresser, confirming that my dreams were actually based upon truth, and I wasn't going quietly mad. The book had come from Eva, presented to me only minutes after returning to Daniel's house, the night of my brief but terrifying adventures in Sebastian's cells. I frowned remembering her words of caution...

'What is it Eva?' I'd whispered, as Eva had handed me a rather battered looking book, which was brown with age and had lost its slip cover, if it ever had one. The embossed design was faded and flattened, and the spine was damaged beyond repair. Yet despite all this it was beautiful, and it drew me in as if calling to me. I held out my hands, a feeling of yearning welling up, and a look of frustration flickering in my eyes, as she held it out of reach, a half-smile dancing about her face.

'It's a book of shadows,' Eva had told me. 'A very old one, and if you're not hunted down for your half-witch, half-vamp status, you'll be hunted down for owning this book. So don't mention it or show it to anyone. This is possibly the only copy in the whole of the UK.'

'You're joking, right?' I'd asked nervously, my hands still itching to get a hold of it.

'When have you ever known me to joke, Jess? This book is worth a small fortune. Even Sebastian couldn't afford it. Luckily I had a favour to call in.'

What kind of favour would buy that? I'd wondered.

'It's fine, sorted,' she said. 'Anyway, it's yours now. Take it,' she added, passing me the beautiful book.

The hammering on the door had started up again. It obviously wasn't some sales rep, and whoever it was clearly had no intention of leaving without giving me a headache, but I'd been forbidden from opening the door or leaving the house...all the usual rules an untrained half-vampire, teen witch had to deal with.

I climbed off my bed and paused by the dresser, my hands drifting towards the book again. In an instant, all my questions were forgotten as my hands touched its leather cover. It felt heavy and somehow warm and after glancing at the embossed pentagram I quickly opened the book to have a quick flick through. A gush of air lifted the hair away from my face, as if someone had opened a window on a breezy day, or maybe a breezy day in Florida, as the air felt warm on my cheeks and stung my eyes.

After a couple of seconds, the wind dropped until it felt like a comforting breeze, making single hairs lift up and tickle my cheeks. I felt calm and in control. I let my eyes delight in the intricate patterns drawn on the title page. My fingers traced a repetition of the same pentagram from the cover, but this one had entwined branches delicately drawn through its lines, and tiny leaves which seemed to dance in the very same breeze I was caught up in. I focused my eyes and stared at them and they immediately stilled, but if I let my eyes wander away from them, I could see them fluttering in the breeze. I *loved* this book!

The visitor's incessant banging started up again. Damn it! What was I going to do? It freaked me out a little. I mean, in the couple of months I'd been living here, the door had only ever rung a handful of times. Now here I was on my own, a rare occurrence, as I was not often left unguarded. So my curiosity was aroused and suddenly I felt the need to prove to Daniel that I could do something normal, like answer a door. I closed the book, placed it back on the dresser and ran down the stairs at vampire speed.

In my head I had it all planned out. It would be easy. If it was a vamp, I'd just say Daniel and Eva were at the club. No vamp would mess with me after recent rumours had gotten around about Aaron's unlucky demotion. If it was a human, I'd simply tell them to call by for Eva or Daniel later, and if it was the gas meter man, I was going to say that I didn't own the house and could he come another time. On no account was I going to let anyone in. Easy! Except it wasn't a vampire, a human or the gas man. It was a *witch*!

I smelled her as soon as I opened the door, so forgive my confusion, but she smelled human and rather tasty at that. But of course, witches are the only supernatural kind with human DNA. However, my questions on her identity were clarified as soon as she opened her mouth.

'Hi, you must be the lovely Jess?' she asked with a strong American accent. This confirmed her identity as the witch sent over to meet me; a representative of my new found family clan in Boston.

'Ehm, yes, I am. Daniel and Eva have gone to meet you at the club. Didn't you get the message?' I asked, wondering what on earth to do with her and knowing Daniel would have a fit if I asked her in.

'Oh silly me! I thought I was to meet you here and go and see the mighty Sebastian later?' she asked her vivid green eyes sparkling with mischief. She opened her mouth in a wide smile and offered her hand to me. 'I'm Susannah from the Malden coven. I guess I must be your cousin, as your mother was *my* mother's sister. It's nice to meet you at last.'

I paused for a second, looking at this woman who seemed so ready to offer me a new family. She didn't look at all as I expected. I thought they were sending an older woman and I'd imagined a greying spinster, but the woman opposite me was in her twenties, with beautiful green eyes and shiny black hair swinging down her slender back. She grinned at me again before cutting into my thoughts.

'Well, are we going to stand here on the doorstep all day? I could really do with a drink, although maybe you don't have anything suitable?' she asked, her smile faltering a little.

'Oh, I'm sorry. Maybe I should just give Daniel a quick ring and let them know you're here. I don't think they wanted me to meet you on my own,' I answered, taking a step back.

'Well it's a bit late for that now, isn't it? You've met me already and I'm hardly a threat. It's not like you're a feeble little human, is it Jess? I heard all about Aaron. We all have.'

I realised this little speech was entirely conceived in order to big up my ego, but after all, what could I do? I could hardly leave her standing on the doorstep for an hour, could I? She was *right*, I thought, after all I am a vampire. I am strong and fast enough to throw a human twelve feet down a dirty alleyway, I can self heal and I've levitated a powerful vamp in the air when he tried to attack me. It would be fine, apart from Daniel being pissed at me when he found out.

'Ok, come on in. I think we've got some coffee somewhere,' I said, as I led her into the hallway, and down towards the kitchen.

'Great, I'm gasping. I hate the airline coffee you get. It really sucks. I don't suppose you've got any real coffee have you?' she asked.

'It's unlikely, but hell, who knows? Daniel keeps the kitchen stocked up for appearances mainly. We had one of the students from next door drop in yesterday. I think she fancies him,' I said, rummaging around the kitchen cupboards until I found one with an unopened pack of fresh coffee in it. I spent the next five minutes looking for a cafetière, which was still in its box, and on finding the milk was five days old, Susannah wisely decided to take it black.

'Right. I'll just go and give Daniel a ring. They must be wondering where you are,' I said, as I placed the mug in front of her and got a delicious whiff of human. Maybe they didn't want me to be on my own with her because *I* was the threat, not her. They still didn't trust me around humans, even though I'd so far resisted even a taste of human blood... well, apart from the processed gloop that came in neat refrigerated packs.

'Sure. Can you direct me to the bathroom? I could do with freshening up after my trip,' she said, following me out of the room.

I took her upstairs to the immaculate bathroom, and returned downstairs to make the call. As I held the handset I desperately tried to recall Daniel's mobile number. Why was it I'd completely lost the ability to remember phone numbers since I'd owned a mobile? Eventually I started tapping it in, and then I realised something was wrong. I brought the receiver to my ear but it was silent. No ringtone. I replaced the handset and checked the power cord. It all seemed to be plugged in fine, so I picked it up and listened again. Nothing. Damn! I'd been complaining to Eva only that week about the shaky broadband connection. It was always timing out on me and now it seemed the landline had died as well.

As I was wondering what to do, I heard the shrill peal of the old pay-as-you-go mobile Daniel had given me a couple of months earlier. Of course! I raced up the stairs, silent and effortlessly, and came to a sudden halt in the doorway to my room. Susannah was standing by my dressing table when I entered the room, and a grim expression flitted across her face as she quickly picked up the mobile and switched it off. A second later she turned around, her surprise at seeing me quickly masked by a wide smile.

'Oooh, hi! You gave me a fright there,' she said.

'Ehm, sorry. Is that my phone you just switched off?' I asked.

'Yes, but I knew you were using the downstairs phone and I guessed you wouldn't be able to get through to him, if he was calling you on this. I didn't want to answer it, because I thought it best coming from you. I'm sorry. Have I done the wrong thing?' she asked, looking confused.

'No, no, that's fine,' I said, walking towards her for the phone.

Before I could take the phone, she swivelled round to face my dresser again and I froze. I watched her fingertips gently trace the outline of the pentagram on my book, Eva's words filling my head for the second time that afternoon.

'if you're not hunted down for your half-witch, half-vamp status, you'll be hunted down for owning this book.'

Too late, I thought miserably as I saw wonder and desire glint in her eyes ever so briefly, before she looked up at me and smiled again.

'So, you have the family book already. That will please the elders. Do the leaves blow in an imaginary breeze for you?' She asked.

'Yes, they do. I thought I was seeing things at first. Is it a family book then?' I asked, relief washing over me, that finally someone understood me and didn't think I was hallucinating. Eva and Daniel never saw the leaves move, not the slightest bit.

'Oh yes, it goes back to the very first coven leader in New England. We have another copy of this at home. We thought this one was lost. How did you get it?' she asked, and again I thought I noticed a hard cold rush of emotion clouding her eyes, but it was gone instantly.

'It was given it as a gift,' I said, not wanting to get Eva in any trouble with the coven.

I walked the last couple of steps towards the dresser and went to pick the book up. It felt dangerous and exposed lying within her reach, and I felt a need to hold it close. Protect it. My hands went out, but she got there at the same time.

Simultaneously, she started muttering something quickly and quietly under her breath and immediately my bedroom ceiling turned into a black thunderous vortex, spinning and swirling its snake-like tail down towards us.

'What the hell?' I shouted, trying to pull the book from her grasp, as she hung on.

'I'm sorry Jess, but the white witches of Malden

cannot claim you, especially now that you have this. We've sought this book for hundreds of years and now we have one who can engage with it. Only direct family members can make the leaves dance. You will join us. It's your destiny.'

All at once several things happened. The black vortex hovered over our heads as Susannah shouted out a final command. I used all my vampire strength available, and yanking the book from her grasp, turned to run when I heard the front door bang. Mere seconds later, Daniel and Eva shot into the room, but it was too late. Susannah's hand hooked around my neck, her long, purple painted nails breaking my skin. Her other arm wrapped around me from behind and with our bodies glued together, the vortex descended and sucked us up into a vast dark nothingness.

CHAPTER TWO

My survival instinct kicked in and I struggled to release myself from her grasp. I wriggled and kicked, but she held on fiercely and yelled into my ear.

'Don't be stupid Jess, you don't know where you'll end up if you fall from the ley lines mid-stream. We don't want to harm you.'

I couldn't take that chance. I didn't have a clue who she was, but I knew for sure that she wasn't who she said she was. She wasn't my cousin. She wasn't from Malden, and if she wasn't a white witch, then presumably she must be a dark witch from a coven that wanted my Book of Shadows.

I felt an encouraging tingle of electricity start to bubble under the surface of my skin, a familiar low humming in my head, as everything began to spin out of control. As I felt my power hum beneath the surface, waiting for an outlet, I scrunched up my eyes and holding firmly to the book, bucked with all my might and sent my elbow ramming into the witch behind me. I wrenched my neck from her hand, feeling her nails leave deep welts across my skin, and threw myself to the side of the vortex. Suddenly I was free falling, plummeting towards a green field, and seconds later I landed with a bone crunching thud as my head spun and I blacked out.

I awoke to find myself lying under the shade of an old oak, its dark green leaves shading the late spring sun from my sensitive skin. I quickly sat up and looked around me. The witch was sitting watching me, cradling my book in her hands.

'Now look what you've done. We'll have to wait here for my sisters to join us. They won't be long,' she said, before adding 'You might want to sort your arm out. It's making me queasy just looking at you.'

At her strange comment, I looked down and flinched. My arm was hanging down at a strange angle, and the bone just above my wrist was jutting out of the broken skin, my dark, almost black blood congealing around it. As my eyes followed the broken arm upwards, I winced again as I took in the strange angle of my shoulder joint, as it pushed forward, straining against the tight, pale skin. All I could feel was a dull throb in my shoulder and a slight burning sensation around my wrist, but I couldn't blame the witch for her queasiness, as looking at it made me heave uncontrollably.

'Oh, for goodness sake! You're a vampire aren't you? Just pop your shoulder back in and push that bone back into your arm. Otherwise they'll heal like that and Carrigan will only make you break them again,' she said, looking up at the sky quickly.

I followed her eyes, but could see nothing. She was right, I needed to sort my arm out, but I also needed to get my book back and fast, if we were about to be joined by the rest of her coven. For the first time since I'd woken, I looked around us. We'd landed in some farm fields and all I could see were miles of yellowish, square patterned, rolling hills. On the brow of the next hill, I could make out a farm and a track winding down to a busy main road. I wondered how long it would take me to run for the house; five minutes, maybe less. I could easily pretend to be a human girl, then they'd take me in, but they'd also be bound to call an ambulance and ask questions. All I needed was a phone to call Daniel. Maybe if I got my arm fixed first I could escape their inevitable questions. I looked down at my arm again and gulping back retches, tried to push the bone back in, but it seemed stuck, and tears sprang to my eyes. I was useless, pathetic! I couldn't even mend myself properly. I couldn't cast spells. I couldn't bring myself to bite people and defend myself. I was nothing, neither a vampire nor a witch.

'Are you crying?' Her surprised voice cut into my thoughts and I glanced up quickly, wiping the tears away. 'Oh my! You are, aren't you. I never knew vampires could cry. Well, aren't you an interesting find!'

Anger surged within me, a maelstrom of emotions giving me the strength I needed. I jumped to my feet and found to my surprise that my arm still worked. I punched forward and then brought it back, swinging it round until, with a sickening crack it found its rightful place in my shoulder joint once again. The bone would just have to wait, as the witch was already clambering hurriedly to her feet, my book clasped to her chest. She had hastily dug deep in her pocket and withdrawn a handful of salt, and was pouring it out on the floor in a circle around her, chanting as she moved.

'I conjure thee, O Circle of Power. A boundary between...'

'Oh no you don't!' I cried, leaping out of the shade of the old oak and into the bright sunshine. My eyes squinted against the light and I could feel the instant warmth against my skin. It wasn't uncomfortable, yet. But I didn't have long.

A second later my hard body slammed into hers and I knocked her back out of the half circle. The book had tumbled from her grip and we both made a jump for it. I was quicker, and though I fumbled with my injured arm, I somehow managed to stuff it into the waistband of my jeans as she flew at me. I hurled myself onto my back, and as she landed on top of me, curled my feet into my body and kicked out hard, flinging her back. I jumped to my feet and made a run for it, as a low chant broke the silence and a hot wind whipped up, blowing my hair about my face viciously. I ran full pelt towards the road and with vampire speed it should have taken moments, but her chanting made my legs feel leaden. I looked down with dismay to see the sun baked ground turn to a thick quagmire of clay-like mud, sucking me in, slowing me down. I turned round to face my quarry. If I couldn't run, I would have to fight.

I bent down, then sprung up, focusing all my strength to power my thigh muscles and jump me out of that bog and back onto dry land. It worked, and I looked up to see Susannah coming at me once again, her face set in a determined line, as she produced a wooden stick and began a slow, menacing chant. I had no idea what her spell would do, but I was pretty sure it wouldn't have a pleasant outcome; so as the dark clouds drew together overhead, mercifully blocking out the bright sun, I unleashed the vampire which I had always kept locked up.

My fangs broke through the surface of my gums, as I let her intoxicating scent wash over me. I felt all the muscles in my body tense for a fight and my eyes flicked around the field, scouting for enemies, searching for allies. But nobody came to help me, as they had no idea where I was. I was on my own.

As Susannah finished her chant, I watched with superhuman eyes as she flicked her wand towards me. A bolt of silver shot out of the air, and had I been human would have pierced my heart within seconds, but I'd seen it coming and easily jumped out of the way. Leaping gracefully over the arched beam of light I landed nearer my quarry. She took a step back tentatively and flicked her eyes skywards again. Relief washed over her face, and I followed her eyes upwards, to see a crazy paving design of electricity skim over the surface of blackened clouds. Then, like a finger placed upon a static electric ball, it condensed, before a lightning bolt shot to the ground. This happened four times. In each of the corners surrounding us, to the north, south, east and west, and from each of those corners, a woman's figure unfolded from a crouching position and began to walk toward us.

I had to do something fast. Knowing I would have no chance of running, I turned back and pounced at Susannah. As my strength knocked her down, a shriek escaped her lips and her scent washed over me, drawing me in. I wouldn't bite her, I wouldn't, I told myself. But she's not human, not *really*, a voice whispered to me. She's not innocent anyway. She wants your book. She lied to you and she's going to hand you over to them.

My eyes flicked up to the swiftly advancing figures, wands drawn for battle. I stood up and dragged her shaking body with me. Holding her in front of my body as a shield, I wrestled her wand from her quaking hand, and forcing her head back I curled my lips back and went in for the kill.

'Stop! Jessie stop. Release her.' His voice brought my head up with a snap and my eyes darted around until I found him. He was standing within the circle of witches, just behind my injured right shoulder. I took in his floppy, dirty blonde locks and saw the monster I had become reflected in his turquoise eyes. With a shiver, I released the witch, and she fell to the ground in a heap and began crawling away to the circle of her coven. Instantly I realised the mistake I'd made and turned on Luke.

'Look what you've made me do. Now we're both trapped and have no bargaining tool,' I stormed, trying to ignore the delicate pink flush to his cheeks, the way his jeans tightened around his thighs, the fact that his beautiful smooth chest was bare, his muscles rippling gently down towards the dark fuzz peeking from the waistband of his jeans. But most of all, I was desperately trying to ignore the white feathered wings unfurled majestically from his back, exuding light and creating a well of luminosity which somehow seemed to soak up the surrounding darkness.

'They're dark witches, Luke. They'll kill us. They want my book,' I added.

'Shhh, I know. I'm sorry Jessie. I shouldn't have walked away from you. I didn't realise your powers had awakened with your rebirth, but I couldn't stay away. You know I couldn't quite leave you, don't you? You've seen me watching over you? I'm here with you now,' he said.

'Right! So if you're going to fly me back home then, now might be a good time,' I said, inclining my head towards the five witches, who were now surrounding us only a couple of metres away, wands all pointing in our direction.

'Oh, don't tell me you've got the angels on side already? Susannah, this wasn't mentioned in your report,' a tall thin woman said, standing directly in front of me.

'I beg your pardon, Priestess. I did not know,' Susannah replied quietly.

'So be it. We have dealt with worse,' the woman answered.

'Luke, get us out of here. What are you waiting for?' I whispered furiously.

'I can't Jess. They'll burn my wings if I try to fly. There are too many of them. I need a distraction.'

'Great! Why did you make me let her go? That would have kept them at bay.'

'If you'd fed from a dark witch your own bloodline would have been polluted. I couldn't take that chance.'

'OK Jess, hand over the book. You can still join us. We can teach you to be strong, powerful. Jessie, come to me,' the priestess said, her words sweet and intoxicating, lulling me, drawing me into her web.

Luke stepped behind me and placed his warm hands on my shoulders, gently massaging the injured one and breaking the spell being cast upon me. I blinked in confusion and shook my head.

'Jessie, he left you. He abandoned you. He has only returned to you because of your powers. You need a mother, to guide you and care for you. Let me teach you. With my help you can be more powerful than all of them. Come to me child,' she said.

I took a quick glance back at the boy I'd once loved so deeply. The boy who had lied to me, pretended he was human. An angel even, who had deserted me when I was attacked by a girl gang and left to die. The same angel who had called me vermin, because I'd been made into a vampire, because *he* had left me. I needed to know his story, his reasons. I needed to know why he was here now, but most of all I needed to know if I loved him still.

'Be ready for the diversion,' I whispered, my lips barely making a sound, as I turned back to face the witch.

'And if I was to go with you? Daniel would track me down with Sebastian and Eva. They wouldn't let you take me,' I said, taking a step towards the witch and away from Luke.

'We can protect you better than anyone else. Your vampires cannot help you learn our ways. They don't see the things you do. Give me the book Jessie. I can protect it better than you.'

'But you need me to read the book, don't you? Only I can see the leaves move, because it's my birth right. You can't, can you?' I asked, taking another step towards her, my hands fiddling with the book still tucked into my jeans, jutting uncomfortably into my hip bone.

A swift look of anger washed across her features as her eyes darted to Susannah, and I realised that my gamble had paid off and Susannah had indeed imparted too much information.

'And yet you cannot make sense of it on your own. We need each other Jessie. Come, let me be your mother,' she answered, as she tucked her wand into her belt and held her hands out to me.

It was the moment I was waiting for and I jumped at it, literally. My feet left the floor and instantly I knocked my quarry over and rolled her onto her front, burying her face in the hard earth, as she struggled to wriggle her wand out from her belt.

Within seconds, the witches were crowding around chanting and pointing their wands at me.

'Do or say anything and I will break her neck,' I shouted at them, as I straddled the witch's back, pinning her to the ground and grabbing her hair with my free hand.

The coven took a step back and I thought for a second that I'd won, until I heard the slow chant begin underneath me and saw the dark thunderous clouds suddenly begin to clear. The sunlight broke through and radiated down upon us.

I squinted through the bright luminous rays to find Luke. Where was he? I felt the sunlight heating up with every chanted line from the tall sorceress. The sun shone down brightly and I imagined a thermometer rising steadily from a nice eighteen degrees to twenty, twenty one, twenty five and up higher and higher, hotter and hotter until I would burn, and slowly but surely turn to ash. I felt a sweat break out on my skin. Now vampires supposedly don't sweat, but I certainly was. I could feel the skin on my neck starting to tingle. How long had the Italian vampire lasted under direct sun torture? I recalled Daniel's famous tale from the early days when he was teaching me about my new life. Six hours, that's right. It had taken six hours before he had burned to death. A slow six hours of torture. I shook with fear and felt a trickle of sweat run down under my t-shirt.

'Luke? Luke, where are you?' I shouted.

'Are you looking for someone? An eye for an eye, an angel for a witch,' Susannah said, suddenly appearing by my side. Luke was standing by her side, seemingly unbound, but his eyes were glassy and his face seemed dead, paralysed.

'What have you done to him?' I shouted. Panic flooded my senses as I squinted through the light at them, trying to ignore the pain now throbbing across my back.

'Oh he'll be fine, he's just a little spellbound at the minute. You see now Jessie, why you need training? You can never beat us until you master your powers, and by the time you have mastered them, you'll want to join us anyway, so you may as well save yourself the pain and join us now,' she said, smiling. 'I really am your cousin, Jessie. I'm family. It would be fun.' She held out her hand, extending it towards me again and as the sun beat down I looked at Luke's dead eyes and felt myself wavering.

What if they were right? I knew better than anyone that 'dark' didn't necessarily mean evil. I mean vampires were supposedly evil and even Luke had called me vermin, yet the vampires I'd come to know were more honourable than the majority of humans I'd encountered.

The high priestess must have felt me waver, for she jumped at the opportunity and with a powerful blast she seemed to evaporate from beneath me, reappearing in front. I felt the slightest touch from her wand, followed by wave after wave of currents slicing through my body. I found myself hanging from an invisible noose, stretched out like a star, several feet from the ground as my body juddered an uncontrollable dance. The pain brought tears to my eyes and I offered up a quick prayer as I glanced at the immobile Luke, wishing he could see my tears and realise I was not the monster he thought.

Suddenly, I noticed an instant relief from the torture, as the sun stopped glaring down on us and the clouds rolled in once more. As the sky darkened, I looked up and noticed luminescent figures slowly appearing in a silent circle, surrounding the dark circle that held Luke and I. The figures shone with unearthly beauty, their skin glowing pink and their eyes dancing. Some held their wings outstretched like beautiful sails while others were already folding them inwards, behind their slender, toned bodies.

It took me a good few seconds of staring before the dark witches took the hint and looked behind them, and when they did an unearthly war erupted around us. Bolts of electricity flew from their wands as the angels jumped forward, pulling beautiful silver swords from nowhere, ancient inscriptions glowing upon the smooth blades.

The angels moved balletically, full of grace and poise. They reminded me of shimmering versions of Eva, and I wished she was here to help. As the priestess's concentration lapsed, her spell broke and I found my body was no longer being used as an electricity pylon. Sighing as the convulsions stilled, I watched as she jumped into the fray and left me hanging in mid-air, in an invisible trap. Luke was still standing immobile several feet away, his eyes glassy. Great cracks and booms thundered in the air and I wondered why the farmer didn't come to investigate. Maybe he had put it down to a bad electrical storm and wisely decided to stay indoors.

I watched helplessly as swords swung and wands spat out spells. The angels were pushing the witches back, rounding them up like a collie rounds up wayward sheep. One witch was slumped in a ragged heap, motionless and I wondered if the angels were capable of murder.

I was fed up of being a helpless child. I pulled at my invisible restraints and arched my body to no avail. It would take more than superhuman strength to break these bonds. I shut my eyes on the surrounding combat, and concentrated as Eva had taught me to do. I dragged up every emotion, every scar, every lost love and I condensed them. I squeezed them together, to form a ball of pure emotion, fiery and full of frustration. I opened my eyes and arched my back once again, sending the power ball racing through my limbs. I imagined it tearing up my arms and down the muscles in my legs, freeing me and breaking the magical bonds. Twice I sent them tearing round my body, and twice I felt the bonds tremble, but they held. I scrunched my eyes up one last time, sure I was doing the right thing, and with an almighty effort I visualised my freedom and screamed. Heat blasted through my injured arm and bound legs, freeing them, and I finally slumped to the ground panting.

As I did so, I felt a hand touch my shoulder and I used the last reserve of energy to jump to my feet, fangs bared. I found myself face to face with an angel. She was pretty in a soft, almost androgynous way. Her dark hair was cropped short in a pixie cut and her delicate features creased into a disapproving frown, as she took in my defensive posture and fully formed fangs. I took a step back.

'I'm sorry. I thought you were one of them. Oh Luke, we need to help Luke,' I said, my fangs receding, as I rubbed at my throbbing arm.

'Shhh! He's fine. He's here. You're safe, for now,' she said, in a quiet lilting voice, with an ancient accent I couldn't quite place.

'Hey Jess, I'm sorry but your plan didn't quite work. Susannah jumped me, the second you jumped Carrigan,' Luke said, appearing suddenly from behind the girl. He held out his arms to me in a gesture that brought back unchecked memories. Memories of lying in his arms, curled up on the sofa watching old films, flashbacks to the last Christmas and skating in the temporary ice rink with the Christmas lights twinkling; of me laughing and stumbling into his open arms. I was human… and he was pretending to be human.

'We need to talk, Luke,' I said.

'I'll leave you guys alone and help with the round up then. Bye Jessie,' the girl said, before grinning at me and winking at Luke. I watched her dance over to the circle of angels, who had finished rounding up the witches into a huddle, under the same old oak I had rested beneath half an hour earlier. Mesmerised, I watched as they held their swords horizontally, each touching the next and then in the blink of an eye a fiery circle encapsulated them all and they disappeared. I looked around confused, but I was alone with Luke, in the middle of a field, somewhere in England. The clouds began to clear and a fresh breeze whipped my hair and tickled my face.

'Where? What on earth... Luke, what happened to them? Was that the witches?' I asked.

'No, they're fine. That's how we transport undesirables back to the courts. Surely the vampires have explained to you about the supernatural court? Well, we're like the police, I guess,' he said, with a wry smile. 'Come on, let's get you back.'

'We need to talk Luke. There's so much I need to know. Daniel said he thought you were with me the night I died, but he said you were gone before he got there. Is it true Luke? Did you leave me, knowing Daniel was on his way?' I asked.

His face said it all, and I saw pain and resentment flash across his features, before he looked at the floor.

'So it's true then? Why? Why did you leave me? I thought you loved me?' I whispered, his pain mirrored in my soul.

'I'm sorry Jess. I'm so sorry. I was weak, selfish, everything an angel should never be. I meant what I said on that bench. I did fail you in every way.'

'Why? How? Tell me. I need to know. Why did you leave me?'

'Because I loved you too much and I couldn't bear to let you go. I knew I should let you die. I knew I should block the vampires. I had a sudden vision of the future and knew I should stop it. I should have let you die and shown you the path to the spirit realm, but I'm an earthbound angel Jessie, and I couldn't leave you. I saw you in that vision, beautiful and full of life. Your eyes sparkled and laughter bubbled from your lips. I wanted you to live. So I left you, knowing he would give you a new life,' he finished in a soft, broken voice.

'Oh!' I didn't know what to say. I was shocked, rendered speechless, but then his harsh words from the cricket club came back to haunt me.

'You called me vermin! I saw the hate in your eyes at the cricket club,' I accused.

He winced, and I watched as the corner of his mouth twitched upwards.

'Vampires and angels don't exactly get on Jess. You bite humans, we protect them.

'*I* don't bite humans. I have never bitten a human and I don't intend to,' I retorted.

'Jess, you're going to have to feed. You can't live off banked blood forever and if you feed much more from Daniel it will only weaken him, pushing him to feed more than necessary. It's a no-win situation. You're a vampire Jess and I'm to blame for that.'

'I will find a way, Luke,' I said, not wanting to accept the inevitable.

'No you won't. We can't be together and you are forgetting your bond with Daniel. He cares for you now, and you care for him I think,' he said.

'There is still more I need to know. You've hidden so much from me,' I said, frowning at his beautiful face.

'Not now. I need to get you home. They'll be sending out the vampire search party soon. Things are out of our control. You belong to Sebastian, and for now all we need to do is to get you home safely.'

His wings suddenly opened out and I watched, dazed as the individual feathers shimmered in the late afternoon sunshine and fluttered slightly against the breeze. I forgot all my questions as he took me in his arms, cradled like a baby and we soared up, high into the sky.

CHAPTER THREE

The sun had all but vanished behind the horizon as we took to the sky and I clung on, squeezing my eyes shut as we climbed higher over the Lancashire farmland. Within seconds we were in a dark cloud mass and I had no idea how Luke knew which way he was going. *Maybe they had a homing instinct like pigeons? Or maybe x-ray vision like Superman!*

A giggle escaped and I realised I wasn't far from losing it. It seemed that my life consisted of a series of increasingly unbelievable and often terrifying events. And whilst a mere six months ago I would have been sitting in my university hall bedroom, probably with my best friend Alex, discussing how we could inject a little excitement into our routine. I now found myself yearning for a little normality, and yearning for Alex. I tried not to think about her, how the last time I'd seen her. She was with Luke attending my father's funeral, whilst I stood hidden and restrained by Daniel, their scents wafting under my newly sensitive vampire nose.

Suddenly I realised the wind had stopped plastering my hair to the side of my face and stinging my eyes. We had stopped. The odd and rather disconcerting thing was, we had stopped hundreds of feet up in the air. Luke appeared to be hovering, yet his wings didn't flap like a bird of prey, nor did they vibrate like a hummingbird. He simply hung in mid-air. I gulped and tightened my grip around his neck, breathing in his heavenly floral scent and trying to ignore the rushing feeling and drumming in my ears, as my fangs started to break through the surface of my gums. *Oh, shit!* I clamped my mouth shut.

'Jessie, we're here, but no doubt *he* will be waiting for you when we land, so I just wanted to apologise again. I am truly sorry I did this to you. I'm sorry I was weak,' Luke said.

'Right! So you'd prefer me to be dead then? Is that it? I suppose it would be less hassle for you. Luke, I'm glad you let Daniel save me. Okay, sometimes I wish I could see Alex and sometimes things are tough, but it's better than being dead!'

'You don't know what you're missing Jess, and that's my fault.'

'No, you're right I don't, and frankly I don't need to know. But what I do know is that I wasn't ready to die, not then. I don't think you were weak; I think you were strong. You let Daniel save me, knowing it went against everything you'd been taught, all because you loved me. What I don't understand is why that has to change now?' I said.

'You're right, you *don't* understand and you never will, and that is why everything has changed. You are one of them now. You...'

'Oh, one of *them*, hey? God Luke, you're so prejudiced. I'm not evil, you know that. Hell, I'm not even a normal vampire. Because of the witch blood genes I'm not even tied to them. I can do what I want, make my own decisions, and you know I haven't bitten anyone,' I said, my voice rising and echoing around the clouds.

'That's a lie! You may have kept your willpower, but Sebastian has other ways of keeping you in line, and you know it.'

'Sebastian's a decent man. He's always been honest with me, which is more than you can offer! They don't kill people, Luke.'

'Jessie, are you so blind? What do they drink? What do *you* drink?'

'Blood, I know, but people don't mind. They give it freely, and I'm not like them anyway.'

'You've bitten Daniel, and it will only be a matter of time before you bite someone else. It's in your blood.'

'How did you know about Daniel? Are you spying on me? Ugh!'

'It doesn't matter how I know, and I don't care. It was bound to happen. You can't help it.'

'I'm not the blind one here Luke, it's you! Take me down.'

'Of course.'

Maybe it was anger, or a desperate need to be rid of me, or maybe angels always descended sickeningly fast to avoid detection, but I was glad I didn't have a full stomach.

I expected us both to end in a crumpled heap on the ground but naturally Luke landed gracefully, and after setting me back on my feet, he shot off into the clouds without a backward glance. I must have really pissed him off! I stared up after him, but even with my vampire vision, he was gone.

'Jessie! You're back? Where is he? Are you alright?' Daniel asked as he came tearing out of the back kitchen door and across the garden to me, which being a vampire took all of about half a second! Luke was right, I thought with a smile, Daniel *was* waiting. He'd always be waiting for me.

'Now t*hat* is disgusting!' Eva's voice was right on cue, half a second after Daniel!

I followed her eyes to my wrist, where the bone was still jutting through the skin, my dark blood congealed and the skin healed all around it. Oh dear! This was not going to be good! Something told me I should have taken the witch's advice, got over my queasiness and fixed it straight away!

'Eva, leave her alone. Let's get you inside, we can fix your arm later. I take it Luke played the *knight in shining armour* role nicely?' Daniel muttered, daring me to tell him otherwise.

'Um yeah, I suppose so. I was doing all right on my own until the entire coven of witches turned up, and then things got a bit tricky,' I said, trying not to think what would have happened if Luke hadn't turned up, just as I was about to have my first human snack!

I followed them back into the house and stopped in the doorway. There was a woman sitting at the kitchen table. She looked up at me expectantly as I entered the room, her eyes a bright, twinkling emerald colour.

'Jessie, this is Francesca, a member of the Malden coven,' Daniel said.

'And if you'd done as we told you and not answered the door, you would have met her a lot less painfully,' Eva added.

'Look, it wasn't my fault. I've got to answer the door one day, and as far as I knew, you were meeting the coven representative at Exodus. Then Susannah turned up, and said she was my cousin. She looked the part and knew all about the meeting. She was really friendly. I could hardly leave her waiting on the doorstep...' I trailed off.

'You could have, and you should have, and then we wouldn't have to reset your arm,' Eva said.

'Did you say the girl's name was Susannah?' the woman named Francesca asked, her brow creased with sudden worry.

'Yes,' I said, nodding.

'It is not Jessie's fault, I think. Susannah *is* her cousin. In fact, her mother, your aunt, was supposed to be the representative coming to meet you, but unfortunately no one knew that Susannah had defected to the Coven of the Blood Moon. She went missing three nights ago, which is why your aunt sent me. They're still searching for her.'

'I think the angels took them somewhere. Luke mentioned the council?' I replied, looking to Daniel for confirmation.

'Yes, they will have done that,' he said. 'I take it they wanted Jessie because they had heard of her half-blood status?'

'Yes. Susannah had of course been told all about Jessie, but I think there must have been another reason for them to take such a risk,' the witch answered.

'The book. She wanted the book,' I said, looking to Eva.

'Don't tell me you showed her the book, after all I told you?' Eva asked.

'I didn't, but she asked to go to the bathroom. I showed her where, and I came to phone you guys. Then I found her in my room, staring at it,' I said with a shrug. There was no way Eva was going to blame me for everything. So, I'd made a couple of mistakes, but I wasn't as inept as she was making out.

'Great! So after all I went through to get that book for you, you go and give it to the worst possible recipient you could find?'

Ahhh! It seemed my day was going to consist mostly of arguments. I looked to Daniel, who stood silently watching us, and breathed in before launching my defence.

'Is that how little you think of me, Eva? Yes, she got the book. She sucked me into some kind of vortex thing and I risked everything to save that book by jumping out of what she called 'ley lines'. That's how I broke my arm. I dislocated my shoulder too, but that went back,' I added with a retch as I remembered the sickening crack, when it clicked back into place.

'You still lost it,' she said with a frown.

'I fought Susannah for it and won. Then the head witch, I think her name was Carrigan, arrived and electrocuted me, and yes, Luke and the other angels saved me. But the book's here, Eva,' I said, pulling it from the waistband of my jeans, where it had made bright red welts along my skin.

'And I suppose you think you deserve a medal?' Eva asked, her frown transforming into a single-browed glare.

I wasn't sure which I preferred, anger or sarcasm.

'Have you ever apologised to anyone Eva?' I asked.

'No, I haven't, and I don't intend to start now,' she said, as she stepped towards me, took the book and left the room.

'Wow! She's got an attitude problem,' I mumbled, as I headed over to the fridge to get myself a fresh blood pack to heat up.

As I crossed the room back to the table, I noticed the witch's eyes following me with interest.

'Why is she still drinking blood packs? I thought only newborns were given those, until they'd learned some control?' she asked Daniel.

'It's her choice. She refuses to feed like us, and as we told you at Exodus we have no direct control over her mind, unlike other newborns,' he replied.

'She looks pale, different,' she added.

'Hello, I am here you know. Or have I turned invisible all of a sudden?' I asked irritably.

'I'm sorry, how rude of me. Let me introduce myself properly. I'm Francesca, as I said before, but you can call me Franny. I'm a good friend of your aunt, your mother's sister, Sally, who is now the High Priestess of our coven. The responsibility should have been your mother's, but of course we now know she ran away and married your father instead, and sadly died in childbirth.'

'I'm sorry, I...'

'Child, it is not your fault; never think that. Laurie would have known the risks she was taking, having you at home and not seeking medical help.'

'But I never knew. I wasn't told any of it. I didn't know anything until last month,' I said.

'It is all such a shame, but now here you are, and we want to help you understand your new heritage.'

'Right, so Sally is the High Priestess and *her* daughter is Susannah, the witch who tried to abduct me, and enrol me into the dark coven. What was it called again?' I asked.

'The Coven of the Blood Moon,' Franny said, shaking her head. 'I can't believe Susannah would join them freely. They must have her under a powerful charm.'

'I don't know, she seemed pretty sure of herself. She really wanted me to join...' I said tailing off, as I saw Daniel frown at me and ever so slightly shake his head.

'Anyway, if my mother should have been the High Priestess, what does that make me? My powers are useless, and I'm only half witch anyway. Obviously my dad wasn't a witch or a wizard, or whatever.'

'The witch blood is only passed down through the female line anyway. Yes, there are Mages, who are men with magical talents, but they are separate from us. Your power will be weak because you are untrained and uninitiated, and I can help you with the both,' she added.

'Hey, hey, hold-up,' Eva said, barging back into the room. 'Sebastian said she was not to leave Manchester without his permission. She's going nowhere.'

'Eva's right. After this morning's sabotage attempt, I think it would be prudent for Jessie to stay in the house. At least until we know she is under no further threat. We can protect her here,' Daniel said.

'Of course, that is what we expected, which is why I have been given leave to stay on a week. I can perform the initiation here and then help Jessie understand her powers. I believe you have found the remaining family Book of Shadows?' She asked.

I looked to Eva before answering, reluctant to earn her wrath yet again, but she nodded for me. After all, Franny had already seen me hand it over.

'There had been rumour of a powerful book of shadows being hidden in London for years. Maybe Laurie brought it with her, and lost it or sold it, but I knew someone who owed me a favour, and was capable of securing it for me...

'The less said about that little deal the better,' Daniel interrupted darkly.

'I thought it could help Jess, but I had no idea it belonged to her,' Eva said.

'You are probably right. The book did go missing around the same time as Laurie, so she possibly used it as payment to secure her passage to Europe. Jessie, have you noticed anything different about the book? How does it make you feel?' Franny asked, looking at me intently.

'Oh! Not you as well?' Eva said. 'It's just a book, an old and rather unusual one I'll grant, but Jess is convinced it's alive, strange girl.'

I shot Eva a wicked glare, and wished I could summon up a spell to seal her big mouth shut.

'I do not! I just feel, well...' I really didn't want to say how the book made me feel, as I knew it made me sound completely wacko. Yet here was another witch, a family member, asking me how the book made me feel, which was a strange question in itself, so maybe I wasn't so nuts after all.

'Go on Jess. Do the pictures move for you?' Franny prompted.

'Yes! Oh yes!' I said, my breath whooshing out as I grinned across at Eva. 'I love the book. I feel a part of the book when I open it... I feel safe. When I said I did everything I could to get the book back from Susannah, it wasn't because of Eva; it was because I wanted to protect the book. The leaves that twist around the pentagram all dance in a breeze which ruffles my hair. It didn't work for Susannah, and she said it wouldn't work for Carrigan, and that's why they wanted me too.'

Franny nodded and smiled at me. 'Show me,' she said.

'Don't you think we should fix her arm first?' Eva asked, with a grin.

CHAPTER FOUR

A couple of hours later I was lying on my bed fighting waves of nausea, as Daniel and Eva stared at me, obviously perplexed.

'I don't understand why you're making such a fuss, Jess,' Eva said.

'Eva, leave her alone. You know she's not like us,' Daniel said, sitting down on the bed next to me.

'Maybe, but she's still a vampire. Her arm shouldn't be hurting, now that we've fixed it.'

'It's not hurting anymore, okay?' I replied, sitting up. 'I just feel a little woozy. I never did like the sight of blood. I fainted at school in Bio once, when we had to dissect a bull's eyeball,' I said, a shiver running the length of my body, making me pull the duvet round in a messy huddle.

'It's still not normal. Vampires can't be squeamish Jess. Here, drink this and pull yourself together,' she said with a smile.

I took the mug of warm, silky blood she was offering and began to drink. When I'd been turned a couple of months back, the blood packs they gave me to drink tasted quite pleasant, chocolaty almost. Then I tasted Daniel's blood... fine, I bit him, but he wanted me to do it, and he tasted like nothing else. The first time was amazing, but for some reason, and I'd never told either Daniel or Eva, the second time I drank from him I'd been violently sick. Since then I'd avoided it, making excuses, which he clearly wasn't happy with. So I was back to the blood packs, which I knew Sebastian, the clan leader, was getting sick and tired of providing for me. I was going to have to tell them, but I didn't know how, and I suspected Eva's solution would be to sample some *regular* human blood, the regular way. It was just a matter of time, and time was running out.

The drink helped and the nausea began to subside. I looked down at my arm and it looked perfect again. I shuddered as I remembered how, after the first attempt Eva had made to fix my arm, and after I had punched her in the face in an effort to escape the scalpel she was slicing through my skin, she had employed Franny to bind me with a spell, so I couldn't move as she worked.

It had only taken a couple of minutes for her to slice my newly healed skin open, rebreak the wonky bone, and push it back into its rightful place, so that it could heal correctly. But I felt every single second. So much for vampire's not feeling pain! It seemed that my half-vampire, witch blood status had awarded me control over my actions and thoughts, but had also given me human pain thresholds. Fantastic!

On the upside, I had at least developed a vampire's healing ability, and now my arm looked as good as new. I threw off the duvet and put the mug on the dresser.

'Better?' Daniel asked.

I nodded my head and smiled at him.

'Good. Well, now that you're fixed, I think Francesca is hoping to have a chat with you, and take a look at the book,' he said. 'I'll be downstairs with Eva if you need us.'

'No funny business this time, okay?' Eva added, as she followed him out of the door. 'And hurry up. I've got a new 'Top Model' episode we can watch when you're done.'

I smiled back and nodded. It was slightly bewildering when Eva slipped from being an arse kicking vampire leader to a girlie best friend, but I was happy when she did. I looked at the book Eva had returned to me, and placing it beside me, waited.

'May I take a look?' Franny asked, sitting opposite me on the edge of the bed.

'Sure.'

Franny spent some time staring at the cover, then again at the front page, but her hair didn't move, and she showed no signs of seeing the leaves dancing. She continued to flick silently through the book until she reached the end, and here she paused.

'Have you studied the back pages, Jess?'

'Um, no, not really. I've only had the book a couple of weeks, and to be honest I don't understand most of it.'

She nodded again and shuffled closer to me on the bed.

'Here, look!' she said as she slid her nail gently around the inner side of the back cover. What appeared to be glued was not. The paper easily lifted up, and underneath was another blank piece of paper.

'Reveal,' she murmured, tracing her fingers across the page, following invisible lines, in the shape of a pentagram.

'Wow!' I said under my breath, as a long list of scribbled names appeared in a column down the page. The names were all written in different handwriting, simply as if each person had written their name in the book one after the other. Some were written very neatly, some seemed scrawled across the page, and the early ones looked to be scratched on it.

'Yes, this is indeed your family book. Look, here is your mother's name, Laurie, and your grandmother's name above that,' Franny said, pointing to the last two names at the bottom of the list.

'So my grandmother is called Sylvie?' I asked.

'She was. She died ten years ago, which is when Laurie should have taken on the role of High Priestess, but instead it passed to her sister, your aunt.'

'So will I have to give her this book back?' I asked, dreading the answer.

'No, it is yours. As High Priestess, Sally owns the other family book, which we keep in the coven. Once you have been initiated into our family, your name will appear in this book, and it will be yours until you die... which could be some time,' she added with a sudden smile. 'Now, show me what you can do.'

'I told you, I can't *do* anything. Well, not unless I'm angry or scared half to death and then I can move things and blow the lights. Some powerful witch I turned out to be!'

'Now, open the book,' she said, handing it to me.

As the book fell into my hands, a sense of contentment washed over me. I opened the cover and the warm breeze immediately lifted my fringe, while the leaves began their merry dance.

'I see the book is happy to be with its rightful owner. I have rarely seen such a powerful energy display with an uninitiated witch before,' Franny said.

'So when are you going to do the initiation? What do I have to do?' I asked.

'I have a few things I want you to practice first, so 'Top Model' may have to wait. I obviously want to initiate you as soon as possible, and whilst Sebastian is being compliant.'

'What do you mean, compliant?'

'Well, let's just say that it isn't necessarily in the vampire clan's best interests for you to become a fully fledged witch, so I was maybe a bit hazy about certain details,' she said with a quick grin.

'I should tell them. *We* should tell them. What details?'

'No Jessie. I can see, even Daniel & Eva can see, that you are not happy as a vampire. You don't drink enough blood and refuse to feed from humans. Now even *you* know that Sebastian is running out of patience with you. He will stop buying blood packs soon and you will be forced to feed, but I think there is another way.'

'Go on,' I said, knowing she was right about Sebastian, and Eva too was fast losing patience.

'Obviously we have never done this before, but I have a feeling, that unlike a normal vampire you managed to keep hold of your soul, which is why they can't control your mind.' I nodded. What she said made sense and had been mentioned before.

'Well, I think that currently your soul and the vampire DNA are battling it out. Sometimes you feel more vampire and sometimes more human, but I suspect that if we perform the initiation ritual, the witch in you may just win out,' she said.

'So I stop being a vampire altogether?' I asked in a whisper.

'I honestly don't know. I discussed it with Sally, and we've never come across it or tried it before. I doubt there will be *no* vampire left, but we hope that it will strengthen you enough to live as one of us.'

'But Sebastian wants me to stay here.'

'Which is why I haven't mentioned it,' she said, the smile creeping across her face. 'But wherever you decide to live is up to *you*. This initiation will just give you more choice.'

'Okay, let's do this. What do you want me to do?' I asked.

'Good. Most witches have years before their initiation ceremony, because we perform it on their fourteenth birthday, and they grow up learning how to ground and cast spells; but you have twenty-four hours. The most important thing for you to learn before the initiation is how to ground. How to draw energy through your chakras, and of course your part in the ceremony. You can learn about casting spells and using your powers *after* the ceremony,' she said.

'Here is a good Wiccan handbook, and even though we are not Wiccan it explains the basics really well, on how to ground and draw energy from the source,' she said, handing me a glossy, modern book of Wicca.

'So you're not Wiccans then?' I asked.

'No, not really. We are an ancient coven. Our powers lie in our blood and have been passed down through centuries, undiluted. But this book makes the rudiments so easy to understand, that we use it to help our children in their studies. You will find it much easier to understand than your own book, because it is written in the modern language which you are accustomed to.'

'Do you want me to read it all?'

'It wouldn't harm you to do so, but tonight concentrate especially on chapters two to four. You also need to practice all the examples they give. You need a full understanding of both techniques.'

'Okay,' I said.

You also need to find some time to memorise the ritual for tomorrow. Pass me a book mark and I will mark the correct page in your Book of Shadows.'

A bookmark? I was a girl who loved books, but I tended to leave my books open, in a tent-like fashion to save the page, or even worse, dog ear them! I had a sneaky suspicion Franny wouldn't be too impressed if I did either to my ancient Book of Shadows, so I cast around until I found an old 'Grazia' magazine, ripped a page out, folded it up into a bookmark shape and handed it over.

'Now, here is the ritual you need to learn. I will leave you for a while, as there is much news I need to tell Sally. I shall come back later tomorrow and we'll perform the initiation at midnight.'

An hour later I sat cross legged on the carpet, the Wiccan guide by my side. I was trying to draw energy from the source up through my root chakra. The problem was, I wasn't good at meditation. I'd tried it before, when I'd flirted with yoga, but it always ended up the same, with me feeling fidgety, my mind wandering.

Franny had said to learn how to ground first, but after nothing interesting happened...I mean, I guess I didn't have any excess energy to get rid of anyway, I decided to move on and learn how to receive extra energy. It sounded more intriguing, and I figured at least then I'd have something to get rid of and *ground with*.

So I followed the instructions and sat, cross-legged on the floor. The book said I'd have more success if I sat outside on the earth, from which I was going to raise the energy, but it had started raining and I didn't fancy getting soggy. Also, I didn't think Daniel would be too impressed if I started doing rituals in the back garden, where I could be spotted by our student neighbours, who seemed to be at their most active after 4pm, so the bedroom floor would have to do.

I was trying to imagine a root running down my spine and plunging into the earth, drawing energy upwards and sending it down my arms and into my hands. I felt nothing. Actually I felt ridiculous, and was only thankful that Eva had stayed downstairs. She would have a field day with this!

Ugh! Get a grip. You have to do this, I told myself. I blocked out all surrounding sound and tried again. Nothing... and again, and again, but still nothing. I flicked through the pages of the book and read a new bit. It was a section about visualising the energy as a ball in your hands, to imagine it floating in the air, and then to visualise it floating between your hands faster and faster like a ping pong ball. I'd try that.

I shifted my shoulders, got comfortable once more and had another go at raising the energy. I squeezed my eyes shut, blocking out the room, concentrated on breathing and imagined the tap root running down my spine, down through the floors in the house, through the foundations then breaking through into the dark clay earth. I visualised the root like a straw, sucking up all the earth's energy, silver traces zapping from the ground, from the plants, from the trees, all drawn into my body and zooming around my veins, making my fingers tingle.

I could feel it; it was working. I could imagine the ball of energy, like a mini sun, bouncing between my hands, faster and faster. My breathing increased and my pulse with it. The energy hummed within me, raw power crackling all over my body, like static electricity on a party balloon. I opened my eyes.

Oh Hell! The mini fireball I'd visualised so well was still there, flying between my hands, faster and faster. Was that supposed to happen? What if I dropped it? I desperately tried to remember how to get rid of it, but I'd only read the chapter through once, so instead I concentrated on not dropping it, and let the fiery glow hypnotise me.

'Jess, what the hell are you doing?' Eva asked her shocked voice startling me and breaking my concentration. Unfortunately, as we both soon discovered, you don't want to be the person who breaks a witch's concentration. The fireball went flying, straight across the room in the direction of my distraction, Eva. Luckily for her, she was a vampire and saw it coming. Had she been graced with regular human speed she would have had no chance. As it was, she dodged the fireball which flew through the doorway, across the hall and unluckily for me hit a mirror. Mirrors it would seem, don't absorb energy, they reflect it. So a second later we found it hurtling back towards us.

'Jess, stop it!' Eva yelled.

Unthinkingly, I put out my hand to catch it, my theory being, that if the energy ball came from me, then surely it could do me no harm? In theory I was right, but let's face it, I didn't really have a clue what I was doing and a couple of seconds later my whole body was fizzing, and from the look on Eva's face, I looked somewhat horrifying.

'I ca..ca... can't hold it anymore Eva,' I stammered. 'I...I...'

As I said the words my body let go, releasing it, and as relief and a soothing chill settled over me, the electric blast shot out across the room in all directions, making everything explode. The light bulbs popped like corn kernels, shattering tiny bits of glass all over my bed. The mirror over my dresser cracked into a million tiny shards, which then proceeded to fall out of the frame and scatter themselves across my carpet. We both winced as we saw the window explode. It happened slowly, like the first cracks on an icy pond, zig-zagging their way across the pane, then more joining the race, until it formed a beautiful starburst which gave a final sigh before its ultimate destruction.

As we watched in horror, Daniel came rushing up the stairs.

'What the...? Oh! Thank God you're okay,' he said, as his eyes roamed the room, taking in the damage. 'I knew this was a bad idea. Francesca should have stayed to help, not left her alone like this.

'Oh, she's fine Daniel. She had to learn at some point. It's me you should be worried about. She nearly turned me into a vampire fireball,' Eva said with a grin.

'I'm sorry, I didn't mean to. Shit! Look what I've done to the room,' I said, my body shivering, as shock crept in.

'Hey, it doesn't matter. You can sleep in another room until we've got it fixed up. I'll call Sebastian; he'll sort it out. There are always worse clean-ups than a bit of broken glass Jessie,' Daniel said, striding over and wrapping his arms around me.

CHAPTER FIVE

That I keep secret, what I am asked to keep secret,
That I will learn and try to master our art,
But never forget our rule,
What good be the tools without inner light
What good be the magic without pure insight.
That I will never use the magic for wrongful ends,
That I consider these vows taken before the Gods,
And understand the threefold law.

Ahh! Why couldn't I get it right? And this was only half of it. I'd been attempting to memorise the ritual all morning, after I'd had a pretty good sleep in one of Daniel's guest rooms. The vampire world being what it is, it didn't shock me when two guys turned up to replace the window at about eleven thirty that night, a couple of hours after my little accident.

'We need a secure house, now more than ever Jess, especially now that news of you and your book has inevitably leaked into the community,' Daniel had explained.

So whilst the men fixed the window, Eva lured me into the back room for a bit of 'America's Next Top Model' viewing.

'You can't keep your nose stuck in a book all night, Jess,' she complained.

'I need to have all this memorised, and somehow I think I should practise that grounding again. I need to be able to do it by tomorrow night,' I said.

'There's not a chance I'm letting you do anymore witchcraft tonight Jess. We need a house to sleep in, and Daniel's only got so many guest rooms. You need a break. You've got all day tomorrow to practice.'

'Okay, okay!' I had relented, and the remainder of the evening passed without mishap.

So far this morning, I'd spent three hours reading and saying the lines in my head, but I'd never been any good at learning things word for word, and being a vampire didn't make me any quicker. I wondered if I should try the power raising and grounding again instead.

'Jess, can I come in?' Daniel said, as he popped his head round the door.

'Sure.'

'How's it going?'

'Fine, I guess. I just keep messing up this last verse,' I said, with a shrug.

'You don't have to do it, you know. I'm a bit concerned that Francesca hasn't told us all there is to tell. We don't know what effect it will have on you. I want you here with me Jess. I don't want to lose our connection.'

'I know, but Daniel, you know I'm not doing so well as a vampire. I have to try this,' I said, wondering if I should tell him what Franny had told me the previous night. 'Anyway, Sebastian's not worried about it, otherwise he would have stopped Franny, but he's authorised it, right?'

'Sebastian and Eva both want you to learn to control your power. You will be much more useful if you become the vampire they foresee. What they aren't taking into account is that you are barely a vampire anymore.'

'What do you mean by that?' I said, stung by his words.

'You know what I mean, Jess. You are all but starving. You won't feed from me anymore, the reason for which I can only presume is something Luke has said to you, but he doesn't care about you anymore. He left you to me and then deserted you.'

'It's nothing to do with that. Sure, Luke knows I fed from you, but he said he didn't care anyway, and I don't care what he thinks either,' I said, my words sounding hollow, even though I desperately wanted to believe in them. Luke was not my future any longer. I had to forget him.

Daniel sat down on the bed next to me, pulling me into to his arms as I breathed out, feeling the welcome comfort that always came from being next to him.

'Jessie, you know I'm not like Sebastian or Eva. I care about you, and only you. I don't want you to do this ritual if it's going to take you away from me,' he said, his fingers finding my chin and gently turning my face to his.

'I'm not going anywhere, and that's for sure!' I said. 'I plan to stay here, with you. *You saved me*!' He leaned in and tingles shimmered down my spine like a waterfall, as our lips touched. The tip of his tongue sought mine and I found myself reaching in, pulling him, and raking my hands through his hair, as I pulled his face even closer.

We lay back on the bed, his hands expertly running up and down the length of my body, increasing the tingles as he covered me in kisses. My fangs appeared with my increased heart rate and everything went a little hazy. I hadn't fed in so long. I was hungry.

Our souls were paired, so Daniel needed no request. He knew what I wanted and he yearned for it as much as I did. He rolled onto his back and pulled me on top so I could feel his heart thrumming and a hardness pushing against our jeans. Turning his head to one side, he bared his neck and pulled my head down to it.

Instinct took over and seconds later I was clamped to his body, rocking myself, grinding against him as his sweet blood poured into my mouth and nourished me. It felt like molten lava pouring down my throat, thick and fiery. All my senses awoke and I suddenly realised how dulled they had become. His scent was exhilarating, driving me on to feed further, bite harder and consume more. I could hear the cleaners chatting in my bedroom across the hall, the television was still on in the front lounge, and the students were stirring in the house next door.

'Jessie, sweet Jessie, you have to stop, my love. Ohhh...' Daniel moaned, as I reluctantly withdrew and looked down at him.

'Oh God! I'm sorry, I'm so sorry. I didn't mean to. I...'

'Hey, it's all good. I'm fine. You stopped just when I asked you to. Many wouldn't be able to.'

'But you look so pale,' I said.

'It's nothing. I will go to the club in a few hours and feed. There is nothing to worry about. But look at you; you are beautiful again.'

I began to pull away from him, but he pulled me back into his arms. His lips found mine once more and I found there were other things to do than feed.

Soon the majority of our clothing was strewn across the bedroom floor and I realised it would only take a couple more items of underwear between us, before we took that final step. There had been a couple of times when things had got pretty steamy between us, but my memories of Luke, and a misguided urge to remain faithful to him had stopped us going any further.

An image of Luke flashed across my eyes, Luke as he had appeared when he thought I was in danger with Susannah, how he'd said he was sorry, and how he would protect me. *Then*, there had been something in his eyes, something I recognised, love. It was only once I was safe that he returned to the cold, new Luke I had come to know, the Luke who wanted nothing to do with me. I did however know one thing. I couldn't have sex with Daniel when I was still so confused about Luke.

I gently pulled back from Daniel, and leaned in to kiss him one last time.

'I'm sorry, I...'

'Jess it's okay. There's plenty more fun things we can do,' he said grinning and pulling the duvet cover back, as he clambered underneath and held it open for me.

I looked at my open Book of Shadows, looked at the book of Wicca which I'd discarded on my desk and looked at the clock; twelve thirty. I shrugged and smiled. I had another twelve hours before Franny would be back.

CHAPTER SIX

'May I come in?' Franny asked, popping her head round my door eleven hours later.

'Sure, come in.'

'My dear, I heard about the accident with your room. I feel responsible, and I know Eva holds me accountable for leaving you unattended.'

'No, it's fine. Look, I'm back now anyway. They fixed the new window straight away and the cleaners came in today. I had it back by five,' I said.

'Hmm, but maybe it would have been best if I had been here. I'm a little surprised by your sudden change of plan regarding diet,' she said, staring at my restored glow and glittering dark eyes.

'That's none of your business. I am who I am. I didn't hurt anybody.'

'Yet... Well, let's hope it doesn't affect our ceremony tonight. I suppose it had the added bonus of Daniel not being here to hang around. I believe he has gone to the club?'

I nodded, unable to think of a suitable retort, especially as I was worrying about quite how much blood I'd taken, and how hungry I'd left Daniel.

'Right then, let's get on with it. We need to prepare and be ready to start the ceremony just before midnight. Have you learned your part?' she asked.

'Yes, I think so, and I had another go at channelling energy. I think I've got it.'

'Good. First I'm going to run you a cleansing bath, then while you are in there I will cleanse this room and set it up.'

'I did actually have a shower this morning, not that I really needed one. You do know that vampires don't really get dirty... or smell?' I said with a smile.

'Of course dear. This is a ceremonial bath to cleanse your aura. Your aura is too entangled with Daniel's currently, and when you attend a coven ceremony you must always be cleansed in honour of the gods.'

'Okay,' I said. I didn't really see how a bath would change my bond with Daniel, but hey, I'm a girl that loves a good soak in a hot, scented bath, so I was *not* going to complain!

The bath was lovely, Franny had lit white candles at each corner of the bath, and a variety of herbs encased in a muslin bag hung beneath the flowing water, and later bobbed gently on the top. Once I was in, Franny stepped next to the bath and poured salt in a circle around me, chanting quietly as she poured.

'As I sprinkle this salt, so I cleanse and purify this water and all who enter. As I sprinkle this salt, I intensify thy power. As I sprinkle this salt, I banish all negativity and unwanted bonds. All is now cleansed and purified...'

I tuned the low chanting out and laid back. I didn't feel any different, maybe a little freaked out, but hey, I was getting used to the weirdness that was my life. I relaxed and let the scent of lavender and sage calm my nerves.

'Right, you relax and I'll cleanse the room. I'll come back in thirty minutes, so don't get out before then, please dearie.'

I closed my eyes and let myself drift, images of Daniel flashing through my memory and making my cheeks burn.

'I don't need three guesses to know what you're thinking about,' Eva said, her voice and subsequent laugh shattering my dreams and making me jump.

'Hey! You scared me half to death. Did anyone ever teach you to knock?'

'If they did, I didn't listen. So what's the witch got you pickling in then? It stinks.'

'It does not. It's lovely. Just lavender and sage I think, with some salt.'

'Salt? Next she'll have the cauldron bubbling! With Dan gone I'd better keep an eye on you, before she turns you into a toad or something.'

'Don't be daft Eva, she wants to help me. This will help me control my powers, and that's what you and Sebastian want, isn't it?'

'Relax, you know I'm only joking. Anyway, Seb's already vetted her, so she's fine I guess. I'll be downstairs if you need me.'

'Sure.'

Fifteen minutes later, there was a knock and Franny popped her head around the door once more.

'It's time to get you out, before you start to wrinkle. I've brought you a clean towel and a ceremonial gown to wear. Take your hair down from that bun and brush it out. We want you as natural as possible.'

I quickly dried myself and pulled on the gown. It looked like an old fashioned white nightdress, made out of a soft clinging material that hugged my new vamp body and made my toned, skinny frame look like it had curves once again. I loved it. It was simple, but hung beautifully.

I pulled my dyed, dark hair out of its bun and brushed it out till it shone, then looked in the mirror. I liked my new hair, but sometimes, like now, I wished I had my old, mousy blonde waves back. Dying it had been part of the transformation that allowed me to move back to Manchester, and actually leave the house. After all, it was still only a couple of months since my very public murder. It wouldn't do to go and get recognised! The rest of the transformation had happened naturally with my new diet. My eyes had turned a dark russet brown, I'd lost my size twelve curves and of course, lost the horrific scars and injuries the girl gang had bestowed upon me.

I walked back to my room and stood in awe in the doorway. The room was a large Victorian bedroom with plenty of floor space, and the cleaners had been in earlier so there hadn't been much to tidy up. Even so, Franny had somehow made it seem huge, and so peaceful. There were no clothes in sight, no books strewn on my bed, no coffee cups (not that they were used for coffee!) on the cabinets. She had lit about twenty candles which were dotted around the room to create a huge circle, and at the four corners of the circle were unlit coloured ones. Incense gently wafted in a spiral towards the ceiling, scenting the room with something I didn't recognise, and catching slightly in the back of my throat.

'Oh good, you're here. We've got five minutes to finish off this circle before we begin,' Franny said. 'Come here, dear. I can see your mother in you now.

It's a shame about the hair, but there's nothing we can do about that yet.'

She held out her hand to me and I stepped across the room, suddenly feeling the nerves crawling up my spine. What if the spell went wrong because of the vampire DNA? They had never initiated a vampire before. I was an experiment.

I stepped into the circle with her and she handed me another large white candle, already lit.

'Now we will call the quarters and close the circle. I'll bring you the corresponding candles to light, and you just say *I honor thee O Fire,* or whichever element I bring you, okay?'

'Sure,' I answered, concentrating on holding the master candle steady, but watching it's flame flicker a crazy dance, as my hands began to shake.

'Air, Fire, Water, Earth, elements of astral birth, I call to you, attend me now,' Franny chanted as she first walked towards the window and picking up the yellow candle, brought it back to me.

'I honor thee, O Air,' I said, as I used my own candle to light it. It sparked and the flame grew tall and thin, before Franny took it back to the east corner of the room, and began to chant again, repeating the lines she had used for Air. Next she brought me the red candle from the south end of the circle for Fire, then the blue candle for Water from the west.

'Air, Fire, Water, Earth, elements of astral birth, I call to you, attend me now,' she said for the final time as she handed me the brown candle.

'I honor thee, O Earth,' I replied, as I watched her return it to its holder and finish the chant.

'In this circle rightly cast, safe from curse, I call to you. This is my will, so mote it be.'

Having returned the Earth candle to its holder she returned to me.

'Jess, the circle's functioning now so you cannot leave it until I say, or else it will break, and no longer protect us. I'll close the circle down nicely when we've finished. Now dearie, you place the Spirit Candle on that little altar there, and I want you to kneel beside it, while I begin the initiation.'

I said nothing, I did nothing. This was all freaking me out a little. I mean, I'd watched loads of supernatural programs, and with my best friend Alex, we'd often thought how cool it would be to do witchcraft, but this was real, and like I said before, I was a little concerned about what would happen to me, being a vampire. My hands shook, as I slowly bent down and placed the candle on the makeshift altar.

'Now Jessie, I've done this ceremony many times. Its white magic, so no harm can come to you. Either, it will work and your own powers will be unlocked, or the vampire DNA will be stronger, it won't work, and no harm done.'

'Okay, let's do this,' I said, pushing my fears away with a grin.

'Good. Now Jess, do you remember your lines? Remember, you can hold no fear in your heart once we begin, so cast it out. As you do so I want you to centre yourself, imagine that tap-root connecting you to the earth and drawing on her power. Let it flow around your body, ridding it of negativity and allowing it to find the human girl inside you, and bring her forth when I ask. Do you understand?'

I nodded my head, as I remembered the ceremony I'd read through about thirty times since the previous day. The words were somewhat scary, but thankfully my part in it was only small. Relieved that I'd practiced a couple more times, I centred myself and felt a calm, cool breeze stir around me.

'You are about to enter a family of power, a place where birth and death, dark and light, joy and pain, meet and make one. You are about to step between the worlds, beyond time, outside the realm of your other life. You who stand on the threshold, have you the courage to make thy bid? Know it is better to fall on my blade and perish, than to make the attempt with fear in thy heart.'

Franny paused, waiting for my reply. She smiled at me and the words came to me easily, as if I'd known them all my life.

'I tread the path with perfect love and perfect trust.'

'Prepare for death and rebirth. As are all first brought into the world, and thus are all first brought into the coven. Are you willing to swear the oath?" she said.

This was the bit I was most worried about. After all, I'd already died and been reborn once, and once was enough for me. I was hoping the words were metaphorical. Franny assured me that they were, but as she'd never initiated a vampire before, we couldn't be sure.

'I am,' I replied, and repeated the lines I had memorised earlier in the day.

Franny smiled at me and nodded reassuringly, before continuing,

'Are you willing to suffer, to learn?'

'Yes,' I said, as she stepped forward, taking a needle from the altar, and passed it briefly through the candle flame, then dipped it into a small bowl of water. I knew what was coming, so I held my hand out to her and watched as she pricked my finger with the needle, squeezing some drops out onto a tiny receptacle, before placing it on the altar.

As she did so the room began to spin, slowly at first, making me feel slightly nauseous, then faster as I desperately tried to keep upright, to stay conscious. I was going to pass out at the sight of a drop of blood, or was it that? And then the ripping began. It was a feeling of something being slowly pulled from my body, my soul. Something was being torn from me. I cried out and clasped my belly.

'Jessie it's alright. It's the witch in you taking over. Jessie, listen, we have to finish the initiation, fast! You need to repeat the last lines after me,' Franny said, kneeling to my level and holding my chin, making me focus. I nodded.

'I Jess, do of my own free will most solemnly swear to protect,'

I repeated her words, my ears ringing and the sickness building in my stomach.

'Help and defend my sisters and brothers...'

'Jessie! Francesca! What the hell is happening? Daniel's in pain. I can feel him. He's coming back now. What are you doing to her?' Eva shouted as she charged through the door.

'Nothing we haven't discussed dearie. We've nearly finished now. Let Jess say the remaining words,' Franny answered.

'Like hell I will! Something's happening we most definitely haven't discussed. Jessie get out of there now!' Eva yelled back.

'I have to finish this. I trust Franny, Eva. It will be fine,' I said, hoping I was right.

'Then I'll have to get you,' Eva replied and launched herself towards us. She hit the circle's barrier at vampire speed, which is pretty damn fast, and when she hit, the noise made a resounding crack, even though there was nothing to see. She prowled the perimeter of the circle, searching for a way in, but there was none.

'Jess, let me help you. You have to break this barrier, we don't know what this ceremony is doing to you, and neither does the coven. You're an experiment, and it's obviously hurting you, and Daniel,' Eva said to me.

'It'll be okay Eva. It's white magic, so it can't be bad. I need to finish this. I need to control my powers, you know that. Franny, let me finish.'

'Help and defend my brothers and sisters, and keep the coven's charge,' Franny said. She leaned nearer and held my shoulder and I felt a new energy pour into me, clearing my head momentarily.

I repeated the words and the dizziness increased. I sat back on my heels and steadied myself on the table we were using as an altar.

'Jessie!' Daniel said, as he suddenly staggered into the room and evading Eva's arms flew at the circle barrier, only to find himself jettisoned back across the room.

'I declare you, Jessica James, part of the Malden Coven, direct heir to Laurie Browning and all her sisters. So mote it be.' Franny said, her voice echoing through the sudden stillness that crept into the room. Eva and Daniel both looked on, impotent as she dipped her fingers first in my blood, then mixed it in the water, before finally flicking it over my head.

I don't remember much directly after that, other than hearing Daniel shout my name, then Eva yell Daniel's name as the world went black and I gave in to it, slumping to the floor.

CHAPTER SEVEN

I was only out for seconds, and when I came to I saw Franny hurrying between the corners of the circle chanting quietly. Eva & Daniel were standing only a foot away, waiting for the circle to lose its power.

'Hurry up woman. I tell you, if Jess is harmed in any way, you'll pay for this,' Daniel said.

'I'm fine, I think,' I said, sitting up and looking over at him. Something felt weird, wrong!

'You have got to be kidding me. What the hell have you done to her?' Eva said, glaring at Franny.

'What? I'm okay. I feel fine...ish,' I said.

'Jessie, your eyes. They're green, bright green. Like Francesca's,' Daniel said, 'and I can't feel you. I can't feel our bond. That's what's different, isn't it?'

He was right. That was what I'd felt being ripped from me. My magical bond with Daniel, which I'd had ever since he'd made me, had vanished. I felt a strange emptiness. I looked across at him and wondered what that meant.

'I'm still me though, right?' I asked. 'Franny, am I

still a vampire?'

Franny finished chanting and the spell broke. Immediately, Eva shot across the room and had her by the neck, her body dangling from her hand, her toes scraping the floor.

'What have you done, Witch?' She said.

A second later, a lightning bolt erupted from Franny's hands and Eva was flung across the room and smashed into the wall with a resounding crack, which being Eva she merely rubbed her head a little and slunk into a defensive crouch, ready to charge again, her fangs at the ready, snarling back.

'Don't be silly dear, the coven wouldn't send an undefended witch into the middle of a vampire's lair now, would we? I'm one of the most powerful witches in our coven, so don't mess with me. Regardless, I've done nothing Sebastian did not want. You saw for yourself, all I did was initiate Jess into our coven. As you said, none of us knew what would happen...and Jess is fine, aren't you dearie?' Franny asked.

'Umm yeah, I think so,' I said, feeling just a little strange, lighter and glad to be back on my feet. I nodded over to Daniel, 'I'm alright, really.'

But I had to get a look at my eyes, so I walked past them all, over to my new dressing table mirror, which had been replaced after the previous night's drama. I bent down and stared at myself. Whoa, seriously! I mean, all my life I had had grey blue eyes to match my dirty blonde hair, then the morning I woke from the vampire sleep my eyes went electric blue and my hair blonder, shinier. However, over the course of a few weeks of vampire diet, my eyes lost their colour and became the two dark pools of chocolate, with the slight reddish tint that all vampires have in common. I dyed my hair dark to match, and to complete my disguise. I looked in the mirror now and saw that once again my eyes had changed colour. As Daniel said, they were a beautiful eerie green, almost phosphorescent. They matched both Franny's and Suzanne's. I had the eyes of a witch.

'That may be the case, but I don't think Sebastian intended for you to break her bond and turn her into a fully fledged witch. Is she even still one of us?' Eva said.

'I have no more idea than you dear, as you are well aware. Jessie, how do you feel?' Franny asked.

'Umm, fine. It feels weird and lighter without, you know, the bond thing,' I said, with a quick apologetic smile at Daniel, 'but...'

'Jess, are you still one of us? Have you still got fangs?' Eva interrupted.

'I don't know, like I said I don't feel much different...'

'Can you still smell her?' Eva asked nodding her

head towards Franny.

'I think so, maybe a bit less, but...'

'Oh, for goodness sake,' Eva sighed and seconds later was standing right up in my face, tilting my head back and pulling up my lips.

'Ahhh, gerr off!' I said, wriggling out of her grasp.

But she hung on, her nails digging into my cheek as she tried to see better into my mouth. I'd had enough.

'Get *off*!' I shouted, and with a surge of frustration and anger I felt a new power well up inside me. The power flowed like red hot lava through my veins, along my arms and out of my fingers. My mouth opened in an 'O' shape, as I saw a similar white light to Franny's flow out and Eva was flung back across the room. Simultaneously, my fangs erupted and adrenaline surged through my body, making me crouch into an offensive position.

'I think there is your answer, but I think it may have been wiser to find it out another way,' Franny said to Eva, as she walked over to me.

'Jessie dear, you have more power than you know how to handle for now. You need to be trained. The vampire's will only teach you war, but you are free to choose you own path now, to come back to your family.'

I looked across the room at Daniel and Eva. Daniel had remained silent. He looked devastated. Eva's eyes flashed and she looked ready to kill, but they were my family. They were the ones who even now wanted only to protect me.

'You're right,' I said, feeling my fangs recede and my heartbeat quiet to its almost-dead rhythm. 'I can make my own choice now, and I'm going to. But I have no intention of leaving Manchester, or you,' I said, turning and smiling at Daniel. 'I want to see Sebastian... later, but now I want all of you to get the hell out of my room, and leave me in peace.'

'But dearie, I need to...'

'And you too. *Especially* you!' I said to Franny, as I saw Eva break into a grin.

I didn't care. I'd had enough of the 'dearies' and there was something I didn't quite trust about her. Everyone had their own motives when it came to me – hell, even Eva! I knew she'd do anything for Sebastian, but the difference was I knew that and she never hid the truth from me. Daniel was pretty much the only person I *could* trust, it seemed. My own father had lied to me about my birth mother, and my very annoying ex-boyfriend had failed to mention that he was *not* the human boy I happened to fall in love with, but an angel placed near me to monitor my magical DNA. Now there was Franny, who seemed all welcoming and grandmotherly – something I deeply wanted in my life right now. However, life had taught me not to trust anymore, and she'd already admitted to pulling the wool over the vampires' eyes in order to fulfil this ceremony, at whatever cost. I was powerful, and the coven wanted me. I'd have to find out why later.

All Daniel had ever wanted was me, to protect me, to love me, and now with the bond gone, I could see if we had true feelings for each other. I remembered our afternoon together and smiled.

'You can stay,' I said, looking over at him.

'You heard the girl... and *you* are going to have some explaining to do to Sebastian about this mess. Out now,' Eva said, as she indicated Franny should leave the room, although managing to keep a healthy distance between the two of them.

'You're gorgeous,' Daniel said, sitting down on my bed, staring at me.

'The eyes are cool, huh? I always wanted green eyes,' I said, with a grin.

'Are you sure you're fine, really?' He asked.

'Yes, I think so. Are you?'

'Yes, it was just a shock, when it happened. It hurt...losing you,' he said.

'I know. It feels hollow now, like something's missing.'

'We might be able to get it back, if you feed from

me again,' he said.

I'd already thought the same, as it seemed likely, but I didn't know if I wanted our bond back. Yes, it felt weird, but there was also a new lightness I could feel. First I needed to understand what exactly had happened to me, what had changed. I'd obviously had my powers released, going off the lightning bolts that came from my fingers and I obviously still had my fangs. So was I really both? Half-vampire and half-witch? Maybe I could eat food now? But more than anything I needed to know what my true feelings for Daniel were; whether my attraction was natural, simply fate as he thought it was, or a product of our bond, and something I had no control over.

'Maybe, but first I want to work out who I am, without being bonded to you,' I told him.

'You mean you want to see what Luke thinks of you, now that you don't have a vampire's eyes,' he challenged.

'No! Actually I hadn't thought about Luke, but it would be nice to find out whether my feelings for you weren't a by-product of our bond.

'Luke may be interested in you, now you've got witches' eyes, but once he finds out you've still got fangs, he won't hang around.'

'I know Daniel, I know, and I meant what I said. I hadn't actually thought about him. What happened earlier...I'm not just going to forget that you know, and anyway, Luke was an ass!'

'Luke *is* an ass,' Daniel said with a grin, as he pulled me over and rolled on top of me on the bed.

'You *are* really sexy with those eyes though. I could get used to that,' he said, leaning in for a kiss, his lips grinding against mine, as he slid a hand under my head and pulled me ever closer.

There was a single knock on the door and Eva popped her head round.

'Ooops! Sorry to interrupt, but Sebastian says he wants to see you tonight and the club's just closing up, so now's a good time.'

'Eva, it's nearly three in the morning. I'm knackered,' I said, pushing Daniel off me.

'I bet you are,' she replied with a wicked smile. 'Still, get your ass in gear, we're leaving in two minutes.'

'Ughh! Come on then. Better not aggravate her wickedness! After all there's only so many times a vampire can take being disobeyed...or thrown against a wall,' Daniel said with a smirk.

'Very funny! You didn't look so clever yourself as you went sailing across the room and into the wall,' Eva replied, as she stalked out.

Half an hour later, I was sitting in one of Sebastian's

expensive leather armchairs in his office, waiting for him to finish a phone call. Eva had gone to find some poor, besotted boy to have dinner with, or rather from, and as Daniel had fed earlier in the evening, he was sitting with me, waiting.

'So, I hear the initiation had surprising consequences?' Sebastian said, as he wandered over. 'What we need to find out is how surprising they seemed to Francesca.'

'I think she knew what she was doing. She set up a magic circle to keep Eva and I out', Daniel replied. 'Once the ceremony was taking place, there was nothing we could do but watch.'

'A protective circle would be set up, regardless of any consequences that may or may not have been anticipated. It's what they do. It protects their magic from things worse than angry vampires, Daniel.'

'Yes, but it's also a happy coincidence, isn't it?' Daniel sneered.

'What? That you weren't able to stop her? Would we have wanted her to be stopped?'

'What do you mean? You knew too? You knew this would rip Jess away from me? I should have known!' Daniel's eyes began to darken, and a low growl burst from his lips, as he hunched his shoulders into an offensive position.

'Daniel, remember your place, or will I need to

remind you? Neither you nor I knew for sure what the effects would be on Jess. How could we? Francesca certainly didn't discuss it with me, but I suspect they were banking on it, and as I am rather more intelligent than they think I am, I considered it as a possibility. It was a chance worth taking.'

'How can you say that? Jess was mine, not yours to experiment upon.'

'Umm guys...hello? I am here, you know. And for God's sake Daniel, I am *not* yours, okay? You know that pisses me off!' I said.

'You know what I mean,' Daniel muttered, not taking his eyes from Sebastian.

'Yeah, I do know what you mean, and I've had enough of it! I don't belong to you, just because you made me. I'm different, deal with it!'

'Fine, so you want to be Sebastian's little lap dog instead?'

'No, I belong to no one, not you and not Sebastian,' I said, hoping that Sebastian wouldn't take it the wrong way and bang me up in one of his cells again. But Sebastian only laughed, loudly.

'I think the best we can hope to get from our little vampire witch here is loyalty born from respect, and Jess you do still have to respect me, as the others do, if you stay on in Manchester. You don't have a free ticket to do as you please,' he said.

'I want the bond reinstated. I believe it will be mended if Jessie drinks from me once again,' Daniel interrupted, his eyes bright.

'And what does Jess say about this?' Sebastian answered.

'What does it matter? I am her maker, we should have a bond,' he replied, refusing to look me in the eye.

'You have got to be kidding me. Daniel, what did I say before? I don't want it reinstated yet. I want to know my true feelings, our true feelings. Don't do this, please,' I said.

'Our feelings were fine *with* the bond intact. You knew perfectly well who you were. We were good together,' he said.

'You're scared. You're scared I'll go back to Luke or not choose you, and I guess there's a chance of that happening, especially if you keep acting like a jerk, but if you force this I *will* leave. I *will* go with Franny, to America, and never come back.'

'Well, I think there's your answer Daniel,' Sebastian said.

'Don't you tell me what my answer is! You should be on my side and you should be more interested in her being a part of our clan,' Daniel stormed, as he leapt from the chair and stood facing us both, fire raging in his eyes.

It was a strange feeling, because I had grown used to the bond between us. I was used to feeling his anger and hurt when I rejected him, just as I had felt his heart leap when I finally accepted him, but now I felt nothing. I could see the anger and hurt, plainly written on his face, yet I had only *my* emotions in my head and I felt free.

'Daniel you are hungry, and I can only hope that it is the reason for this highly irregular behaviour...' Sebastian said, before I interrupted him.

'He only fed a few hours ago. He was out when the ceremony was taking place.'

'Yes, but Jess, we are not all like you. You may only need a minimum amount of nourishment, but from the looks of it you nearly drained Daniel earlier and it will take more than one meal to satisfy his needs,' Sebastian answered.

'It's not her fault. I let her feed a little longer than I should, but that is not the reason I...' Daniel said, pausing as Eva walked in the room.

'Sebastian, I think it may be best if I take Daniel out again, if you agree of course?' she said.

'Of course. You go, Daniel. Eva will talk to you, but you need to understand the situation we are in. I know this is not what you planned when you turned Jess, and you are one of the youngest, yet it seems we have to accept certain changes...for the time being at least,' he said with a small smile.

Once they had gone, Sebastian turned his eyes back to me and said nothing, staring, so I felt like I was suddenly falling down a black, bottomless wormhole in space, and this time Daniel would never hear my thoughts...or even my screams.

'You're making me nervous,' I stated, breaking the silence.

'I hoped as much. It is always imperative to have the upper hand when dealing with a witch, even a young witch,' he said with a smile. 'And you certainly look like a witch to me.'

'I've still got fangs,' I replied, with a half-smile.

'So I hear, but I have yet to see them for myself. Your eyes are dazzling green, your skin is flushed, pink...'

'That's because of feeding from Daniel earlier,' I said, hoping to distract his strange, hollow gaze.

'Maybe, but your scent has changed too; the witch in you is much stronger now. It reminds me of...ahh never mind. Let us move on,' he said, abruptly giving his head a very slight shake, and relaxing his shoulders.

Who was the other witch he had known, years earlier? The same witch who had given him his powerful, protective charm. The same charm that had destroyed his head henchman, only a couple of weeks earlier when he was caught trying to rape me and overthrow Sebastian's position. Did my scent now remind him of her?

I shouldn't have paused, as his eyes were once again glued to me, drawing me deep into their inky depths.

'Sebastian, I am still a vampire. I'm just a witch too, and that's what you wanted, wasn't it?'

'Hmm,' he sighed. 'Your scent; I can't seem to get over it. Do you remember the first time Daniel brought you to me? Do you remember how *useful*, and how pleasant my little experiment was?' he asked.

Oh no! I wasn't liking the sound of this. I remembered only too well how he had insisted on tasting my blood when he first took me into his clan. How Eva had said he had the singular talent of gauging someone's motives and personality through their blood. How his fangs felt as they pierced my flesh, and how hot certain parts of me had become during the brief second he drank from me. And how Daniel had read my mind and jealously stormed off down the corridor.

Oh Daniel! But Daniel wouldn't know what was going on this time, and yet this time it would feel wrong. It had taken a long time for me to accept that Luke was no longer a part of my life, and gradually my feelings for Daniel had grown. We may have gone further this time than the others, but this had not been a one-off. I did care about Daniel, I was sure of it, even without our bond, and even if he *was* acting like a possessive idiot! I didn't want to go messing it up, by getting hot with Sebastian.

It seemed that I had spent too long in my head, because suddenly I jolted back into the present to find Sebastian leaning in close, his eyes shining brightly, his fangs protruding and heading towards my neck.

CHAPTER EIGHT

'Sebastian! Getthehelloffme...Gerroff...ugh!' My words came out as a jumble, as his full weight pinned me down and compressed my chest.

He pulled back a little, and I sucked air back into my lungs and glared at him.

'Come on sweet Jessie, my little witch. You know it won't hurt and it's the best option all round. I get to trust you, and we'll both know just how much vampire is left in there.'

'It's not that, and you know it. Daniel will freak when he finds out, and this is hard enough for him anyway,' I said.

'Hmm. He let out almost a groan, as he once again pushed against me. Why had I chosen to sit on the only two seater sofa, and not the chair?

'Well, as I'm his master, I'll just have to force you, then you won't be held accountable,' he said, and in one swift movement, quicker than a human could blink, his hands gripped my head, both cradling and forcing it to the side, exposing the thick artery running down my neck.

As his fangs pierced my skin, goosebumps shivered up and down my spine and I heard myself let out a low moan of desire. Damn! He heard it and was spurred on, pulling me underneath him on the sofa, pinning me below his body as he too groaned and dug his hand into my hair, crushing his mouth into my neck.

The first time I'd met Sebastian he had tasted me and turned me on simultaneously, which vexed Daniel as much as it mortified me. But this time he set my body on fire. His cool, hard skin felt delicious pressed against me and as he drank, he ground against me. Everything seemed to happen so suddenly, and it was only minutes before I realised he wasn't going to stop, or wasn't able to stop. This was not the same Sebastian who had once politely pulled away, leaving me panting, after only the briefest bite. Something had changed the status quo... I was now a fully fledged witch, and he was addicted to my taste. Hadn't he mentioned a witch who was a 'very good friend', a powerful witch, he spoke about with obvious affection...a witch who was now dead?

The heat coursing round my body stilled and I felt cold. How much had he taken already? I pushed against him, but it was like having a thousand year old lump of granite pinning me down. I couldn't budge, and every movement I made seemed to spur him on. Shit! I needed magic. I tried to focus, as the book had taught me. I needed to work fast because the very energy I needed was being literally sucked out of me. I drew it to me, and closing my eyes, focused on connecting to another energy source. I tried the taproot meditation, imagined myself connecting to the earth and drawing up her energy, taking it into my body, and letting it flow up my spine and along my arms.

As the extra energy entered my body, he obviously noticed the difference because he let out another, louder moan and his fangs penetrated even deeper.

'GET OFF ME! GET OFF!' I shouted, concentrating all the energy into my hands, and not really worrying about the consequences, I imagined it firing from my palms, catapulting him across the room, sending him as far away from me as possible.

It worked. In one swift movement his body was whipped from mine and flung across the room, electrified by an invisible current, where it slammed with an almighty crack into the far wall. A human would be dead, but of course Sebastian was a thousand year old vampire and not quite as easy to kill.

Seconds after the impact, the door burst open revealing Troy and Isabelle, two of his bodyguards, who took one glance at him and then launched themselves at me. I really needed to take the time to learn a protection spell, and I certainly didn't have the time to conjure a circle, in fact by the time I'd finished thinking about it, they were on me.

'YOU TWO, OUT! NOW!' Sebastian was on his feet, and with his command forcing them to retreat, they dropped me, confusion dancing across their faces, as they backed up and left the room.

It seemed I was the only one left round here with any free will, and I wondered why he allowed it. I still expected retribution. A very pissed off Sebastian stared at me from across the room. Had I pushed him too far this time? Hell no! He was about to drain me, and what about the other witch?

'You drained her didn't you? You killed her,' I said, wondering if I was in my right mind. 'You would have drained *me*, if I hadn't done something,' I added.

My words seemed to have a strange effect on him. His anger dissipated, and crumpled. I didn't quite believe it could be true, from the mighty Sebastian, but was that a single dark tear, hanging on the edge of his eyelid? He turned his back on me, walked swiftly back to his desk and sank down. He looked at me briefly, nodded and stared towards a small high window.

'Her name was Alba, she was only fifteen when I

smuggled her out of Italy, in 1647. She was to be tried for heresy and sorcery. Her mother had already been beheaded and burned at the stake a week before.'

'Oh God! I… but she was only fifteen, you say?' I asked.

'Do not begin to judge me, Jessica. You are only two years older than her, and as it happens I was in love with her mother. It was Caterina who cast the spell which protects me still, knowing she was going to die, and to help me get Alba out of the country.'

'Oh!' I said. 'But I thought you killed her? I thought that was what was going on here?'

'I did. Not Caterina. I killed Alba. You are right of course. I drained her, and she died later in my arms.'

'But how? I don't understand. If you loved her mother…you wouldn't have done that. Why would you have done that?' I was rambling now, afraid of the answer, yet also sure I needed to hear it. Sebastian was scary as hell, sure, but he'd always been fair to me. He was not the monster I was picturing in my mind.

'We made it out of Italy, all the way to France, but in the sixteen hundreds the Inquisition was all over Europe. It was the opposite of today - *everybody* readily believed in demons, vampires and witches. We were ambushed just outside Paris, not by witch hunters this time, but vampire hunters. They knew what I was, but the first we knew of it was my head being half-severed from my body. Luckily for me they had a blunt axe, and I had the shield. Jessica, you look very pale, can I get you something?'

'No, I'm fine. I'm sure Daniel will be back soon. What happened then?'

'The shield fried two of them, and the others ran away. They could see I wouldn't last the night,' he shrugged, his face etched with memories. I said nothing, and waited.

'I told her to run, to leave me and go back to the city, but she refused. She stayed with me for the hours it took for my neck to heal, by which time I had no blood left and no energy to even rise to my feet. Again I told her to leave me, as dawn was fast approaching, and with it a new army of hunters would arrive to finish the job.'

'But she didn't go did she? She let you feed from her instead?' I asked, knowing the answer to be true. He nodded.

'She lay in my blood, next to me and told me to drink. I was weak. I had no control. I told myself I would take just enough for me to get us both to safety, but she tasted so pure, so sweet. I could not stop. I failed Caterina, I murdered her daughter, and I fled France and came to England.'

'But if you were in love with her mother,

presumably you had tasted her? Then why were you not able to stop with me? I am not pure, not like Alba would have been,' I said.

'You *are* special Jessica, maybe not in the same way that Alba was, and yes I was used to the taste of Caterina, but I have not tasted witch blood for five hundred years. Yes I had a taste when you were first brought here by Daniel, but his blood was strong in you then, and I purposely only took the tiniest bite. Your blood was merely laced with witch blood. Now you are an initiated witch, and any vampire who comes across you will want a taste.'

'Fantastic! But what about the rest? Could you still detect vampire blood?' I asked.

'Yes, the blood bond may be broken, but I could still taste Daniel's blood within yours. You are a vampire Jessica, but we will have to wait to find out which one is stronger. In the meantime, thank you for stopping me. It would have been most unfortunate to lose your exuberant will from our clan, but I think we will tell Troy and Isabelle you were practising defence magic, yes?' he said.

I nodded back, grinning again.

'Now, our last little problem is putting some colour back into your cheeks, because if Daniel sees you looking all pasty again, we could have an unfortunate display of protectiveness on our hands. I could get you your usual bottled type, but I'm not sure of its effectiveness in such a dire situation. I feel it only fair that I repay my debt to you in kind, so to speak.'

'No! The bond. Daniel would kill us if I bonded to you, and I don't want to be bonded to anyone right now,' I said.

'You can only bond to Daniel, of that I am sure. You are already a vampire Jess, and Daniel remains your creator, so it will be safe to drink from me, and also the quickest way to get your blood back,' he added with his typical slow, sexy smile.

Damn! 'Okay then,' I said, knowing what he said was true. Even if I had a couple of bottles of blood, Daniel would know the difference immediately.

In what seemed like one fluid movement Sebastian left his desk chair, crossed the room and sat himself next to me on the couch again. And here we were again! However, this time he was gentle, his eyes focused on the window, controlling his inner demons as he pulled my face towards his neck.

I sighed. It had to be done, it really was the best way. His scent was musky, heavy and masculine. I paused, breathing it in and waiting for my vampire instincts to take over and my fangs to break out, but it didn't happen.

'Um Sebastian, I have a little problem...no fangs,' I mumbled. 'I had fangs earlier, when I threw Eva across the room, I know I did, I just can't seem to access them now. I...'

'Here, how about now?' he said, as he ran a sharp nail through the skin, making a small incision and letting his blood pool at the surface.

Seconds later, the scent of the fresh blood assaulted my senses, the hungry vampire took over and losing my inhibitions, I jumped on him. My arms wrapped around his neck, my hand pulling at his dark, almost black hair. I clamped my mouth to his neck, feeling my teeth bite down hard into his flesh. He moaned with pleasure and pulled me round, so I was sitting in his lap, his hands running up and down my body. A moan of desire matched his own, but the fire didn't burn quite as hot as with Daniel. I untangled my fingers from his hair and still greedily gulping down his blood, reached for his hands and held them still. This wasn't about sex, this was about dinner.

A couple of minutes later he gently brought his hands up to my face and holding my jaw, he pushed me back. I climbed off and sat back, embarrassed as I attempted to wipe my mouth with a handkerchief he handed me. I was buzzing, alive, and wanting Daniel.

'Daniel and Eva will be here any minute. It appears there has been some trouble,' he said staring into the distance.

'How do you know? Oh your bond...of course. Will

Eva know what we've done?' I asked.

'No, I made her, so she only knows what I want her to.'

What's happened? Is Daniel alright?'

'Yes they are fine. Eva will explain when they arrive. Ahh, they're here now.'

The door swung open and Eva, followed by Daniel, Troy and Isabelle entered the room. Troy and Isabelle were the first to glance warily across the room, but at a stern glance from Sebastian, neither said a thing.

'What happened?' Sebastian asked.

'The police have found a body a couple of streets away, a young girl, one of our regular feeders. We believe she's been drained, but we couldn't get there in time. The police are all over it,' Eva said.

'Well, there'll be no proof we need to worry about. The teeth marks should have disappeared almost immediately. Who was the girl's favourite?' Sebastian asked.

As I watched them from Sebastian's side, I noticed a quick glance pass between Daniel and Eva. Something was being said through their bond. Something I wasn't supposed to hear, but then Eva shrugged, and Daniel took a step forward.

'A while back she was known to be a favourite of mine. I haven't seen her for weeks though.' He glanced at me, concern etched in his eyes. Daniel had a favourite? He had promised me he didn't, but then he did say this was weeks ago…

My thoughts drifted off, as I thought about what was being said, what Daniel had told me, and all that had gone on over the last twenty four hours. A yawn escaped my lips and all eyes centred on me.

'Right! Well, Daniel, you take Jess home. She's had a busy day and needs to rest. For the time being I am happy to let her be; bondless. I don't want to hear any more about it, and it seems like we have a new problem to fix now anyway,' Sebastian said.

'Daniel was with me all night. He is blameless,' Eva said, her eyes flicking between Daniel and Sebastian.

'*Nearly* all night,' the vampire known as Isabelle said. 'There was the ten minutes you were feeding with that young pup that follows you round.'

'You know quite well Daniel wouldn't drain anyone, so stop making trouble Izzy, you bitch,' Eva said, menace flashing in her eyes.

'Now girls, I'm sure we all know Daniel is not to blame for this, so let's get it sorted as soon as possible. Daniel you take Jess. Eva, Isabelle and Troy, I'll chat to you, each in turn. Eva first. Daniel I'll catch up with you tomorrow.'

CHAPTER NINE

On our return to the house Daniel paced the ground floor, back and forth until I stopped him and asked the words he'd been expecting to hear.

'Hey! Stop a minute. I know it wasn't you, okay? Sebastian knows too, or else he wouldn't have let you come home with me,' I said, sure of his innocence. 'When did you last see her anyway? Have you fed from her...since me?'

At my final question, Daniel stopped pacing and looked at me. We were standing in the back living room, the girl's room, and he took both my hands and pulled me down so we sat next to each other on the couch.

'Jessie, I swear it wasn't me. You know I wouldn't, don't you?'

I'd already answered that question so I nodded again, and waited for more.

'Her name was Sophie, and yes she was a regular before I met you. The last time I saw her was actually the night before you awakened and we took you to

Cumbria. I told her that night I was going away. She was fine,' he said.

'And you haven't seen her since? Doesn't she know you live here?'

'No, honestly I haven't, and we never tell feeders where we live, as sometimes they become too dependent. It complicates things.'

'Right, so you have nothing to worry about then. Eva knows you haven't seen her either, and she was already vouching for you tonight.'

'It's not just me I'm worried about. She was a sweet girl Jess. She didn't deserve to die, and the fact that she was also drained leads to more concern. *Why?*'

'Oh! Of course. I'm sorry.' I didn't know what to say. Shit! Of course this girl obviously meant something to him, and I was acting like it was nothing. It wasn't nothing, but I didn't know the girl. I mean if you let vampires feed from you, there had to be a risk factor involved. My concern was Daniel, but he had other ideas.

'It's fine. Look, I'm sure you've got some spells to be learning anyway. I need some time to think, Jess. I think it means something,' he said, and with that he left the room.

I wanted to run after him. I didn't like to let things go, not until I had them sorted out in my head, but instinct told me to give him time. So deciding there was nothing more I could do, I headed upstairs to get some sleep.

It seemed the dead girl had caused a furore within both the human world and the supernatural one, and whilst Daniel was called to interviews with both Sebastian and the Council, I watched the human story unfold on the television. Obviously the police, doctors and forensics were stumped, as living in the twenty first century no one was able to admit to believing in *monsters*. Equally there were no wounds to be found on the girl; bite wounds would have healed even before her death. Consequently, they were bewildered as to how she had lost three quarters of her blood. Requests were put out for information, but it seemed no one knew the girl, or where she was from.

With the distraction all of this caused, I was relieved to find that for the time being, Daniel let the subject of our bond drop. I spent the time studying my Book of Shadows, and the Wiccan handbook Franny had brought me. Franny herself had returned to Boston, realising for the time being that she needed to steer clear of Eva and Daniel.

Daniel was quickly cleared of suspicion within the Council, but continued to act strangely; quiet and withdrawn. We needed to get out.

'Daniel, let's go to the club tonight. Eva mentioned

she was going to meet up with some friends, and we need to get out,' I said.

'I didn't think you liked Exodus, Jess. Are you sure you can handle it, after last time?'

'Sure, that was months ago now. I have to move on, just like you. We live here, and we can't hide forever,' I said.

Exodus was Sebastian's nightclub, and the club where I had first met Daniel. It was also just round the corner from the alleyway where I'd been attacked and left to die by a girl gang, after losing my best friend and deciding, rather stupidly to walk down a shortcut to the main road. That night Daniel had found me and given me his blood, and the next time I visited Exodus I was a new born vampire, with rather unsettling DNA. Every time I visited the club something went wrong, be it me coming face to face with old friends – who luckily didn't recognise me – or me unleashing uncontrollable magic and destroying Eva's nineteenth century dressing table. Then there was the time I decided to seek revenge on the girl gang, and ended up in Sebastian's cells, and of course the final time when Sebastian nearly drained me and we found out Daniel's feeder had been killed! It didn't bode well, but something told me my luck had to change.

It was a Thursday night, student night at Exodus, which meant cheap drinks and jeans. Not that we'd be drinking the drinks, just buying them for show. Then again, maybe tonight with my green eyes glowing under the lights, I'd give my old favourite a try.

'Hi Johnny,' I said, to the only vampire bartender in the place, the guy who Alex, my best friend and I had decided was 'Manchester's Best Looking Bartender', before I was turned into a vampire myself and forbidden from contacting Alex again. She thought I was dead, and I missed her like crazy.

'Wow Jess, those are some awesome contacts you've got there. How'd you get them past Sebastian? Thought we weren't allowed to change our eye colour?' he said.

'Erm, haven't you heard? They're not contacts. My initiation…' I trailed off, unsure as to how much Sebastian's staff had been told about me.

'Oh right! Wow! So it's true then.' He suddenly took a step back and his eyes flicked nervously from side to side.

'Hey Johnny, get us some drinks will you. She's not going to turn you into a toad,' Eva said, coming up quickly behind me and giving me a quick hug.

'Erm, I was going to try a rum and coke,' I said, wishing I could sound more confident.

'Later, okay? We don't need any dramatics just yet. Let's relax. Thanks Johnny,' she said, grabbing the fake beer bottles and striding off to the corner table where

Daniel and a couple of other vampires were sitting.

As I sat down, all conversation stopped and all eyes zeroed in on me, searching my face, gazing with wonder at my eyes. I tried to ignore it and pulled up a chair next to Daniel.

'So, what's new?' I asked.

As an attempt to shatter the awkwardness it worked and everybody laughed.

'Right, let me rephrase that, what's new apart from my freaky green eyes?' I asked with a grin.

As conversation returned to normal I relaxed and settled back. My bottle of slightly warmed blood nourished me, but didn't excite me; in fact it tasted worse than usual.

'Eva, is this blood different? It doesn't taste great,' I said.

'Oh! So you're finally developing tastebuds now are you? No, these are the same, they always taste rank.'

After we'd finished our drinks, I noticed Daniel had relaxed and was engrossed in conversation with Troy about the latest football league results, so I grabbed Eva and we headed to the dance floor.

I'd always loved dancing, and Alex and I had danced till dawn most weekends of our first term at university. I missed her, but Eva was a great substitute, her movements fluid and sexy, and we developed that intuitive link girls have when they dance together. Our bodies moved in time with both the music and each other. We laughed and smiled as we watched the boys around us circle, their eyes fixed on our writhing bodies. How easy it would be to take things one step further and choose one to take somewhere quiet, to kiss him, hypnotise him...bite him. Whoa! What was I thinking? I'd never thought that before. The one thing that really stood me apart from my fellow vamps was my unswerving dislike of feeding from humans. I had never bitten anyone but Daniel, and as I told Luke, I had no intention of changing that.

'Hey, what's up?' Eva asked, pulling me off the dance floor.

'Nothing. I'm fine... I err.. just thought I saw someone from Uni,' I said, quickly thinking of an excuse. If Eva knew what I'd been thinking, she'd have me upstairs in her room with a tasty boy before I could shout *'vampire'*! She'd already tried, unsuccessfully, to tempt me with a hot, young hypnotised lad once before, and I knew if I showed the slightest bit of interest she'd do it again. Both she and Sebastian were desperate to get me off bottled blood, and I could see it wasn't fair –and maybe it wasn't safe – to feed too much from Daniel either. I needed to sort out my diet. Franny had thought it possible that becoming a stronger witch would allow me to eat normal food, so why was I now having strong cravings for human blood?

As we moved away from the dance floor and pushed our way through the crowds of students, my eyes constantly searched the area. I'd already spotted Gemma, Lucy and Tom here on a previous occasion. Gemma had locked eyes with me, and I wondered if she'd recognised me in that split second before I blew the lights, but I'd never seen Alex, and now I wanted to. Now I was ready.

Not that she'd believe me. She'd probably think I was a crazy girl. After all she'd been to my funeral, and she'd seen the horrific pictures of the blood stained alleyway in the papers…but then again, Alex was my best friend, and if anyone could see past the new eye colour, skinny frame and dyed hair it would be her.

A couple of hours later, I decided I needed a new plan. We were on our way home, Daniel and Eva chatting easily in the front and I was relieved to see that Daniel had relaxed and appeared to be much happier again. In contrast, I felt a strange sense of foreboding, and stared out of the window, watching the dark empty streets roll by, wondering what Alex was doing. I'd scoured the club for her, sure she'd be there, and after all it *was* student night, and it was long enough after my death for her to be out again. I told myself I was stupid. It was three in the morning, she'd probably be sleeping, and after all it must be getting near exam time. There were loads of reasons for her *not* to be out.

If I wanted to see her, I was going to have to start doing things on my own. I was a witch now. I was powerful, more powerful than Daniel and Eva probably and they would have to learn to give me independence and trust. Trust I would have to break, if I wanted to see Alex again.

However, when we got home someone else was waiting for us, for *me*.

As Daniel opened the front door, both vampires stood immobile for a second before launching themselves down the corridor, slamming open the kitchen door and coming to a comical halt before a figure who was seated at the table, a glass of water in his hand.

'What the hell do you want, and what made you think you could enter our house without being asked?' Eva demanded.

I had of course closed the door and sprinted up the hallway after them, entering the kitchen only seconds after they had. I stood and stared. Luke was sitting at the table, his face arrogant and unapologetic, his wings thankfully hidden beneath his clothes.

'I came to speak to Jess. I didn't think you'd want me hanging around outside and raising suspicion, but then again, I forgot how jealous you vampires can be about the whole 'entering a house' rule.'

'Oh shut up! Don't be ridiculous. It's nothing to do with that. Just common decency, which you angelic ones seem to think is an outdated commodity,' Eva said.

'What are you talking about?' I asked, pushing my way into the kitchen and standing opposite Luke.

'So, it's true? The initiation worked then?' Luke said.

'Well it's made my eyes green, if that's what you mean, but I'm still a vampire. That's not changed,' I said, thinking back to the scene in the club, and my thirst for the boy's blood.

'What do you want?' I asked, looking at his arrogant features and wondering what had happened to the boy I once knew.

'Alex has gone missing. I saw her a couple of weeks ago, after she came back from her parent's house at Easter break. She missed most of the previous term because of you, as she'd gone back home after your father's funeral. I wanted her to change universities, but she said she was coming back,' Luke said.

'And she did? She came back?' I asked.

'Yes. I helped her move her stuff into a new room in Fallowfield two weeks ago. Lucy said she saw her in lectures that week, but no one's seen her at all this week. I wondered if you had anything to do with it?' he said, his eyes hardening and searching all our faces.

'You have got to be kidding? After everything I've told you, and all you've seen, you still think we might hurt her?' I said, my voice beginning to tremble. 'I'm not allowed to see her. I haven't seen her since Dad's funeral. Oh God! Is she okay?'

'What is *that*?' Eva interrupted. A quiet *miaow* was suddenly heard, as we all glared at each other.

'Oh yeah! So, I brought your cat. Alex had been looking after him, but she's not allowed pets in her new house, so I said I'd take him. I thought you might like him?' he said, his tone suddenly softening as he reached down to the cat basket by his feet.

'No way!' Eva said, as I simultaneously threw myself round the table to the ground and popped open the latch on the basket.

'Murphy!' I crooned, as I pulled the sleek, beautiful Siamese stray out of the basket and into my lap.

CHAPTER TEN

'Err Jess, cats don't get on with vampires so much,' Eva said, eyeing the cat with suspicion.

'He doesn't seem to mind Jess though,' Daniel said with a smile, as I rubbed under Murphy's chin and sent him into an ecstasy of purrs.

'So is this the stray you told Sebastian about?' Eva asked.

'Yes, he just kept turning up at our flat window, and he was so skinny we started feeding him. I called him Murphy because he must have been so thirsty that first day we let him in, he stuck his head in this Irish lad's glass of stout and had a taste. It was so funny... he got all the foam on his whiskers,' I laughed.

'Hey Murphy,' Daniel said, holding out his hand as he approached.

But Eva was right, cats didn't like vampires, and he leapt from my lap, hissed at Daniel and ran from the kitchen, into the house.

'Oh dear. I guess you'll have to choose, Jess. Daniel or Murphy, who's it to be?' Luke sneered, the corners of his mouth turning up.

'What's got into you lately, Luke? You're so mean,' I said.

'*You*, dealing with you. Having to see the mistake I made every time I see you.'

I let out an irritated sigh and hoped Daniel would be able to restrain himself, because I was sure that he would be visualising breaking Luke's neck in 3D technicolour, with every word he said.

'Look, Murphy will be fine. He'll get used to us, and thanks for bringing him, but hadn't we better find Alex?' I said, my hurt feelings squashed by daggers of irritation.

'She probably just went home. Maybe she decided she couldn't take it, being back in Manchester?' Daniel said, helping me back onto my feet and leaving his arm around my waist.

'Do you not think I would have checked that before I came into this vampire infested lair?' Luke drawled.

'No one invited you angel-boy, and you heard Jess. We haven't seen Alex, so you can go do your sleuthing elsewhere,' Eva said.

'Do you think I could talk to Jess alone, without her two minders, for one minute…or are you too important for that now?' he said, turning to look at me.

'Why do you need her on her own?' Daniel asked, his arm creeping up and pulling me to him, his fingers digging into my shoulder.

'It's fine. You guys go and watch TV. I'll be in in a bit,' I said.

'What is wrong with you?' I hissed, turning on him as they reluctantly left the room.

'Nothing. What do you mean?' he said, with a quick shrug of his shoulders.

'I don't know you anymore Luke. You're so... angry.'

I looked at him, and stepped towards him, and suddenly he looked up, tears in his eyes. He took my hands and stared into my eyes.

'I'm sorry, I just... I can't take it. I can't deal with it... what I did to you, what I made you. Everything has gone wrong. It shouldn't have been like this,' he said.

'Luke, *you* didn't make me what I am, Daniel did.'

'Yes, but it was my decision. You know that. I left you to him...'

'Yes, because you didn't want me to die.'

'But you did die Jess, and what's worse, you're one of *them*.'

'Oh, not that again! Please Luke. I am what I am, and yes, that's a vampire, but really I am no more evil than you, and *you* are apparently an angel, so I can't be all that bad,' I said with a grin.

'I'm sorry. I guess I was taken aback when I saw your eyes. You look so beautiful… human again,' he said.

'But Luke, I'm not. I'm still a vampire. I just have much better control of my powers now,' I said, pulling my hands out of his.

'How do you know? Have you even tried eating normal food? I bet they wouldn't let you, would they?'

'No, I haven't tried yet, but I will, I promise, and it's not about what they will and won't let me do. I make my own decisions, okay, but you need to know, I can still *smell* humans. I still *want* to bite them,' I said, not able to meet his eyes.

'So that's it then, my final hope destroyed.'

'If that's how you see it, fine. I love Daniel, I think. He doesn't care whether I'm a witch or a vampire. He's hurting because the spell broke our bond, but I can show him that we never needed a bond. I'd like to be friends Luke, I really would, but more importantly I'm worried about Alex. We need to find her,' I said.

As I'd spoken, he looked at the floor, and when I finished he nodded.

'I'll ask around the campus again, see if I can come up with anything new. If I haven't seen her by Monday, I'll let you know.'

'Thanks Luke, and thanks for bringing Murphy. I

missed him. I miss you all.'

He nodded again, briefly. With a quick duck of his head he stood, turned abruptly and exited through the patio doors, disappearing into the garden, where the sun was just beginning to appear on the horizon, casting out the murky shadows of the night.

The following afternoon I was dressed for action, running through my proposal, with Murphy purring contentedly in my lap. The previous night, I had found him waiting for me when I'd gone up to my room, curled up, right in the centre of my bed, so I had to fit myself around him in order to sleep. I'd still managed a good eight hour sleep though, and for the first time I felt like I could put Luke behind me, filed under 'ex-boyfriends worthy of keeping in contact', unlike a few creeps which were filed under the 'biggest mistake ever/what on earth was I thinking' title.

As I'd slept through the morning, I woke up to find that Daniel had gone out, apparently doing some work for Sebastian. I still wasn't sure what all Sebastian's clan members did for him. Obviously some were bodyguards and some worked in the club, but it was unclear what other members like Eva & Daniel did for him to pay back their 'loans'. The loan system was the money and new identity which Sebastian handed out to the newly created vampires, made by him and his 'family'. I had yet to receive my 'loan' and identity, and obviously I couldn't use any of my old details. Officially I was now dead and buried!

After about two hundred and twenty years Eva had paid back her loan and was now a free vampire. She had her own investments and stayed with Sebastian's clan through loyalty and friendship. She'd been about to start a fashion design course, until Daniel had changed me, and found he had taken on more than they both anticipated, but now that things were settling down she spent her days lazing on our couch, watching mind-numbing television and bossing me about. Things were going to change.

'Hey Eva, I'm going out in a bit. I want to head over to some of my old university haunts, and see if I can find anything out about Alex,' I said, gently lifting Murphy from my lap and standing up. I said the sentence perfectly; after all I'd practiced it for about half an hour, practised to sound confident, in a tone she wouldn't question.

'I'm sorry, what?' Eva said, jumping from her seat and following me into the kitchen.

'Okay, so I know I've never been out on my own, blah blah blah, but you've got to let me do it one day. You know I don't bite people. You know no-one would recognise me, and you know I'm in control of my magic now, so what's the problem?' I said.

'There's a fairly good chance Alex would recognise you, and maybe some of your other friends too if you started poking round all the places you used to hang out. You know I can't let you go.'

'First, Alex is gone, so she's not going to see me. Luke thought it might have something to do with *us*... but what if it has something to do with another vampire? What if it's the girl gang that killed me? I need to find her,' I said.

'He just wanted an excuse to come and see you, Jess. She'll be fine. The other vampires would know not to go anywhere near Alex, because of the connection to you. Seb would kill them.'

'Well there's one vampire on the loose that doesn't worry about Sebastion. He drained Sophie, didn't he? What if he's got Alex?'

'Look, you're worrying about nothing Jess. Whoever drained Sophie was probably just a rogue vamp passing through. We'll catch him, but he wouldn't have seen Alex. She's probably gone home. Maybe Luke just missed her. Maybe she's got a boyfriend Luke doesn't know about,' she added with a grin.

'Eva, I'm going. If you want you can come with me, but if you try to stop me I *will* use my magic. Please Eva, just let me do this. I don't want things to go bad between us. Just come with me.'

With my mention of magic, Eva's face momentarily fell. She looked hurt, and I knew I was wrong, but I needed to know that Alex was okay.

'Fine, I'll come, but make sure you've had breakfast before we go,' she said, and saving face she walked from the room.

Breakfast, now there was a thought! Obviously Eva was referring to the bottles of blood packs neatly lined up in the secret refrigerator in the utility room, but instead I headed over to the 'show' fridge. Daniel kept a 'human' fridge just for show, in case of any sudden visits by our student neighbours, or any unwanted visitors. I opened the door and peered in. There wasn't much to see, in fact it seemed pretty typical for a student; beer bottles, coke cans, a pint of milk, two days old and some cheese. I was about to close the door again when my eyes caught sight of something vacuum packed on the top shelf. I reached up and lifted it out... a sirloin steak. Steak for breakfast?

I smiled as I imagined just how freaked out Eva would be when she smelled frying steak wafting through to the lounge. I quickly unwrapped it and hunted through the drawers for a frying pan. Bingo! I didn't expect to find any olive oil, or oil of any kind, so I just turned up the gas and slapped the steak in the pan. Suddenly, as it began to sizzle the rich earthy scent hit my nostrils, and my mouth filled with saliva.

A few seconds later, I watched as the red juices began to ooze out of the meat and smiling, I ran my tongue gently over my fully formed fangs. I decided I was going to try my steak rare and bloody!

'Oh my God! What has gotten into you today?' Eva asked as she stormed into the kitchen seconds later, to see me lifting the barely browned steak, still dripping blood, out of the pan and slopping it onto a plate.

'I'm having breakfast, like you suggested,' I said, grinning.

'And this I've got to watch,' she said, pulling up a seat opposite.

'You're not going to rant?' I asked.

'Nope. Jess, you're a vampire. If you want to make yourself sick by eating cow, then that's for you to learn.'

'Fine. This looks good actually,' I said, and grabbing my knife and fork I started to eat.

The meat really was rare, I could taste the blood running over my tongue as I chewed, but irritatingly I found the act of chewing difficult with my fangs fully extended. A vampire was meant to bite once, and then drink. With each act of chewing, my fangs rubbed uncomfortably against my gums, scratched my lips and caught on the meat. Maybe a bloody steak wasn't the best idea, but it satisfied both my personas, and though awkward to eat, I enjoyed the taste more than the previous day's bottled blood. It satisfied me, being able to feel real food in my mouth, which I could swallow. It made me feel normal.

As I finished the last mouthful Eva sat back, one eyebrow raised.

'I didn't think you'd manage it. I mean we can eat human food if pushed. It won't harm us on occasion, if forced, to have a mouthful or two, but it tastes awful. It feels like swallowing lumps of coal, our stomachs feel leaden, full of hard pebbles that won't digest. For you to eat all that… Jess?… Jessie, are you okay?' Eva asked, as I suddenly let out a groan.

'Ughhhh, I think I'm going to be sick!' I said, running with all the vampire speed I could muster up the stairs and into the sanctuary of the bathroom.

Five minutes later, Eva knocked lightly on the bathroom door.

'Jess, are you alright? Can I come in?'

'Sure,' I groaned. I'd emptied the contents of my stomach, flushed and cleaned up. I was now sitting on the floor, my head resting on the cool tiles, feeling more than a little stupid.

'Hey, try this. It will help,' Eva said, handing me a mug of warmed blood.

'Thanks.' I took the mug, breathing in its soft chocolaty aroma, grateful not to be laughed at.

As I sipped at the liquid I felt my stomach settle, and I looked up again, my lips curving into a small smile.

'I guess I'm still not able to eat human food then,' I said.

'I don't know. I mean it was something that you actually cooked and then you ate the whole thing. Most vampires wouldn't manage that,' she said with a shrug.

'I think it was just the smell of blood that enabled me to eat it all. It was really difficult actually, I kept biting myself with my fangs,' I said with a laugh.

'Crazy girl! I thought the last few months were interesting, but I have a feeling things are only just getting going,' she said, as we both looked at each other and laughed. The ridiculous situation hit me and still giggling, she grabbed my hand and pulled me to my feet.

'So where were you planning on going then?' Eva asked when we were back downstairs.

'First I thought I'd go back to our old flat, see if I can get in, if it's still empty and have a look around. Maybe she went back there, or left something there?'

'I don't know. If it's empty I guess we could have a quick look, but quick, okay? I don't want us to get caught,' Eva said. 'And if there's nothing there, or new tenants? What then?'

'Hmm, not sure. Maybe just check out a few old haunts - a coffee shop, the students' union maybe?'

'The coffee shop yes, but we can't go in the union without passes and we can't use your old one, it's too much of a risk.'

'Right, let's start with the flat,' I agreed.

Due to Alex only officially moving out of our flat a couple of weeks earlier, and it being mid-term, it was still unoccupied. I had found the original key from my old keyring, which Eva had kept after my transformation, and now I found myself slowly pushing it into the shiny lock and turning it, giving it a little jiggle as I had done so many times, to get it to open.

I half expected to see it fully furnished, our colourful Ikea rug covering up the disgusting old carpet that had served a decade of freshman occupants. The old sofa would still be covered with Ikea throws and blankets, while a couple of little square coffee tables would be covered in coffee mugs and beer bottles the lads brought around and never cleared away.

Alex should be curled up on the sofa with her latest murder mystery novel in her hands...but she wasn't. The flat was empty, gutted. The rug was gone, as was all our furniture, and our overstuffed bookshelves were bare. The old stains on the sofa and carpet stood out like blood spills at a murder investigation.

'I don't think we'll find anything here, Jess,' Eva said, startling me out of my daydreams.

'I know, I just want to check...' I said, as I walked through the tiny lounge area towards the two bedrooms.

I went into hers first, to see if she'd left anything, even though I had no idea what I was looking for. Where would she have gone? As Eva said, home was the likely option. Maybe Luke had just missed her, or maybe she'd been staying with a different relative. But why had she gone to the trouble of moving flats and staying in Manchester, if she couldn't hack it after only a week of lectures? Alex was tough, she watched forensics programmes nonstop on television, and was studying forensic psychology at university. If Alex had decided she was up to returning to Manchester, she wouldn't have left after just one week.

Her bedroom was empty, with just a bed in the middle, stripped down to the old, battered mattress. Alex had left nothing behind and had never returned. After a brief check under the bed, I walked across the tiny hallway and opened the door to my old room. Like Alex's it had been stripped of all my possessions, the wardrobe door hanging open on one side, revealing its empty interior. The small desk had been cleared of my towering pile of books and coffee cups, the bin emptied of my record breaking amount of Crunchie wrappers. But as I walked through the door I didn't see any of this, because my eyes were instantly drawn to the bed, which like Alex's had been stripped down to the bare mattress, only where the pillow should have been was a small bunch of hand tied daffodils. They were dead now, but only just. Their petals dry and colourless like an old woman's cheek, their green stalks browning and sticky.

Whilst white winter pansies may have been my favourite flower to get me through the dark, cold months of autumn and winter, daffodils were a sign of spring, a signal of sunshine, warmth and new life. I always bought them by the dozen, filling pint glasses with them and lining them up along the window ledges.

'Someone's been here,' Eva said, looking over my shoulder.

I nodded and walked over to the bed, but there was nothing else, no note.

'These can only be a few weeks old, I think,' I said.

'Yes, but I don't think Alex put them there, do you?' Eva said.

'Well, who? Oh! I didn't think. Do you think Luke brought them? But why? I mean... he hates me now.'

'No he doesn't. Don't be stupid. He hates *us*, he

hates what you are, but he doesn't hate you. Who planted the pansies at your grave, Jess?'

'Oh! It never occurred to me. After I saw him at the cricket club, he was so awful...I forgot all about the pansies.'

'Well, anyway, that would be my guess. I think angel-boy is having a hard time letting go of the old you, but doesn't like the new you, which works in Daniel's favour,' she said, one corner of her mouth turning up in an ironic twist.

'It doesn't matter in whose favour it works out, it's *my* choice and I *do* choose Daniel. Not that I've had much of a chance to tell him, since he went all weird about our bond. Too much has passed between Luke and I, and he lied to me for so long. He could have told me about my past, my DNA, but instead he waited till it was too late. And that's not even counting how much of a jerk he's been recently,' I said.

'Good. Let's get out of here. There's nothing to see.'

We headed to the coffee shop just down the street from the student accommodation, and ten minutes later we were sitting in the corner by the window, our mugs of tea steaming in front of us.

'Remember, this was your idea Jess, so drink up,' Eva said with a wicked grin.

'Very funny! I didn't want to have a drink, but I

don't think the owner would be too impressed if we just came in, sat down and didn't order anything.'

'True, but we could have just gone home and drunk something more nutritious,' she said.

'But, it's nice to feel normal, do normal things. I used to have a coffee here with Alex every Monday morning before our ten o'clock lecture, and a full breakfast every Sunday.'

'Yes, but she's not going to magically appear Jess, and if she did you wouldn't be able to speak to her,' Eva said quietly.

I sighed. I *was* going to find Alex and when I did, I was going to find a way around the whole non-disclosure policy Sebastian had warned me about.

'Great! Looks like we've got company,' Eva said, frowning.

Looking up towards the door I saw Luke, dressed in his usual human jeans and rugby shirt combo, wings hidden, student stubble making him look irritatingly attractive in a relaxed, unkempt way. His face was barely concealing the anger as he wrenched open the door and barged through the nearby tables to get to ours.

'What are you doing here?' he hissed.

'I'm looking for Alex, same as you,' I said, instantly annoyed.

'You can't come here anymore. Are you stupid?' he

continued.

'No, I'm not stupid. No one's recognised me, and no one will. Have you seen her?'

'No, I haven't. I said I'd tell you on Monday, when I've done looking.'

'Where does she live now?' I asked.

'I'm not going to tell you. You can't go there. She's not allowed to know about us anyway,'

'Us?' I asked, confused.

'Not *us,* us… Just me being an angel, and you being…one of them,' he said under his breath, nodding at Eva.

'A vampire you mean,' I said.

'Shush will you! This is the exact reason why you can't come here. You might have bought some tea and be sitting here thinking you look all normal, but you don't. Your eyes are *not* a normal green…'

'So they could be contacts. I've seen people clubbing with much stranger ones in,' I said.

'You're not drinking your tea, they're both full,' he said, driving his point home.

'I could if I wanted too,' I said, as I nonchalantly picked up the mug in front of me and had a sip.

I looked at it. It sure looked like strong tea, but to me it tasted really bland, like very weak tea, too milky. The milk covered my tongue, and I fought the urge to gag. Instead I smiled up at his shocked face, and took another mouthful.

'Eva, let's go. He's ruined the atmosphere,' I said, as I stood up and waited a second for Eva, before leaving the shop.

'Please tell me you're not going to start drinking tea now?' Eva said once we were alone again, walking back to her car.

I smiled and momentarily considered fibbing, but in the end I giggled and pulled a face.

'No, I don't know what was wrong with it, but that was possibly the worst cup of tea I have ever tasted in my life. It shocked the hell out of him though, didn't it?'

CHAPTER ELEVEN

Thanks to British Summer Time, and the clocks going back, the sun was still up when we returned to the house, and while Eva and Daniel had grumbled about it for the past month, I had revelled in it. Even before I'd become an initiated witch, I had preferred the light to the long winter nights. Sure, the sun would burn us to a crisp if we stood in it long enough, but the English sun was rarely hot enough to do that. There were always shadows to seek out and dappled tree shade to cool off in. It also made a good excuse to nip into the odd cool shop or two. Back home I had already persuaded Daniel to order a gorgeous patio set with a huge canvas sunshade for the garden, and I was looking forward to chilling out in the fresh air.

'Has the patio set been delivered yet?' I shouted through the house when we closed the front door behind us.

'No, but this has,' Daniel said, walking out of the kitchen with an envelope in his hand. 'Who have you been talking to, Jess? Who knows you're here?'

'No one,' I said, shrugging my shoulders. 'Maybe it's from Franny?'

'It has not got a stamp Jess. It was hand delivered before I got back,' he said.

'Oh, weird! Let me open it then.'

'You don't know who it's from?'

'No, I told you that already, but if I open it I can find out.'

'I think I should open it Jess,' he said.

'No way! It's my mail; it's for me. I'm not a child. Give me my mail,' I said, feeling hot and irritated all at once.

'Jess, I really think… we don't know who it's from,' he insisted, backing off a couple of steps down the hallway, holding tight to my letter.

'Give it to me… now!' I yelled, looking at the letter. I wanted the letter and in that split second I decided to put my magic to the test and show them not to treat me like a child.

I imagined the letter leaving his hand and sailing through the air to me, a bit like something out of a Harry Potter movie. Maybe I should shout *Wingardium Leviosa* I mused, but it turned out that I didn't need to.

Seconds later Daniel let out a primeval howl, and I watched, horror struck as all the fingers on his hand uncurled from around my letter and straightened out.

Unfortunately the spell didn't stop there, and his fingers carried on stretching backwards, until one by one they started to break, and the sound of his finger joints cracking reverberated through the shocked silence, as my letter left his hand and fell to the floor.

'Stop,' I yelled, running towards him.

'Jess, what the hell have you done?' Eva shouted as she flew past me and blocked Daniel from my view, protecting him.

Luckily, it seemed that as the letter had been released the spell had broken, and Daniel cradled his broken hand to his chest.

'Daniel, I'm so sorry. I didn't mean to. I...'

'What? So you didn't mean to break all his fingers one by one, or you didn't mean to perform magic that you know nothing about, on the one person who sticks up for you through everything?' Eva said, glaring at me.

'Look, I'm sorry. Daniel please...' I said, trying to push past Eva to see Daniel and apologise.

I looked at his face. The pain had made his fangs protrude, and I could tell he was struggling with a very real fight urge, as his vampire instinct told him to attack his assailant. His eyes burned bright, the red flecks in them glittering. His vampire blood had rushed to his cheeks, flushing them, as his muscles tightened, contracting, ready to pounce. He glared at me. This was one pissed vampire.

'How could you Jess?' he snarled, before pushing past me so forcefully, he knocked me flying into the wall. I steadied myself and rubbed my arm, as Eva followed him into the front lounge, sending a quick look of contempt my way, before slamming the door in my face. His bones would heal, quicker than our relationship, so I needed to give him space. I picked up the abandoned envelope and took it into the kitchen.

Dear Jessica,

Recently I have become acquainted with a friend of yours. She is very sweet and most interested to find out about your big deception. However, unfortunately for her, I am becoming bored with her teenage youthfulness. There is only so much sugar one can consume before needing a shot of something bitter. Therefore I am proposing a swap. She may return to Manchester, but you will need to come and fetch her, as I fear she is too weak to make the journey by herself, and of course Sebastian has forbidden me to pass Birmingham.

Yours Affectionately,

Cole

PS: I fear that if you involve those pesky, winged control freaks, she will not survive the delay.

'Daniel,' I shouted. I jumped up from my chair, knocking it flying, as I charged from the room. I might be a witch, but thankfully, I had kept my vampire speed, and I didn't wait for a reply before I exploded into their room. They both shot out of their seats. Eva, obviously thinking I had lost the plot and was going to attack again, went immediately on the defensive, but Daniel knew from my face that something was up. I flew into his arms.

'He's got her, Cole. She's in London, with Cole,' I said.

'Wait, wait, calm down. What do you mean he's got her?' he asked.

'The letter, it's from Cole. Here,' I passed it over, into his perfectly healed hand and sank into the sofa they had both jumped up from. I couldn't believe it. Why would Cole, leader of the London clan, bother with Alex?

Daniel read it quickly, his eyes darkening as they passed quickly over the words before he passed it to Eva and sank down next to me.

'Jessie, it's a ploy. Cole must have heard about you by now. You know how he and Sebastian are always vying to have more power. He knows that Sebastian has you, and now he wants you,' Daniel said.

'He probably hasn't even got Alex. Like Dan says, it will be a ploy to get you down there. You can't go,' Eva added.

'He *has* got her, or where else would she be? Even Luke can't find her,' I said. 'I have to go for her.'

'No way! It's too dangerous. We'll tell Luke and he can get his cronies to fetch her back,' Eva said.

'We can't. You've read what he said. He says not to involve the angels, or else she won't survive,' I said, trying to be the strong, powerful vampire Sebastian said I could be, and not crawl sobbing into Daniel's arms as I wanted to.

'It's all empty threats Jessie. He wouldn't dare. The council would be on his back in minutes. We'll give Luke the letter and let them fight it out. It's too dangerous for you to go.'

'Jess, you can break every bone in my body, but I'll heal and come straight after you. You're not going, and that is that!' he said.

'And after you've broken all his bones, you still have to get through me,' Eva said. 'I know Alex is your best friend and you miss her, but *you* are *my* best friend, and I'm not about to let you go hang yourself in Cole's lair.'

'I thought you said he wouldn't dare harm anyone? So why is it so dangerous for me to go?' I asked.

'Daniel said he wouldn't dare kill *Alex*, as she is human, and the Council would get involved; but as you are a vampire, they would probably let us sort it out ourselves, unless it got too messy…', Eva said, trailing off with a shrug of her shoulders.

'The last thing we want to start is a full scale vampire war, with you stuck in the middle,' Daniel added.

'Okay, look, I don't mind telling Luke and seeing what he says, but I don't want all the angels and the Council involved. I don't want to risk Alex,' I said.

'It will be up to Sebastian,' Eva said, 'but I suspect he won't want to involve the Council either. I'll go over to the club in an hour and see him before it opens. I need a snack anyway. I still feel sick from watching you drink that tea.'

'You what!' Daniel said, one eyebrow disappearing under his floppy waves.

'We bumped into Luke in a coffee shop. He thought we shouldn't be there and told me I couldn't drink the tea,' I said, remembering the foul taste it left in my mouth.

'So she showed him,' Eva said, winking at me.

'But I could do with a proper drink now,' I said, still feeling the claggy milky residue on my tongue.

Without waiting for Daniel's predictable lecture, I left the front room and went to the kitchen to find myself a blood pack. It was an improvement on the tea, but it left me feeling unsatisfied, with old memories resurfacing of the scents of the human boys in the night club, and my thoughts about drinking from them; tasting them.

A couple of hours later, I was curled up on the sofa talking to Daniel. I needed to talk to someone, and Daniel was the only person I knew I could trust one hundred per cent. He might be bossy, he might be pig-headed and over protective, but I knew he would listen and never betray me. I was suspicious that the initiation had done more than release my magical talents, and I needed to discuss it.

'Do you remember when I first saw Luke after becoming a vampire at the cricket club?' I asked.

'Yes,' Daniel said, pointing the remote at the screen in front of us and muting the music.

'Well, do you remember when he said that he'd been placed to watch over me when I was a teenager, to monitor my dormant witch DNA, and that once it kicked in he was supposed to help guide me to become a white witch, as opposed to a dark one?'

'Yes, and obviously it didn't matter, because it didn't kick in until you were made a vampire. It would have been pretty useful for us to know before we turned you,' he said with a smile.

'Would you have left me to die; if you knew what you know now? If you knew I wouldn't do what you wanted, be who you wanted?' I asked, not daring to meet his eyes.

'I don't know Jess, but I do know that if I knew everything I know now… how you are worth every broken finger to me,' he said pulling my face up so my eyes met his, 'I would fight both Sebastian *and* Eva tooth and nail to have you by my side.'

I smiled and pulled him in for a kiss, feeling my insides somersault, my heart quicken, and my fangs push outwards through my gums. It would be all too easy to forget this conversation and lose myself in his kisses. I gently pushed him away.

'Daniel, I need to talk…'

'About Luke? Again?' he asked.

'No, not really about him. I mean, what he said that day. I was thinking… I haven't got anyone to guide me now. The magic I performed today, I didn't mean to. I didn't even think about hurting you. I was thinking about Harry Potter…'

'Who?'

'Harry Potter, you know, the books? The films? Even if you haven't read the books, surely you've seen the films? Please tell me you know who Harry Potter is?' I said, not quite believing that there was someone in the western world who didn't know who Harry

Potter was, and more to the point, that I was falling in love with him!

'Urm, that would be a no. Who is he?' he asked with a grin.

'Oh never mind, but next time they're on TV, you're going to watch with me. He is a boy wizard, and until the last book he goes to this magical school where they learn spells. He does this one spell, called Wingardium Leviosa, where they make things levitate through the air, and I was thinking of that when I wanted the envelope. I just imagined the envelope floating out of your hand and into mine,' I said.

'Well, I guess you need a bit more practice then, and I am not offering to be the guinea pig,' he said, looking down at his hand and flexing his fingers in and out.

'That's just it. I did dark magic, without even trying. What if being a vampire has automatically turned me into a dark witch?' I asked blurting out my new fear.

'Don't be ridiculous Jess. You just have to learn to control your magic, that's all.'

'But that's not everything. Franny suspected that initiating me into their coven would quieten the vampire within me, if not eradicate it. She mentioned me moving to the States and even eating food like them,' I said, knowing I had to tell him everything.

'I knew it! Those conniving bitches.'

'Don't you mean *witches*?' I said with a smile.

'I bet Sebastian wasn't aware of that,' he said.

'No, I don't think so.'

'So that's why you ate the steak today, and the tea?'

'Eva told you about the steak?' I asked.

'I had smelled it when I came in the house, so she told me about it when she was mending my hand,' he said, pulling a comical 'injured party' face.

'Okay, okay, and I suppose that was part of the thinking behind the steak. I also wanted to shock Eva,' I said with a smile.

'You certainly did that, but she said you threw it all up after. So you can't eat human food then? And if you knew that, why did you drink the tea?'

'No, I can't. The steak tasted alright, but it was *really* bloody. I think that's the only reason I got it all down. The tea was disgusting. I did it just to shock Luke.'

'Why do you care what he thinks, Jessie? After how he's treated you, how he talks to you?'

'I don't care. I really don't. I just wanted the upper hand, that's all,' I said with a shrug. 'But that's not all of it. The witches thought I'd be able to eat food, but I can't.'

'And?'

'And I think the initiation has not only made my magic dark, but made my vampire side stronger too. Don't freak out alright, and please don't tell Eva, as she'll race straight over with Gavin again, and I *really* don't want that, but I keep thinking about biting people!'

'Ha! Jessie, sweet, sweet Jessie, you are a *vampire*. You are supposed to think about biting people. Is that all you're worried about?' he said, the clouds of concern clearing from his features, his gorgeous, full lips breaking into a wide smile.

'Look, they might say that men think about sex every seven seconds or something similar...which we don't by the way, but when I go out into town, or the club, and am surrounded by human scent, I probably *do* think about biting someone every seven seconds. It doesn't mean I act upon it,' he added.

'Really? Wow! Hmm, but something must have gone wrong with me. I have never been like that. The initiation was supposed to quash my vampire appetite, not strengthen it. The blood packs are alright I suppose, but all I can think about is what it would be like to drink fresh blood.'

'You're appetite has certainly improved. Although I suppose it has been two weeks since you fed from me,' he said.

And Sebastian! I thought.

'I don't want to keep taking blood from you, but however much I might be thinking about feeding from humans, I still can't get my head around it.'

'Jessie, I think you've accepted who you've become now. You are a vampire and you *do* need to drink blood. If you could only try to feed as we do, I think you would soon realise it is not as bad as you are making yourself believe. I think we should tell Eva when she returns and between the three of us work towards gently weaning you off the blood packs.'

'I know it's something I have to do, but I'm terrified I won't be able to stop and that I'll kill someone.'

'You won't Jessie, I know you. I know you could stop. You're stronger than you think, and Eva and I will be there to stop you, if you want? There's still time. We could go out now, as it's barely midnight?'

'No, not tonight. I need at least another night to prepare. I want to drink plenty of packs before I go, so I won't be too hungry,' I said.

'I can think of a more pleasant way to stem your hunger,' he said with a wicked grin.

'No Daniel. I took too much last time. I made you weak…and hungry,' I said, thinking of the drained corpse that had turned up the following day. I one hundred percent believed Daniel would never be capable of draining a human girl, especially one he had a bond with, but the death had brought home how easy it would be to take one pint too much; for dinner to turn into murder. I didn't want to prove Luke right and become a murderer.

'So this time I'll stop you earlier,' he said with a shrug. 'You've fed from me before and not taken too much. It was only last time it had an effect.'

'Maybe it was a cumulative effect?'

'No Jessie, it will be fine. I was planning to go out tomorrow anyway, and if you are going to lose your vampire stabilisers and start feeding like the rest of us, we won't need to do this anymore… I'll miss it. One last time? You know you want to!'

'What about the bond? Are you doing this to re-establish our bond?' I asked, suddenly suspicious that maybe he had planned this all along.

'No, I'm not. It hadn't occurred to me, but I won't deny that if it does mend our bond I will be a very happy man… or vampire.'

'I can't take that risk,' I said.

'Why? What was so awful about being bonded to me? It saved your life once before remember? You wouldn't have held Aaron in mid-air long enough to escape being raped and then, probably not so accidentally murdered. Without our bond, Sebastian and I wouldn't have gotten to you in time, and Sebastian wouldn't have been able to save you.'

'I know, but I like having my thoughts kept private, I...'

'Jessie, you were already learning how to shut me out of your head, before our bond broke. How else would you have managed to get all the way to Didsbury and the cricket club for your birthday? Now your magic is much more powerful, you could easily learn how to block me, and I wouldn't stop you. It might not even work anyway. Magic broke the bond, so magic may be needed to fix it,' he said.

I nodded, evaluating the pros and cons. I desperately wanted to feed from Daniel again. I wanted to taste his blood, like the dark addiction it had become, have him set me alight and feel his hands running the length of my body. My fangs began to extend, and my pulse quickened. He slid his hand softly down the side of my face, trailing a finger down my neck, lingering for seconds over my artery which throbbed beneath his touch. His hand slid lower, stroking the silky skin covering my collarbone, sending tingles down my spine, and spreading heat between my legs. I sucked air into my lungs, my breathing becoming jagged with desire. What was the worst that could happen? So I ended up bonded to him again? He was my saviour, my best friend, my boyfriend. As he said, I would just have to learn to block him, to shut him out of my head, and I knew I could do that. If I could break all his fingers, then I could definitely learn a simple blocking technique.

I leant forward and kissed him, smushing my lips against his, clawing my fingers along the back of his neck, and winding his shoulder length waves around my fingertips, as I climbed onto his lap. My other hand dropped lower and slid beneath his t-shirt, feeling his abs tight and hard, his skin smooth, like alabaster. He let out a gentle moan and I pushed his hair away from his neck, pulling back from his kiss. The vein in his neck stood proud, my fangs were ready and saliva gushed into my mouth as I sank into him, a fast, flurry of emotion following, reopening our bond, a second soul connected to mine. All his thoughts, fears and emotions streamed past, accessible to me. His slow, steady heartbeat connecting to and aligning with mine.

CHAPTER TWELVE

'So, Daniel says that you've restored your bond with him, but you've attached yourself to the cat as well. I thought you didn't want to be bonded?' Eva asked me the following evening, once we were settled in our girlie den, feet on the table and the credits for Project Runway rolling.

'I hadn't wanted it back initially, but I guess over the last few days I've missed it, and as he said, I can always learn how to block him. I can already filter him out on a normal level. Now I just want to use my powers to choose whether to block him completely on demand or not. I just wanted some privacy, that's all,' I said, pausing before mentioning my surreal experience with Murphy.

'Like you said, you learn pretty fast to filter them out. I'd go insane if I had Sebastian in my head 24/7, and Daniel too don't forget, but I guess I've got used to the lack of privacy. If I had the choice though...' Eva smiled at me and gave a shrug. 'So, what's with the cat?'

'I don't really know what happened. Daniel thinks it's because I'm a witch, and he's my familiar or something. It was weird, I was just stroking him last night, and he did this weird kind of shudder, and then suddenly I felt connected to him,' I said, giving a little shrug.

'What? He speaks to you?' Eva asked, her eyebrows disappearing into her hair.

'No, not like specific words. It's more like I get a feeling from him. I knew he was happy he found me, and he likes the name Murphy,' I said grinning.

'Weird!' Eva said. 'Do you think you could persuade him to like *me*? As cats always hate vampires, I've not had a cuddle since I was fourteen and lost my Persian when we fled from Paris.'

I would never had guessed Eva had a soft spot for cats, and made it my mission to convince Murphy of Eva's cat-loving qualities. For now though, let him hiss at her and leave the room, his tail stuck up like a lightning rod.

'So after Daniel had stopped raving about your bond being back, he mentioned you might have something to tell me?' she ventured.

Daniel had gone out to the club, and I was fairly confident I hadn't left him too hungry after our previous night's exertions, but with my renewed energy, glossy hair and skin, I was reminded that fresh blood was indeed what I now required, no matter how the change had occurred. I needed to tell Eva that I was coming off the bottled blood, and I looked forward to seeing her reaction.

'Um, yeah... You know how I tried eating steak the other day?' I asked.

'Yes, and how violently it made you vomit afterwards... please don't tell me you are going to try something else. You tried drinking tea, and admitted *that* tasted disgusting. You're a vampire Jess, and I know you're also a witch and you desperately don't want to drink blood like the rest of us, but if your body can't manage raw, bloody steak then it's not going to cope with anything else,' she said, a frown clouding her features.

'Well there was one other thing I wanted to try,' I said, enjoying dragging it out a little.

'Oh God! What? I can't think of anything else. Jess you've got to stop this and accept who you are, and you can't keep feeding from Daniel. It's not fair.'

'I know, you're right,' I said, looking her straight in the eye and smiling.

'Uh...what?'

'You're right, about everything. I can't rely on Daniel for food, I don't like the taste of the processed blood anymore, and as I said to Daniel last night, I think the initiation made the vampire part of me stronger. I think it's time to try and feed properly.'

I watched as her face transformed. Her jaw dropped and her eyes widened. For a moment no one spoke, until I laughed at her and her whole face lit up.

'Have you been thinking about biting boys Jess?' she asked with a laugh.

'Uhh yes, and the odd girl too,' I laughed, 'but I don't want to hurt anyone.'

'Jess, Jess, you must know by now, that we don't hurt them. They love it, and come back for more. Our saliva stimulates their happy endorphins, and the bite wound heals within seconds. Oooh! I'm so excited. Now we can go out for dinner together.'

'Hey, slow down a bit. I want to take it slowly. I thought that maybe we'd do what you tried to do last time with Gavin... but not him, okay?' I said, cringing at the memory of his spaced out, loved up face.

Eva nodded enthusiastically, almost bouncing off the sofa.

'I think I'd feel safer in your room at the club, and Eva...would you mind staying with me, and not Daniel? It just feels wrong in front of him. I'd feel under too much pressure, in case I enjoy it too much...' I trailed off, looking at the floor.

'Sure, good idea. We don't need him getting all jealous, though I can't believe he didn't tell me about this. Boy am I going to have a word with him later,' she said.

'I made him promise not to tell you. I wanted to tell you myself. I knew it would be good fun,' I said, grinning.

'So when do you want to go out? I take it you're feeling quite full currently.'

'Yes, but I don't want to be hungry for my first time anyway, so I thought maybe we could go tomorrow night?' I asked.

'Yes, that could work. Oooh, Sebastian will be thrilled with you. He has a soft spot for you anyway I think, you lucky girl,' she replied.

'He likes you too,' I said.

'Yes I know. We're both lucky then,' she said with a laugh.

'Why lucky? He is quite gorgeous I suppose, but I just can't get over the fact that he's about five hundred years old, and treats me like a little girl.'

'I know, I don't mean it like that. We had a brief fling when he first turned me, thought he was the most gorgeous male alive...or undead, ha! But I'm over that now. I meant lucky because life is so much easier when you have Seb on your side,' she said.

'He would kill you if he knew you called him that,' I said laughing.

'I know, I have occasionally been caught out. You know how I shorten everyone's name. It's an affliction. I can't help it,' she said, her grin widening. 'And life is so much more difficult if he doesn't take to you. Look at poor Amelie.'

'Who's Amelie? I've never met her,' I said, running through all the names of the vampires I had met at Sebastian's club.

'Exactly! She's never at the club. She doesn't get on with anyone and ends up with all the worst jobs Sebastian doles out. It's definitely better to be on his good side.'

'So, have you heard back from Sebastian about contacting Luke? Has he found out anything about Alex yet?' I asked.

'I believe Daniel spoke to Sebastian last night and I'm sure he'll be working on it. Don't worry Jess. She'll be fine. Like I said, I'm sure she's probably not even with Cole. Oh for effing sake!'

'What?' I asked smiling at Eva's refusal to swear, and following her eyes out through the patio doors into the dark night.

'Your *ex*-lover boy is here. Seems he can't keep away.'

'Why are you here, Luke?' I asked, a couple of minutes later, when I had let him in through the kitchen door, and we were seated around the table.

'Sebastian informed the Council about your letter from Cole, so myself and a couple of others have been to London to speak to him,' he said.

'How could you Luke? You might have put her in danger,' I said.

'If you were that bothered about her safety you would have gone to London yourself, instead of running to Sebastian,' he answered.

'I wanted to, I really did, but...'

'We wouldn't let her. It would be madness to play into his hands and send Jess to London. That's just what he wants, and we can't go there unless we want war breaking out. It's not our territory,' Eva interrupted.

'But you went to London with Bradley, only a couple of months ago?' I asked Eva.

'Yes, but Bradley was flying back to Texas from Heathrow, and Cole was notified and gave us permission. The point is, he wouldn't be giving us permission to enter his territory this time. He's heard about you Jess, and he wants you.'

'Right, so you put Jess's life over a human girl's?' Luke asked.

'Yes we do. Jess is special, as you know. Would you want her terrorised by Cole and forced to submit to his rule, because that's what he'll do,' Eva said.

'Don't be so overdramatic Eva. Cole would do nothing of the sort. How could he? That kind of torture is illegal, and has been for the last fifty years. That is why the Council have us higher beings to keep the peace,' Luke said, looking scornfully at Eva, who in return looked like she wanted to punch him.

'I don't know how you had a relationship with this creep, Jess. He's so far up his own ass, he can't see the reality that's in front of his eyes. I'm going in the back room for a break.'

'Luke, why do you have to wind her up? Can't we work together?' I asked.

'No we can't, and she winds me up, and you don't bother,' Luke sniped.

'Never mind. So you went to London? Did you find her? Is that why you've come?'

'No...and yes. We didn't put her in danger Jess, I promise, and I'm sorry, I know you couldn't go. I mean, I'm sure Cole wouldn't hurt you, he wouldn't be allowed, but I can see how they wouldn't permit it.'

'So...no, you haven't found her?' I prompted.

He shook his head and looked at his feet.

'Initially we did a recon. We went to London and nosed around his bar and his area, listened in to conversations, but there was nothing. Cole has plenty of rich human girls hanging around his club, but none of them had heard of a girl called Alex, from Manchester.'

'Rich girls? That seems weird,' I said, thinking of the hangers on in Exodus, the students, the goths, the clubbers and the loners.

'Cole doesn't have a night club, like Sebastian. He owns an elite members only club in Mayfair, called Mayfair Moon. He's owned the place for over a century and has quite a reputation for fashionable charity events in the city. He also owns all the exclusive apartments in the Georgian building above the club.'

'Oh!' I said, actually feeling somewhat intrigued, the more I heard about him. 'So, no sign of Alex then?'

'It's not that simple. Beth and Adam both believed that it would be worth talking to Cole, and asking him about the letter. They believed it would be safe to do so, as we had heard nothing of Alex…'

'But he specifically said not to involve the angels on his note,' I interjected.

'I know, but we couldn't have found out anything more unless we did speak to him.'

'So what did he say? He's not going to admit to it, is he?' I asked, frustration building in my chest, making me feel as if someone was wrapping my torso in bandages, mummifying me with fear.

'He admitted to writing the note, said it was a personal joke between the two of you, that he wanted to meet you, and had never seen Alex. He laughed it off and apologised for any bad feelings.'

'But Alex still hasn't turned up has she?' I asked. 'Don't you think that is a little coincidental?'

'Yes Jess. I'm sorry I came here with bad news and I don't know what we can do about it,' he said, his blue eyes blurring with unshed tears.

'He's got her, hasn't he?' I asked, already knowing the answer.

'Yes. When Beth and Adam walked on ahead of me and left the building, a guard blocked my exit, with the excuse of tying his shoelace. At the same time, Cole walked swiftly past me and whispered in my ear. He said, *Sometimes letters speak more truth than words*.'

'Oh God! He means that the note is true and everything he said to the angels is untrue, doesn't he?'

'I think so,' Luke said, nodding slowly.

'Did you tell the others?' I asked.

'No, because I honestly don't know what we can do. He would deny saying it and it could put Alex at more risk...'

'You told Eva that Cole wouldn't dare hurt her?' I accused.

'I know, I'm sorry. I don't think he will; he can't. I cannot believe that he would test the Council in this way, but I wanted to be sure. Alex was my friend too, you know.'

'Right, so we need a plan. Could he have her in his apartments?' I asked.

'No. We interviewed Cole in his private suite, and most of the apartments belong to billionaire Europeans anyway. He would never risk his business and reputation, if he is indeed doing something illegal.'

'So where can he have her? Does he have any other businesses?'

'None in this country, and I don't think he'd try to take her out of the country. Again it's too risky,' he said.

'Have you followed him? To see if he goes anywhere?' I asked.

'No, not yet. I could try that. After the meeting, Beth and Adam wanted to come back and didn't see the point in following him, other than to antagonise him. Jess, if he catches me following him, Alex could be in real danger.'

'So don't let him catch you then,' I said. 'We need to know where she is.'

'Right. I'll go back tonight, before dawn,' he said.

'I'm going to tell Daniel tonight when he comes home. I want to go to London, and if Daniel and Eva can't go, then I could go with you.'

'I don't know Jess. It's likely that Eva is right to some degree, and Cole is after you, not Alex. You should probably stay here.'

'Damn right! It's a relief to hear you say something sensible for once,' Eva remarked from the kitchen door.

'I thought you were in the back room?' Luke said, his eyes sparking with irritation.

'Ahh you see, you might be *higher beings* but we have better hearing than you, better eyesight, scent and speed as well, now I come to mention it,' Eva said, her mouth tilting upwards in a slow, sarcastic smile.

'Stop fighting you two, or else I'll go and join Cole's clan just to get away from you both,' I said. 'So, did you hear everything he said?' I asked Eva.

'Yes, and you're not going on a mad-cap rescue mission to London Jess, but I'll let Daniel tell you that when he gets back.'

'You can't stop her wanting to save her friend, so if she wants to come with me, she can,' Luke challenged.

'You said yourself, Jess should be kept safe. It's not about controlling her,' Eva answered.

'It doesn't sound that way to me. Do you actually ever listen to the needs of the vampires below you, or are they just slaves?' Luke said, his eyes glinting.

'Luke, they never treat me like a slave. They care about me,' I said.

'That's because you're different. You're a prize worth keeping happy. It's the other poor souls I meant,' he said.

'They aren't like that!' I said, my anger forming a hard, solid ball in my tight chest.

'How do you know Jess? Have you met any others?'

'This is ridiculous! Get out of our house before you force me to test the law,' Eva snarled.

'Jess, I'll be back at dawn to see if you want to join me,' Luke said. 'Remember, it's your choice; your choice only.'

'Just go Luke, I'll see you later,' I snarled through gritted teeth, as I desperately tried to control my frustration. I didn't want any more fireballs breaking Daniel's windows, and I needed to prove to myself that I could control my anger. Why the hell couldn't they at least *try* and get on!

'Damn!' I shouted, my irritation needing an outlet, as I banged my fist onto the table.

With a crack, the wood splintered beneath my fist and a fissure snaked its way from the six inch thick oak edge, half way across the smooth surface. Ugh! Why was I always breaking things? I'd just had enough. I had gotten over the incredible sadness and grief that had threatened to engulf me over the previous few months, and now I was left feeling angry. My anger bubbled at the surface like a feral cat, spitting and biting, eager to escape. I ignored Eva's raised eyebrow and looked down at the table. I placed both hands flat on its surface and I felt a warm glow between my palms and the wood, throbbing slightly as the anger dissipated, leaving my body. My heartbeat returned to its undead, barely beating state and the frustration poured out, through my chakras, down my arms, and fingers. I had channelled it out into the wood. I had grounded, this time without the book's help. A smile crept across my face till it reached my eyes and I looked up at Eva.

'Any chance you've learned any mending magic yet then?' Eva asked.

'No, sorry. I'll go and see if I can find anything in the books while we wait for Daniel. And Eva, I'm going to London, whether you help me or not.'

Daniel came back just past midnight, by which time I had Eva back onside, after earning serious brownie points for my new magic skills. In the hours while we waited for Daniel, I had indeed kept my word and flicked through my Book of Shadows until I came across a transmutation spell. I found it early on in the book, in the section which Franny had suggested I start working with first... the beginner spells.

It only took two attempts to master it, and even then it was all down to concentration. Eva sat opposite me at the table, instructed to stay perfectly motionless and utter not a word. I zoned her out and concentrated on breathing. Now, as a vampire, it is true that I didn't need to breathe, but it was a habit that being a new vampire, I'd not lost. This was convenient, because it was certainly easier to relax when you could hear yourself breathe. It still freaked me out when Eva occasionally stopped for minutes at a time, until I gave her a quick jab in the ribs.

To be fair to Eva, the only movement she made throughout the whole half hour was a movement so slight, but so full of expression it made me giggle. Luckily by then, I didn't need to concentrate so much because I had already grounded, drawn the energy through my body, down into my hands which rested on either side of the fracture. In a low tone, I quietly chanted the simple, ancient lines that had been printed in the book, and watched as I turned the wood under my hands to a jelly-like substance. In my head I envisioned the wood growing again, weaving its now softened splinters together. I stroked the pliable, dough-like wood back together, caressed it and smoothed out any bumps. Her jaw dropped open enough for me to notice the movement out of the corner of my eye. I smirked, pleased with myself, and once I was sure the table was as good as new, I let the excess energy leave my body and looked up.

'Woah! That is serious magic, witch-girl,' Eva said. 'It would have come in useful when you first broke my mirror at Exodus, wouldn't it?'

'I think this was an easy first attempt, as I only had a single crack to sort out. A shattered mirror would be a different story.'

'When do you think Daniel will be back? He's out later than usual,' I asked.

'Any minute now, and from the vibes I'm getting he's in a mood. Something's up...just be warned!'

'Great! I bet Sebastian's grilled him. That's all I need, before I tell him I want to go to London,' I said.

'Jess, I know you're going to go anyway, but I think it's a really bad idea. I will try and get Sebastian to allow me to follow you, but without Cole's invitation, Daniel and I would be on dangerous ground.'

'Eva, I don't want to risk getting you in trouble with Sebastian, or Cole. I'm sure Luke will be able to watch out for me. After all he can fly me out of trouble, can't he?'

'Why will Luke be needing to fly you anywhere? What exciting plans are being made behind my back then?' Daniel said quietly from the door frame, making me jump with sudden guilt.

'Daniel, you're late, where've you been all night?' I asked.

'You know where I've been and stop avoiding the question. Have you seen Luke?' he asked as Eva took one look at his face, set like marble, pushed back her chair and left us to it.

'Yes, I have. He came here. I didn't invite him but...'

'Oh, so that makes it okay then! When were you planning on telling me your plans to fly off into the sunset with him?'

'Oh, shut up and stop being so damn jealous of me! I've told you there is nothing between Luke and I anymore. I've also told you I want to be with you, so chill out and back off, before you make me break some more of your bones,' I said, placing my palms flat on the table again. I could see I was going to need to ground again very soon, as my annoyance was already brewing.

'Fine, so why were you talking about him flying you out of trouble, when I came in?' he asked, sitting down opposite me.

The next half hour thankfully passed without the need to break anything or to ground, and he managed to keep his temper, as I explained what Luke had come to tell me, and what I had discussed with Eva. He remained adamant though. He wouldn't let me go, and certainly not at dawn, with Luke.

'Did you tell Eva about your plan to feed?' he asked.

'Yes, it was rather fun watching her face,' I said, smiling at the memory. 'But I can't go to the club tomorrow. Not now. I need to find Alex first.'

'Jessie, that is exactly what you *should* do tomorrow. If you are intent on going to London, you should do it with your full strength. He will be expecting you sooner rather than later, and if you put it back a couple of days, feed and then go, there is a chance you may have the upper hand.'

'And there is also the chance she could be dead by then,' I said.

'He won't kill her Jess, he wouldn't risk everything he's got for one human girl, I promise you.'

I didn't know what to do, as I desperately wanted to find Alex. I could only hope that Cole's vampires behaved better than Sebastian's chief bodyguard Aaron had. I shivered as I remembered the vampire ripping at my top, my bra, pinning me down. My breathing became shallow, and faster.

'Hey Jessie, it's okay. We'll work it out. It's not your fault. The angels should have done something about it, but as usual they don't want to get involved in vampire politics.'

'It *is* my fault. She's been through all this because of me.'

'Jessie, who left you at the club? Who walked home, leaving you to get attacked by the girl gang? It's not your fault. None of this is.'

'It's not hers either. She was just drunk. She would never have left me alone if she was thinking straight, and she doesn't deserve to pay for it like this,' I said.

'She may still turn up. He may not even have her. Luke said they hadn't heard any of his staff or peers mention a girl. It could all be a ploy.'

'He *has* got her. Even Luke thinks so now.'

'Luke again!'

'Yes, and you better get used to it, because Luke was her friend too and he wants to find her as much as I do. I don't love him anymore and he certainly doesn't love me, but he can help us find Alex.'

'Fine, but you're not going with him at dawn. He can go and scout London, follow Cole or whatever, and I will find a way to take you to London myself, *after* you have fed properly in Exodus tomorrow night.'

I badly wanted to leave that minute. I was concerned that Cole could already have taken action, after his warning not to involve the angels, but what

Daniel said made sense, and even though Cole had warned me not to involve the angels, he had not forbidden me to bring other vampires. It *could* work, if Luke went on ahead and scouted possible locations, spied on Cole, and then I followed with Daniel in a couple of days, hopefully strengthened by my first real feed.

'Okay. I would prefer to leave tomorrow night, straight after the club, but Monday at the absolute latest,' I said.

'Deal!' he said, the tiny red flecks glittering in his dark eyes as his full, sexy lips widened into a smile that could hypnotise a thousand girls. 'Let's go and tell Eva the plan before lover-boy returns.'

'*Ex*-lover-boy,' I said, getting up from my chair and moving over to him for a kiss.

A loud banging on the door interrupted us, and we heard Eva's angry words as she tried unsuccessfully to bar people from entering the house. I leapt from Daniel's lap, and we both shot out of the room and skidded to a stop in the narrow Victorian hallway, which was now uncomfortably full of supernaturals.

The kitchen end of the hallway contained myself, Daniel and Eva, who had now backed towards us. The rest of the hallway contained no less than five angels, in the same green hooded robes I had seen when they had come to Luke's and my rescue, a couple of weeks previously. They held their long, beautifully crafted swords close to their bodies, and their faces were drawn with barely concealed anger.

'We have come to arrest Mr Daniel Bailey for the suspected murder of human girl Tillie Rose, tonight between the hours of ten and twelve. Your maker may accompany you to the cells and advise on your behalf.'

CHAPTER THIRTEEN

It had been an hour since Daniel and Eva had left with the angels. For one long hour I sat pretty much motionless in the back room, Murphy on my lap, staring at the wall. I was trying to get my head straight and decide what to do. Daniel had gone willingly, his eyes betraying a sadness he refused to emote. Eva had accompanied him, telling me not to worry, that it would all work out. I didn't know what to believe. I was in shock.

It turned out that whereas Daniel had apparently been telling the truth about not seeing Sophie since before he made me, he had lied when he said that he didn't have a regular human girl that he fed from. Tillie Rose was a nineteen year old vampire groupie, and she *had* been his regular. Even Eva knew that he had been seeing her the entire time he had been with me. Why hadn't he told me? We'd had the conversation before and he had assured me that he fed from different people each time.

In the five minutes this all came out, before he left

the house, he told me it was because I wouldn't understand, as I hadn't yet fed from a human. He promised me he was innocent, that he hadn't killed her. He pleaded with me to believe him when he said that all he did was feed, that she meant nothing more to him, and when he'd left her tonight he swore she'd still been alive.

As I ran my hand the length of Murphy's back, caressing his soft velvety fur, I could feel him connecting with me, soothing me. He took my confusion and pain and fed me hope and belief. He strengthened me and allowed me to think. I began to feel bad for the jealous words I'd shouted at him, asking him if he'd had sex with her, because I hadn't been ready to. This poor girl was dead and yet I felt cheated, jealous. I needed to get my priorities straight. He begged me to believe him, to accompany them both to the courts, but I was confused. If he had lied to me so easily about having this regular girl to feed from, to see at the night club, when I wasn't there, what else could he lie about? Could he have drained these girls? I was sure I hadn't left him too thirsty this last time…but maybe I was wrong.

I didn't think it was possible for Daniel to commit such a crime. When we found out about Sophie, we all thought it must be a horrible fluke, but now a second girl had turned up dead. A girl who, as his regular, he had admitted to feeding from this very night, the night she died. Her blood must be in his system, making him strong and again it was his first feed after a night with me. I simply didn't know what to think. Why would both girls be linked to Daniel, if he hadn't drained them? I couldn't think of why anyone would want to set him up, as he seemed to get on with everyone in the clan. It just didn't make sense. Why had he gone with the angels, so willingly, so submissively? The only thing he had fought for was to have me with him, and I had refused. I needed time. Murphy purred and shifted in my lap.

A light knock on the patio window disturbed my thoughts and I found myself staring into those azure blue eyes I knew so well. I flicked the latch and he opened the door, and as I didn't move from my position I soon found myself being gently pulled from my seated position into a bear hug, and the tears were unlocked. After a few minutes my sobs subsided and he pushed me back and sat down next to me.

'I heard. Jess, I'm so sorry. I don't know what to believe,' Luke said.

'Neither do I. I can't believe he'd drain anybody, never mind a girl he cared about. He just wouldn't Luke, but he lied to me about her. I'm so confused.'

'I tend to agree. I don't like the bloke... obviously, and a blood sucking parasite has definitely drained these girls. It was lucky we got to this one before the human authorities, otherwise we'd have a full scale cover-up mission on our hands.'

'He wouldn't do it Luke,' I said, feeling more certain with every word.

'Then why didn't you go with him?' Luke asked. 'I was sure I'd find you in the courts with them both. When you weren't there, I came straight over.'

'I don't know why I didn't go. He begged me to. I was confused. I still am, but it's more about the lie surrounding him seeing this girl, having a regular. I guess I'm jealous,' I admitted, looking at the floor.

'But why would he lie to you about this, if he was innocent? After all, it's what you guys do… you bite people, you suck their blood. Why wouldn't he want you to know he fed from this girl?' Luke asked, his voice growing colder.

'Because once I got jealous, and I worried about what happened when he fed from girls. I wanted to know if it turned to more. I haven't fed from a human remember?' I said, almost adding 'yet' onto the end, but knowing he was mentally adding it anyway.

'So you wanted to know if he was shagging you and the girls he fed from at the same time?' he sneered.

'I haven't had sex with him Luke, but yes, I guess I was worried about that, not that it's any of your business,' I said.

'You haven't...? Wow! Uhh, I mean...I thought... you *are* a vampire aren't you, Jess? Oh never mind, what does it matter... So he told you not to worry, blah, blah, blah, and that he fed from different people each time?'

'Yes, pretty much, and now it turns out he did have a regular, probably gorgeous, nineteen year old vampire fan. I guess she adored him. Oh, what am I turning into? I hate this!' I needed the kitchen table. My anger was building. I could feel it simmering beneath the surface, and I didn't think Luke would be too impressed if I nuked something right now.

'Jess, are you alright?' Luke asked, concern etching his features as he took my hand.

I snatched it back, afraid I'd burn him or something, jumped up and began pacing. What I needed was a girlfriend to mull this over with. An ex-boyfriend, who happened to be a vampire despising angel, was never going to give me a straight answer. Eva was a good friend... and a girl, but she was also Daniel's maker and therefore biased. I needed Alex, now more than ever before.

'I'm coming with you,' I said.

'What? Where? To court?' Luke asked.

'No, to London. I want to find Alex. You're going at dawn, aren't you?'

'Well... I'm supposed to be back at court in a couple

of hours. This is a huge thing for the whole supernatural community. We haven't had serial drainings for decades, since it was outlawed… with a death sentence,' he added quietly.

'Death sentence? They can't kill Daniel!'

'They can if he has been killing humans, and they will,' Luke replied.

'But he hasn't. Shit! What am I going to do? I can't leave Daniel if they are going to kill him, but I can't leave Alex with Cole either…'

What I needed was Hermione's time turner from 'The Prisoner of Azkaban', but I had a very strong feeling that I wasn't going to find a spell for one in my Book of Shadows. I wondered how Susannah had opened up that vortex. If I could travel in the ley lines I could get between London and Manchester in record time… and maybe I could bring Alex with me.

'Luke, do you know how to use the ley lines to travel?' I asked.

'Sure. Angels can use them for quick transportation across the globe. It was also how we transported the dark witches to court the other week. Personally I prefer to fly, after all that's what God gave us wings for,' he said smiling.

'God…wow! So you mean… of course, duh! How stupid of me. You are an angel after all…'

'Jessie, your waffling. I'm concerned. What's the

matter?' He asked.

'I mean *God* and you're an *angel*! So He does exist... I was never sure. Do you see him?'

'Still pretty incoherent there Jess, but no, I haven't ever seen the 'Him' you mention. We're *fallen* angels Jessie. There are a couple of the originals, so to speak, who remember the ancient times, but the rest of us have been born here on earth. We have no contact with that realm, so I couldn't tell you whether he still exists or not. Sorry,' he said, with a shrug.

'Oh!' There wasn't much else I could say, at least for the couple of minutes it took for the endless stream of questions to start pouring out of my mouth.

'But you must surely believe in Him? You can't just shrug Him off?'

'Of course we believe in Him Jessie, we're angels! But as I have no proof of Him existing, and I've never spoken to or seen Him I wouldn't try and enforce my view on others. And after all, *you* are a vampire, so I don't think it would do you much good believing in Him anyway...' he said trailing off quietly.

'Why? Because all vampires are damned?' I said, heating up again.

'Pretty much, sorry.'

'Whatever! Anyway, if you're *fallen* you can't be all that godly yourself,' I retorted, feeling more than a little smug with myself.

'Look, *fallen* just means we're earth-bound, that's all. We weren't banished to Hell with Satan. We do His work here, that's all.'

'You tell yourself that, if it makes you feel better, but I know that I have no intention of going to Hell anytime soon, or for the next few hundred years.'

'Look, this wasn't a conversation I wanted to have...'

'I know that. I mean, you much prefer to pretend you're a *human* boy, don't you, and then you don't have to talk about who you *really* are at all!' I said feeling my voice begin to raise a little.

'Jessie, can we just get back to Alex? You were saying about ley lines?'

'Okay,' I said begrudgingly, not really wanting to drop the subject or stop bickering just yet. I felt too hot, too frustrated. I had too many niggles and questions… but they would have to wait. For now.

'So, I thought if you have to be back in the morning at court, then maybe you could whizz me up to London tonight via the ley lines and then use them to get back in time? I haven't had anyone teach me how to use them yet so I need you to take me,' I said.

'Well, I'm afraid I can't teach you, because witches use them differently than us, and I don't want to take you and leave you there. We'll just have to wait a couple of days,' he said.

'Alex could be in danger, Luke. By then she could be dead.'

'He won't kill her, I'm sure. He wouldn't risk it, he has far too much to lose.'

'But if he has got her locked up somewhere, it's likely she's being watched by someone other than Cole, seeing as he is always visible in Mayfair, and that someone may not be as careful as Cole.'

I decided to tell him about my brief experience in Sebastian's cell, the night his bodyguard tried to bite and rape me. He was suitably shocked and went immediately into 'defender' mode.

'You should have told me sooner Jess. We could have arrested them. Sebastian had no reason to lock you up...'

'He did. I attacked the girl gang who murdered me. I showed them my fangs and scared them halfway to Hell and back,' I interrupted with a grin, as I remembered their white faces.

'Jessie! You can't do that. You put the whole supernatural community at risk. Why on earth...'

'Calm down will you? I know that *now*, but then I just wanted revenge. I still do actually, because Sebastian had all their memories corrected, so they didn't remember anything I did. Then, he put me in the cell, whilst he talked to Daniel about it. He didn't intend to harm me, but unfortunately his flunky guarding my door had other ideas. If it hadn't been for my powers enabling me to protect myself, and my bond with Daniel which ensured he heard my attack and could come running, it would have ended very differently. Basically if I had been Alex, he would have raped me, bitten me, fed from me and possibly killed me, before any help arrived.'

I waited in silence whilst I let my words sink in and do their job. I knew Luke cared about Alex, and he wouldn't want to risk putting her in jeopardy.

'Okay, I'll take you to London, but you have to promise me that all you'll do is stay well in the shadows, scout around and wait for me to come back. We'll arrange a meeting place and once I get out, around midday, I'll come for you. But you have to promise Jessie,' he said.

'I promise. I won't find Cole, and I'll stay in the shadows... hell, I certainly won't be seeking the sun, will I?' I said, grinning. 'Let me just change and write a note for Eva, so she knows where I've gone.'

'Were they going to let you come with me, or did you make a stand?' he asked.

'No, of course they weren't,' I grinned, 'but Daniel had actually agreed to take me tomorrow evening instead, so I'd agreed to wait.'

'I thought Sebastian's vampires weren't allowed in the Southern area without an invitation?' Luke asked.

'They're not, but I guess as Cole had invited me and not explicitly banned them from coming, we were banking on that. It was you guys he said not to involve, remember?'

'So why do you want me to take you, if Daniel was going to play super hero?' Luke asked his tone beginning to cool again.

'Daniel isn't here now, is he? And believe me, if I knew how to travel the ley lines by myself, I would *so* be doing this on my own. There is way too much competitive testosterone flying about between you guys, but I need you Luke. I need you now. I need you to take me to London so we can find Alex.'

'Okay, sorry,' he said, a guilty smile playing across his lips.

'Good, give me ten,' I said with a quick smile, as I raced from the room.

Nine and a half minutes later I was in the kitchen with Luke, wondering whether he was going to get his wings out, or zap us into the ley lines some other way. To be fair it hadn't actually taken me ten minutes to get ready. I had changed my jeans, thrown on a clean, warm hoody, pulled a brush through my hair and yanked it back into a don't mess with me ponytail... or that's what I had hoped to have pulled off, just in case I came face to face with Cole's henchmen. I'd spent another couple of minutes writing a short and somewhat apologetic note to Eva. I was sorry to be deserting her, and leaving Daniel in court, knowing they would totally freak out about my disappearance, but also knowing that I couldn't chance leaving Alex any longer.

The last five minutes I had spent sitting on my bed staring at the floor. I was still gutted that Daniel hadn't told me about Tillie, and for the entire last hour I had studiously closed off any bond between us, knowing that he would immediately send Eva back to the house if he knew what I was about to do. But for those last few minutes, I cautiously reached out for him. I blocked out all my fears for the impending trip and instead allowed him the frailest of connections.

'Jessie? Is that you? Are you alright?' His words formed in my head, and as I reached out to him, I could almost picture him in my mind.

'Yes. Are you in a dark room? In my head it looks like a dark room... I thought it would be a cell, like a jail?' I asked.

'They hold us in rooms, but their opulence belies their impassable walls. I'm fine, Jessie. Eva has gone with Sebastian, to work on my defence. Come to me, please.'

I could feel his pain. He was as confused as I, about why both dead girls were linked to him. As he allowed me deeper access to his thoughts than I let him have over mine, I knew instinctively that he was innocent. Either that or he was exceptionally skilled at deception.

'I'm sorry Daniel, I can't come just yet. I need a little time...' My thoughts drifted and I shut him out quickly, before he understood why I needed that time. For now he would have to believe me to be upset over his relationship with Tillie, but by tomorrow Eva would have found my letter and he would know the truth. Just before I pulled away, I saw the flash of a memory, a memory of his last meeting with Tillie, several hours earlier.

Tillie was a normal girl, she wasn't Hollywood gorgeous. She'd had average, mousy blonde hair, like mine had been before my change. As it was his memory, I felt the emotion that went with it... it was brotherly. He cared about this girl, but it wasn't anything more. What's more, she knew about me, and was asking if he had told me about her yet. I didn't catch his reply, or anything more, before I was pulling away, feeling uncomfortable for spying on his memories... this was exactly the reason why I hadn't liked the bond relationship. It was too intense.

I was left feeling guilty. Daniel needed me and not only was I deserting him, but I would be adding to his stress and worry the moment he knew me to be gone.

I could only hope that Luke and I could find out where Alex was being kept, then Luke could get the angel army in to rescue her and I could wing it back to Daniel, before they cast any sentence that would terminate our relationship forever.

'Okay, so how do you do it then? I take it you don't conjure a swirling vortex like Susannah did?' I asked Luke, back in the kitchen.

'Nope, we fly up and jump aboard midstream,' he said with a grin.

'Of course you do! I'm not sure which method sounds worse, but as the vortex was no fun on my stomach, I can only hope your method is easier,' I said.

But it wasn't. What I'd failed to account for was the speed with which angels can both ascend and descend when they want to, and as dawn was fast approaching, I guess Luke was concerned about the neighbours witnessing something they shouldn't. After I had pulled the kitchen door closed behind me and stepped out into the crisp cool morning, I found I barely had time to take a breath before Luke had pulled me in to his side, wrapped his arm around me and shot up into the air. I'm not altogether sure that I could have counted to two even if I had tried, but as it was, all I did was yelp slightly, and two seconds later I found myself, once again in the magical ley lines that circle our planet.

'Umm Luke, how do you know which way to go?' I asked, noticing for the first time the different, ethereal threads and wisps of glowing currents that crisscrossed each other like a handful of colourful ribbons.

'You just concentrate, and think about where you want to go. Link your mind to the stream, connect, and once your consciousness makes the connection it takes you where you need to go.'

'So if I started thinking about...'

'Jess I need silence, shut up!' He interrupted.

'Oh, sorry.' I took the hint and instead watched the dizzying patterns unwind around me. Some lines seemed thicker than others, some seemed frail and delicate. Some glowed with phosphorescence, whereas some were barely wisps of white matter floating on the breeze.

From kitchen door to London backstreet it took no more than fifteen minutes, and as I looked at my watch, I marvelled at the new mode of transport open to me, and wondered why I hadn't seen the air filled with witches and angels. If humans ever worked out a way of using it, it would soon be overrun. I looked over at Luke and the reason became apparent. He was slumped back against the wall of the back street we had landed in, a sheen of sweat on his slightly paler face.

'Are you okay?' I asked.

'Yeah, I'll be fine in a moment. It's hard work on your own, which is why angels usually only use it for transporting undesirables in teams, working together.'

'Oh, sorry!'

'It's fine. See, I'm better already,' he said with a weak smile.

So where are we then? I thought we'd be going to Mayfair?' I asked.

'No, I want you to stay as far away from Cole as possible. This area is popular with the young goth crowd… Emos, or whatever you want to call them. There are loads of vampire fan clubs here, so now wouldn't be a great time to change your mind on that biting ban you've given yourself,' he said softly.

I decided not to tell him of my recent change of heart, after all, I certainly wouldn't be putting that particular plan into action until Daniel was safe and Eva was able to escort me to the club. With that plan on hold, I didn't see the point in telling him and making him pissed at me sooner than necessary.

'Fine, but what can I do here? Especially as it's dawn. The clubs will have closed.'

'I believe there's a café around the corner called Dawnbreaker,' which is open for the post-club crowd. You can mingle there and make friends. See if you hear anything interesting. Cole may behave perfectly for us in Mayfair, but if he indulges his darker side…

which let's face it, he's a bloodsucker, so I can't see him not doing... he'll come somewhere like this.'

'What if I get recognised by other vampires?' I asked, suddenly worrying about his impending departure.

'Thanks to your new green eyes, you don't look like a vampire any longer Jess... at least, not until you get close up. They will probably be able to smell you if they get too close, or get you on your own... so don't let them,' he said.

'But we don't smell. It's you guys that smell!'

'Exactly! They'll know you aren't human by your lack of scent. We should have thought of it and doused you in perfume before we came. In fact, once it gets to nine o'clock, go and find a perfume shop and spray yourself. That will help a little.'

'When will you be back?'

'I'm expected on court duty between nine and two pm. I'm going to set off now and fly back, which should take me a couple of hours, so I have the energy to catch a ley line back to you at two. We can meet here at two fifteen.'

'Um Luke, if you see Daniel... be nice, okay? He *is* innocent, I saw his memories. I can and *will* vouch for him once I get back,' I said.

'Fine.'

'And don't let anything happen to him, promise?'

For a second he didn't say anything, in fact, he looked pretty pissed, but then he looked up at me again and nodded.

'You really care about him, don't you? Even when you weren't bonded?' he said.

'Yes, I do. So don't let them kill him. He's a good man.'

'Bloodsuc... vampire you mean. He's not been a man for decades,' he said with a smile.

'Look, just go. I'll see what I can find and meet you back here at two fifteen. Don't be late, or else I'll worry.'

'Ditto,' he said, and after a quick furtive check around us, he shot up into the air and was gone. I was on my own, in London.

CHAPTER FOURTEEN

If only Alex was next to me, sharing a greasy breakfast, as we planned the day ahead. If only I wasn't a vampire with half the supernatural community after my powers, and if we had a wallet full of money to shop till we dropped, the hours stretching ahead could hold so much potential. As it was, I was a seventeen year old, in a capital city that I'd never before visited, with a super scary agenda to follow. I didn't have a single clue where to begin, so I figured I'd better find the place Luke had mentioned.

'Dawnbreaker' was a dingy café on the corner of two main streets. Even at six o'clock in the morning, the traffic pouring around the junction formed an unbreakable torrent. Mindful that zipping across the roads at triple speed would be the same as wearing a neon light on my forehead, flashing 'vampire' to anyone glancing my way, I decided to cross at the pedestrian crossings, which also gave me time to assess the café before I entered it.

As I approached the café, I was surprised to see it still half full. I pushed open the door and ignoring the scowl from the waitress with black rings under her eyes, I found myself a table on the edge of the crowd of clubbers.

'We're closing in half an hour,' the waitress grumbled, as she stopped by my table, hands on hips.

'That's fine, I just wanted a coffee,' I replied, knowing even the sight of another milky tea would finish me.

The waitress scowled at me, muttering something under her breath as she walked back over to the kitchen area and poured me a stale coffee from an old percolator, returned and placed it down in front of me, her eyes daring me to ask her for a fresh pot. Luckily for her I didn't plan on drinking it, so I said nothing and waited till she slunk away.

I warmed my hands on the lukewarm mug and watched the groups in the room. Initially, I felt self-conscious, sure I would stick out as a teenage girl on my own, but then I soon realised no one was bothered. The majority age group in the room was between seventeen and twenty five. Half of them were dressed in black; black hair, black eye makeup, black dress, black boots, black nails... but the other half weren't so obviously goths. They were young, all of them, but some were dressed in jeans like me. A couple of girls wore tiny dresses more suitable for the Ibiza scene, and some girls dressed with nothing but their own style in mind, a mish-mash of colours, textures and prints splashed together and worn with a grace I knew I didn't have. A couple of girls glanced my way and smiled, but the majority drank their drinks, ignored the ever increasing glares from the waitress and talked as if I wasn't there.

I pulled out my iPod, which I'd grabbed at the last minute before leaving the house, and put the headphones in my ears. With the machine switched off, I was free to listen in to the conversations around me without appearing rude. So coffee in hand, head nodding slightly to a non-existent rhythm, I settled back in my chair and concentrated on the group nearest me. The group consisted of five stereotypical goths, two girls and three boys, all dressed head to toe in black, with matching eyeliner. They were all discussing the band they had seen at the club – the girls discussing the varying delights of the lead guitarist and the boys raving about how pumped it was.

I switched groups and tuned into a group I hadn't noticed initially, as they were seated at a table just behind the goth group. There were two girls dressed similarly to those I'd seen hanging around Exodus after closing time; skinny jeans, knee high boots, revealing tops. Their skin was a little too pale to be healthy, their eyes bright and smiles adoring. They were sitting with two slightly older guys, maybe in their late twenties, wearing designer labels, their almost black eyes giving away their true nature.

I strained to hear what they were talking about, but without staring at them and lip reading, it was tricky siphoning out all the surrounding conversation. The bits I did hear were pretty meaningless, but I stayed with them, sure they'd be my best hope of a lead.

'You're not drinking that? Is it too cold? I can make the girl get you a fresh one if you like?' The voice came from behind my shoulder, making me jump slightly. I turned and found myself face to face with a vampire. He was dressed to blend in, fashionable with a slightly gothic twist, but like the vampires I'd been watching, it was more couture than Camden.

'Oh, um thanks, I'm fine.' I took a tentative sip, trying not to grimace as the now cold coffee coated my tongue. I hadn't liked coffee before I was turned, and it seemed the taste hadn't improved with my change.

'Cold, huh?' he said, pulling out the seat opposite me and sitting down.

'Yeah, I guess, but I didn't really come for the coffee… I was umm... early for a meeting and so I was just wasting some time. It's cold outside.' I knew I didn't sound convincing. I'd always been terrible at lying and this guy had caught me off guard.

'Sure, so where's this meeting you're going to?' he asked with a slight smile.

'Oh, just round the corner, not far,' I said, trying to sound as vague as possible.

'Right, well if you want any company, come and find me,' he said, before standing up and sauntering over to the group I'd been watching.

I let out a sigh, not quite believing I'd got away with it, and smiled when the group all turned to stare at me, before turning back to their conversation. As other groups were now breaking up and leaving the café in twos and threes, I decided I should make a move as well. I didn't want to hang around and cause more suspicion with the vamps.

I followed a group of three goth girls out of the café and onto the street. Where would I go now? I wasn't even sure whereabouts in London I was. I guessed I was a fair way outside the centre, because I couldn't see any of the landmarks, the Thames or any of the typical brown tourist signs. I followed the group of girls a short way along the busy road and back around the main junction. I stopped and stared in front of me as a gorgeous old building with a domed roof loomed ahead of me. The sign above it said Brixton Academy. Right, so I was in Brixton then.

I decided to hunt around and look for the nearest tube station, where I should at least be able to find a map and have a look at the surrounding geography. I was currently standing at a big junction with three main roads, one of them bound to lead to the train station, but which? Suddenly I heard a muted giggle and whipping my head round I saw the three vampires with their girls come around the corner, the way I'd just come. I looked for my group of girls, but they'd gone. I needed to move, so I picked the road to my right and started walking, listening hard to the noises from behind.

I started to realise, as I crossed the street, that I was probably going in the wrong direction, as the road seemed to be going away from the centre and there was no train station in sight. The traffic was much lighter here as well, and there were no pedestrians about at all. The good news was that the group behind had presumably broken up and weren't following me, as very little sound now came from behind. I decided to take the next right turn in the hope that it would loop back onto the parallel road leading back to the junction.

As I crossed the road to take the narrow residential street that ran off it, I took a quick look behind me. The group had indeed split up and now there was just one vampire and one girl walking towards me, but on the other side of the road. They didn't seem interested in me, so I shrugged it off as a fluke and disappeared round the corner.

The street I was now on was lined with expensive, well-maintained houses on one side and a strange mixture of shabby council houses on the right. Further on, there were sparse areas of wasteland, with rubbish and industrial bins piled up against each other. My route didn't look hopeful, so I took the next left and picked up speed, finding myself on a narrow alleyway. It surely led back towards the junction as it appeared to back onto the same street, with the backs of warehouse and commercial buildings lining each side.

I was out of luck, as I soon found myself at a dead end, my route blocked by a large warehouse with fifteen foot high wire fencing which cast long shadows in the early morning gloom. I turned back to retrace my steps and felt my stomach lurch. The vampire and his mate had stopped at the end of the alleyway and were talking to somebody through the window of a large black Mercedes. The Mercedes had turned into the alleyway and was facing me, its engine purring as it blocked the route in and out.

I had the warehouse behind me, which had a fence I could surely scale, but security cameras would film me and land me in trouble with the supernatural community, for revealing my nature. To my right were the blank backs of buildings, their paint peeling off like rust on an old bicycle. The left seemed more promising; with three wooden gates and the back entrances of the shops I had seen lining the high street. If I could jump the gates and the doors were unlocked, I could potentially escape that way. I still wasn't sure that they knew who I was. I told myself it was still possible they thought I was easy prey, and if I was right, they'd be in for a shock.

I couldn't risk finding out, so I ran over to the nearest gate and felt relief flood my system as the hinges creaked open against my touch, and I fell into a small courtyard littered with pizza boxes and takeaway rubbish. I dodged the bins and ran to the door. Of course, as it was barely seven in the morning, the business was closed and the door was locked. Dare I use magic to open the door? Could I? I mentally scanned the spells I had learned so far, but with the sound of the car screeching to a halt behind the gate, I couldn't think of anything useful and resorted to banging on the door instead. Maybe someone lived in the flat above, who could open the door for me...

'Jess, you're going to be late for that meeting you told me about,' the vampire from the café said, stepping into the courtyard.

'Um, I didn't tell you my name... I'm not Jess,

you've got the wrong girl,' I said, mentally kicking myself for being so lame.

'Oh, silly me, and here I was thinking you were here to meet up with a girl called Alex. No wonder I scared you. My mistake, goodbye.' He turned and suddenly left through the gate. I heard his steps retreat and the car door open.

Damn! This was it, my chance to find Alex. Clearly they knew who I was and yet they hadn't attempted to attack me, as everyone presumed they would. Maybe Cole meant what he said in his letter. Maybe he *did* just want to talk... then again, no, I was kidding myself. I knew it. I knew I was walking into a trap, but *they* knew where Alex was and I didn't. I felt my body turn from the door and towards the gate. I could hear the engine idling, before it suddenly revved as the car manoeuvred in the alley, to drive back out. I ran the last few steps and bounded out of the gates, skidding to a stop in front of the car.

'I want to see Alex,' I said.

'Jump in then,' he said, leaning across and opening the passenger door for me.

I could hear Luke, Daniel and Eva all screaming at me in my head. They would all kill me if I got in this car... if Cole didn't kill me first, but I didn't have a choice. If I refused, I wasn't at all sure they'd let me go, and if they did we may never find Alex. I also had no idea what Cole would do with a redundant girl whose life was a threat to his reputation. I didn't want to find out, so I got in the car. I figured if I needed to, I could telepathically contact Daniel and then he could tell Luke where I was, but for now I didn't see the need in panicking my friends.

'So, I gather you must be Sebastian's new pet half-breed, Jessica?' the vampire said to me from the driver's seat.

I didn't know how to answer, as I would have loved to make a snappy retort, but I wasn't sure either who he was, or what he was capable of. I was outnumbered, so I decided the best course of action was to stay silent.

The couple that had followed me were still guarding the end of the alleyway, and the other couple from the café, I now noticed, were sitting in the back of the car. I'd been mistaken about the two girls, as only one of them had been human - the one in the car was a vampire. The guy asking the question was the same one I spoke to in the café. His hair was glossy brown and swept to one side, more like an Armani model than a Justin Bieber look alike. He looked young, maybe early twenties, and his couture skinny black jeans and faux goth t-shirt did little to hide his perfectly defined body. As he appeared to be waiting for an answer, I resorted to a teen's best defence... I shrugged!

'Well Jessica, I'm very pleased to meet you, and pleased you heeded my little note and came alone. Good girl. By the way, I'm Cole.'

'You're Cole? But you're so...' I was going to say young, and then it dawned on me as to how stupid that would sound. I already knew he was hundreds of years old, but looking at him I just couldn't match the Cole I had heard such stories about with the cute, posh boy sitting next to me.

As I faltered, Cole grinned and raised a single eyebrow.

'So? What exactly?' he asked.

'Um sorry, you just don't look how I expected,' I mumbled. Feeling my cheeks flushing, I turned to stare out of the window.

'Do we ever? But I shall take it as a compliment that Sebastian and Daniel obviously think so highly of me as instil such fearsome visions of me in their pets. Now you see, I am not so different from them after all,' he said.

'Why did you take Alex then? And why did you threaten me with your note?' I said, suddenly feeling braver, 'Will you take me to see her?'

'I'm sorry if you took my note as a threat, but I didn't want the inconvenience of an army of angels accompanying you. I know Sebastian has not yet made you take an Oath of Fealty, and I have heard you are free of your bond with Daniel, so as you are free to do as you please I thought we should be acquainted.'

'I have no intentions of leaving Manchester,' I said, realising my impulsivity was a mistake from the moment I opened my mouth, and watched his eyes harden.

'You shouldn't be so impulsive, young one. Remember, I have much to offer and much to take away,' he said, suddenly putting the car in gear and taking his foot off the brake.

'Where are you taking me?' I asked, beginning to panic.

'To see Alex, where else?' he replied, his smile returning.

When we got to the end of the alley, he raised his hand at the waiting couple and with a quick nod they turned and walked off. Cole then took a right, in the opposite direction to that which we had walked, and after a short distance we went right again and then left. I stared out of the window and tried to memorise the route the car took in case I found myself needing an escape, hopefully with Alex in tow, but it was impossible. Brixton, it seemed, was a maze of back streets and Cole seemed to take every possible turn. It dawned on me that he was purposely taking a convoluted route in order to confuse me, and it was working. I had soon lost count of the rights and lefts, and had no clue of the general direction we had come from.

We ended up driving along a main street, but I hadn't been able to find the road name, as he seemed to bypass corners and junctions by cutting down side streets. We finally turned off the main road and slowed to a stop in another alleyway, at the back of a dilapidated church, which appeared to have some kind of nineteen sixties concrete box structure added on to the side of it.

The instant the car stopped, I opened the door and leapt out, but it was pretty hopeless... after all, they had the same unnatural speed I did, and were only seconds behind me. And really, what was I planning to do?

'Where are you going Jess?' Cole asked as he sauntered around the front of the car, holding a large hypodermic needle in one hand, while the vampire couple closed in from the rear.

'You don't need to use that, drugs don't work on us anyway... and I'm clearly outnumbered,' I said, holding my chin high, and meeting his eyes. I refused to let him think he could so easily threaten me. They might outnumber me, but I had my magic, and I needed to find Alex before I used it. The syringe didn't bother me, as Eva had told me months ago, in Exodus when we came across a creep with date-rape drugs, how our fast metabolisms would burn up any drugs too fast to be a concern to us. Cole was obviously only playing with me.

'My problem Jessica, is that you are a witch. It is clear from your eye colour that the initiation was a success, and if you managed to neutralise Aaron *before* you were initiated, it would be reckless of me to ignore your potential newfound abilities. So I apologise for this measure, and you are right of course… this dose would do nothing to you, but act as a very good decoy…'

Pain stabbed momentarily into my thigh, piercing straight through my jeans, sending freezing liquid coursing through my veins.

'You see, Alison's syringe is filled with industrial strength horse tranquiliser, from a helpful veterinarian. This should put you out long enough for us to safely transport you to your accommodation.'

A wave of fear and panic unfurled and coursed around my body. This I had not planned. As my eyes widened with terror, a hand clamped over my mouth from behind, just as I tried unsuccessfully to scream. Seconds later, a strong arm encircled my waist to catch my weight as the tranquilizer began to take effect. Desperately I tried to contact Daniel, open my mind and reach out to him. It was my last chance, to save myself and to save Alex.

'Jess where are you?' His voice came to me, panicked, mirroring my total terror.

The drug was working too fast and my brain wouldn't work. All I could do was open the barriers I had so carefully built up to keep him out and let him read my memories of the past few hours. I stared at the building in front of me, willing him to see all the details in and commit them to his memory.

'Jess, Jess...use your magic. Do whatever you need to do to get out of there. Stay awake Jess...' Daniels words echoed far away, as I felt him slowly fade from my mind.

As my body began to slump, my captor lifted me from the ground and I used what was left to arch my back and kick my legs, a last show of defiance before my world went black.

CHAPTER FIFTEEN

I awoke to find myself underground, in the cellars of the old church. To three sides I had two feet thick stone walling with one tiny, iron barred window, looking out at ground level. The fourth wall comprised the same vampire proofed iron bars I had come across in Sebastian's cells.

Where was Alex? Was it all a hoax as Eva had suggested?

I strained my eyes against the gloom. The daylight barely broke through the tiny window, due to overgrown shrubbery, which would have perfectly concealed its location. I had been laid on a narrow bed, with a grey blanket and pillow. I smiled slightly when I saw that they had left me both a glass of water and a glass of blood... they still weren't sure what I was... or what I drank. The tranquiliser had blurred my vision, giving me an almighty headache, and my mouth felt parched, as if I'd been walking for days in the heat of an Indian summer. My skin felt dry, cracked, and I yearned for blood, but I resisted. Let them keep guessing a while longer.

I stood up and rubbed my fingers through my hair, massaging the pain in the back of my head, as I took in my surroundings. My cell was bare, and all I could see beyond the bars was a stone passageway, and another set of bars, fitted to the opposite cell.

'Jessie?'

I looked across my cell through the bars, in the direction of the voice I knew so well. *Could it be? How could she recognise me? What must she think of me?*

'Alex?' I asked, as my supernatural eyesight finally sorted itself out, focused through the murk and found the friend I'd been waiting months to see.

She stood at the bars of her cage, peering through at me, her eyes wide, her face emaciated. Alex had always been skinny compared to me, but now she looked ill, her shoulders jutting out through the grubby thin sweater she was wearing, her cheeks hollow and black rings circling her eyes.

In a second I had cleared the distance between my bed and the bars, stretching my hand out towards her, but she pulled back quickly 'Can it be true? I thought they were lying to me. Are you really one of them?' She whispered, her eyes sparkling with tears which began to spill onto her cheeks.

'Yes, it's me, Jessie. Don't be scared please... I've wanted to see you so much,' I said quietly. 'I came to find you Alex.'

'Are you... Jessie, you don't look like them. Your eyes, they're green, but they said you're one of them. Hell, I don't believe this. I didn't believe any of this until they started... feeding. Jessie, they bit me... over and over again.' She sunk slowly to the floor, folding in on herself, tears now falling unchecked as she avoided my eyes.

Anger coursed around my body, anger at everyone. They'd been feeding from her, biting her, harming her, unchecked for three extra days because Daniel, Eva, Sebastian and even Luke refused to believe that Cole would allow a human to be harmed. As if he cared about their damn rules. I was going to get us out of here; they wouldn't touch her again.

'Alex, look at me. Alex, I'm going to get us out. I'm so, so sorry they got to you. It's me they want, and I'll tell you the whole story later. It's pretty strange I guess, but basically, yes I am a vampire... but I haven't bitten anyone yet, I promise,' I said quickly, as I watched the new hope fall from her face with her remaining tears.

'Why are your eyes different? Why do they want you? Why did they get me, when you haven't even seen me? You let me go through all that pain and grief after I thought you died. God Jess, your dad killed himself because he couldn't bear it anymore,' she stormed, sudden hatred blazing in her eyes.

Alex, I'm sorry, but I promise I did try to see you, but I wasn't allowed. I wasn't allowed anywhere near you, or anyone I knew, but I saw dad just before he died. It was really weird, a bit like a dream, but I saw him... I saw him die.'

'You were there? In the hospital? But how?'

'It doesn't matter, not now. I've got so much to tell you, but first we have to work out how to escape. When did they bring me down here? How long have I been out of it?' I asked.

'Not long, a couple of hours possibly... it's hard to tell. I think I've been here five nights, but I'm not sure. What day is it?' she asked.

'Um... it's Sunday... I think. It's all been pretty hectic the last few days. Luke came to tell me you were missing on Thursday night, and then...'

'What, Luke knows you're alive too? You've seen him? Did he know about you and not tell me? That lying son of a... why though? Why would he hold me, crying, night after night and not tell me? Why Jess?'

I felt awful. I thought I'd been through so much, but I'd failed to realise just how much it had affected Alex. I wasn't going to keep any more secrets. I didn't care if Luke and The Council got pissed at me. She already knew about vampires, what did it matter if she knew the rest as well?

'Alex, Luke couldn't tell you because *he* isn't human either, and don't worry, I didn't know that either. All those years I knew him, and the months I dated him and thought I loved him, he was lying to me. You're not going to believe this, but he's an angel!' There, I said it, and it felt really silly, so silly in fact that I let out a muted giggle. Alex caught my eye and her mouth twitched upwards, crinkling her eyes in the way I loved, and we both laughed out.

'You're joking!' she exclaimed, looking at me as if I was demented.

'No, I'm not. He's really an angel, a fallen one apparently, and I'm warning you, he has some serious vampire issues. According to him, he loved me so much that he couldn't bear to let me die, so when the girl gang attacked me, he could sense that Daniel and Eva were around the corner; they're the vampires that turned me, and he left me to them. That would be great, if it wasn't for the fact that he now regrets it, hates what he did and has a massive chip on his shoulder about me being a vampire. Apart from him managing to fly me up to London this morning, and bring Murphy back to me, he's been a right royal pain in the rear!' I stopped talking, aware that Alex had gone silent and was just staring at me, her jaw slack, her eyes wide.

'Sorry, have I freaked you out? I forget what a weird world I live in, but I am going to get us out, okay?' I said.

'Jess, why do they want you? If vampires are the norm around here, why did they go to such lengths to get you?'

'Well,' I said, taking a deep breath, 'Luke wasn't the only one lying to me, when I was alive...'

'You're alive now Jess, you are, aren't you? I'm not dreaming this?'

'No, I'm here, but you know what I mean, before the attack. My dad and mum had both been lying to me, my whole life. She *wasn't* my mum you see, not my *real* mum. My real mum had died in childbirth, and here's the bit you might want to stay sitting down for, because she was a witch.'

'A what? A *witch*?' Alex shrieked.

'Yes, again something new I've learned these past few months is that there are real witches, and when a witch gives birth they pass on their power to their child, as it is born. The power splits and can cause a massive heart attack. My mum had run away and refused to go to a hospital, so she died. My dad didn't know she was a witch and remarried and they decided not to tell anyone, including me. So I get turned into a vampire, and in doing so they awaken this latent witch DNA which means I'm not a normal vampire.' I sighed and studied Alex. I knew I had so much to tell her, but for now we needed to get through the basics for her to understand and not be too freaked out, when I started putting my plan into action.

'So you're a witch too?' she asked 'Is that why you've got green eyes?'

'Bingo! Yes. Actually they only turned green a couple of weeks ago, when I was initiated into my family's coven. Turns out I'm half American as well!'

'Whoa! Information overload. Is this for real?' she demanded.

'Yes, I'm afraid so. My life for the past six months has been just that... information overload, one thing after another. But I am a witch, I can work spells, and *that* is how I intend to get us out of here.'

'So that's why these vampires want you, because you're a witch? But they've got a witch here. I've seen her,' Alex said frowning.

'What? Are you sure?'

'Yes, I think so. I mean, I didn't know what she was before you came, but now I've seen you I realise what she was. She came in with that tall, young, posh vampire...'

'Cole?' I asked.

'Yes, I think that was what she called him. Anyway, they came down here last night. They switched the lamps on, so I saw them quite clearly. I think they thought I was asleep, because one of his friends had just been down to... see me.' I felt crushed as I watched the shadows pass over her face, hoping beyond hope that feeding was all they had done to my dearest friend. After a slight pause she carried on, 'The girl had green eyes, just like yours, but she wasn't as pale, she had a tan, looked Spanish or something. Anyway, they both went in your cell and she chanted something, they laughed a bit, and then they left.

'Oh! I wonder what spell she cast in here?'

'What were you planning?' she asked.

'I'm not sure. I was kidnapped a few weeks ago by a dark witch, she created a vortex in my room and pulled us both up into it and carried us away. I escaped, but if I knew how to create a vortex that would work.'

'But you don't?' Alex asked with a smile.

'No sorry. I've only been a witch a few weeks, and believe me, I've not had much practice time, or a tutor. However, I did a really cool transmutation spell the other day.'

'A what?'

'A transmutation spell. I broke a table by accident, so I used this spell to transmute the matter, turn it from solid matter to liquid matter, then I concentrated on pulling it back together and smoothing it over. It worked, so what if I could turn the iron bars from solid to jelly?' I grinned back at her.

'Fine, but then how are you going to get us out of the building? There are at least four vampires up there, because I've seen four different ones.'

'Are they two girls and two boys?' I asked thinking back to the two couples I had seen with Cole at the café.

'No, I've only seen the one you call Cole and three other male vampires.'

'Right, well, there's definitely another female vampire hanging around as she was a passenger in the car they brought me in, and knowing vampire leaders, I bet there are more up there. I wonder if I could make these windows any bigger?' I asked gazing up at the tiny windows.

'That would be the best bet, because then we wouldn't have to get past any of those creeps upstairs,' Alex said with a visible shiver that coursed the length of her body.

'Okay, I'll give it a shot. I'll do yours first and then if that works I can do mine. If I do it, will you be able to climb up and get out, if you push your bed underneath?' I said, taking in her skinny frame and wondering how much energy she had left. 'Have you got some water? Here have mine. Drink it now, because if we get out we might need to run,' I said, passing her my water through the bars and pushing it across the smooth, stone floor, so it was just within her reach.

'Thanks. They haven't refilled mine today,' she said, as she sat back on her bed and began to drink.

I pulled my mattress off the bed and pulled it over to my wall of bars, where I was directly opposite Alex's window, and sat down. This time I wouldn't be able to touch the object, so I had to concentrate with every atom of my being. I crossed my legs and grounded. It came immediately, maybe because I was underground and so close to the earth, but I felt my body fill with energy and power, which I directed out at the window ahead of me. I imagined the stone wall crumbling, the window expanding, the bars falling out like rotten teeth in a recurring nightmare; except this wasn't a nightmare, it was a dream, we *would* escape.

'Jess, it's working,' Alex said, with a high-pitched yelp of excitement that broke my concentration, so the shimmering window frame wobbled back and solidified.

'Ooops! Sorry,' she whispered.

'Shhh,' I said and concentrated once more.

This time the magic worked quicker and the window frame doubled in size, just large enough for

Alex's skinny frame to squeeze through. I intensified my magic and watched, as the shimmering outline solidified and took shape. I breathed in, realising that whilst concentrating I hadn't taken a single breath, and Alex was watching me, somewhat freaked out.

'Sorry, it's a vampire thing,' I said taking another gulp of air. 'Do you think you can squeeze through that?' I asked.

'You bet. I'd climb through that if it meant having to chop my arm off. I'm not becoming a vampire's dinner again today, no way,' she said with a smile that brought back the old sparkle to her eyes. 'Now you.'

'I just need a minute. I want to see you pull that bed over and climb out first, and then I'm going to drink this blo... erm drink. I need some more energy before I do mine,' I said.

'But I thought you said you didn't feed like they did?' she said, her face falling again.

'I haven't bitten anyone, but Alex I am a vampire and I do have to drink blood to stay alive. This will be from a blood bank.'

'Oh, I guess. I think I'll just turn this way and erm, move my bed then,' she said quietly.

I drank the blood they'd left for me and watched Alex struggle to pull the little camp bed across the cell. Her arms were so skinny and she looked so frail, I just wished I could offer her some of my strength, but eventually she did it.

'Right, you climb through,' I said.

'No, you do your window first,' she said.

'No, I want to see you out first. You know, it won't take me long to do and I will be able to jump through easily once it's open. You climb out and then crawl around the perimeter of the building. It won't be far till you reach my window, but stay low down in case there are any ground floor windows. Once you're outside my window I'll open it and we'll be off. I don't think there'll be many vampires about, as it must be midday by now, and they'll prefer to stay indoors.'

'But what about you?'

'I'll be fine, we can go out in daylight. The sun burns us, but slowly and it's not too bright today, thankfully. Don't worry. You get out.'

Whilst I kept an eye on Alex slowly pulling herself out of the window and wriggling through onto the grass, I pulled the mattress back onto the bed and dragged it under my own window. This window I could touch, so it should be a simple matter of enlarging it, moulding it, and climbing through. I waited for Alex, aware that my near dead heart had sprung to life and was beating much faster than usual.

'I'm here.' Alex's hand poked through my bars and her face grinned down at me. 'There's no one about, and I can see the road.'

'That's great. Now just stand out of the way so the magic doesn't hit you,' I said, with a nervous giggle.

Once again I grounded and drew up energy, the blood had revitalised me and given me the boost I needed. I took hold of the bars with both hands and willed my magic to do its thing.

Except it did something else. As I pushed my magic into the bars I noticed they began to glow green. A strange green luminosity sparked beneath my fingers, causing electric currents to spit and snap. Suddenly an eerie, wailing siren started up, vibrating around my cell, getting louder and louder with each second. They'd alarmed my cell against magic.

'Alex run, run down the road and find someone human. Don't tell them who you are and don't tell the police, but get them to tell you where Brixton centre is. Find Luke. He'll be there to meet me at two fifteen. Just get away from here, please. Run, now.'

She paused momentarily, unsure what to do, before finally her common sense took over and she ran. I had seconds to try and cover her escape. I concentrated all my energy onto her window, reached out with my magic as I pulled it back together. Then I thought back to my old lessons in telekinesis. This time it was easy, as since my initiation I only had to tell things to move and they did. I picked up the old blankets and pillow and manoeuvred them into a person shaped lump on her bed. I couldn't do anything about the bars lying on the floor of her cell, because the door at the top of the stairs creaked open, but maybe, just maybe, this would buy her precious minutes.

I watched as a pair of smart black shoes descended down the stone stairwell and Cole's body came into view. His witch girlfriend was just behind. Neither hurried, as both were secure in the knowledge that her magic would put an end to my escape.

'Well, well, well, so my estimations of your magic were accurate then, Miss Jessica. You see, that is why I have done so well for myself, and from such a young age,' he smiled, as I scowled at his perfect teenage face. 'I never take anyone for granted, and I *always* over accommodate for their potential skills. It never lets me down.'

Shame you didn't think to ward Alex's cell then, isn't it? I thought to myself, allowing a small smile to escape.

'You're smiling? Do you like a challenge? You didn't expect me to put the girl who is supposedly the most powerful magical girl in the UK in an unwarded cell did you?' he smirked.

I wasn't playing his games, so I glanced at the girl and shrugged.

'So, have you had a chance to reconnect with your friend yet, or has she been sleeping the whole time? I'm afraid her fresh, sweet blood was almost too much for some of my staff last night. We shall have to wake her for you,' he said with a smile. 'I am so looking forward to seeing her face, when she realises we have been telling her the truth, that you are indeed one of *us*, whom she despises so much, almost as much as your poor old boyfriend. You can see the regret in that angel's eyes, every time he thinks about you.'

Whoever said that girls were bitchy, had yet to see the male supernatural community in full flow. It seemed these men had spent centuries perfecting their cattiness and they seemed to take pleasure in verbally assaulting each other. It was tiring to say the least.

'You can of course wake her for me, if you wish,' I said, knowing that asking him not to, would be a sure way to speed up his discovery, 'but I thought it was me you wanted here and now you've got me, what do you intend to do to me, because I have many things I intend to do to you?' I glared at him, staring him down, refusing to play victim.

'Well that sounds very appealing,' he said, his eyes roaming the length of my body, lingering on my chest, then slowly drifting down over my hard stomach to the tops of my thighs. How very boring. I decided to shake things up a little. They may have warded my cell but his witch clearly didn't have the power to bind my magic. I planted my feet on the floor and drew up more energy from the ground until I could feel it tingling in my veins and surging like an electrical storm. I threw everything I had at them both. I didn't want them dead, just disabled and out of my way. I wanted out.

Cole was instantly flung across the room, his eyes wide with shock, hair standing on end as the electrical energy ran through his undead body. He smacked into the stone walling with a crack that resounded around the cellar, and I watched as a crack snaked its way up the wall from where his head had landed. If only he wasn't a five hundred year old vampire I might have gotten somewhere, but as it was he picked himself up, dusted himself down and smiled at me.

'I like a girl with a bit of fight in her,' he said. 'Next time I would appreciate it if you extended your protection to cover your boss, as well as your lovely self,' he added, casting a cold glance towards the witch, who had remained in the same spot. 'I fear we will have to tame your spirits a little, before we continue our discussion. Bind her Brit,' he said.

Before I had time throw a protection spell around myself, I was hit sideways, the blast knocking me off my feet, so I landed on my butt. Within seconds I was back on my feet throwing my hands out, trying to lift her off her feet and slam her head on the stone ground. If I knocked her out, her magic would be disabled, but her wards held. She lifted her hands and chanted, magic pouring out of her fingers and slithering through the bars, settling on me, around me, tightening my chest, wrapping around my throat, my wrists and my ankles. I was held fast, and then slowly, excruciatingly pushed backwards where I fell onto the bed.

'Now then my dear, I can do all those things to you that you talked about,' Cole said, his eyes sparkling with desire. 'I have developed quite a taste for witch blood recently,' he said, glancing back at the witch. 'But I have heard mixed blood is a taste quite unlike anything else.' The witch frowned, her eyes flashing with jealousy as she watched Cole move towards my cell, retrieving the keys from his jeans pocket.

'You may go now Brittany, but I may need you later on to set up some camouflage wards around the club, to protect us from any prying eyes that come in search of my little conquest.'

CHAPTER SIXTEEN

Brittany scowled at me one last time as if I was the lucky one, stealing her prize. *Weird!* As far as I was concerned, she was welcome to him. I scowled back and couldn't resist one last try of my magic. As she turned her back on me I tried to trip her up. I wanted to see her on her ass, but alas nothing. Her magical bonds squeezed tighter around my aura, an invisible anaconda holding me fast in its coils. Terror now began to edge in, creeping around the edges of my confidence, tearing down my walls. I was helpless, but luckily for me Cole appeared to be hesitating at my door.

'Hmm, I do think maybe a little three-way might make things a little more interesting,' he said, casting a quick glance at Alex's cell, and then grinning back at me. 'Not that she has much left to give, but it might make things a little more exciting, don't you think?'

I shuddered, he was truly despicable. My heart jumped as I realised what he was about to uncover, but I knew that Alex had hopefully had enough time to get somewhere safe.

'You wake her,' I said smiling.

This clearly wasn't the answer he expected, so he stared at me a moment longer, obviously wondering if I was bluffing. I grinned some more, feeling true happiness that I had at least succeeded in foiling a part of his plan.

'I will, and you will now pay for your attitude by watching as I gorge myself on the last remaining drop of her blood.'

'I'd like to see you try,' I said.

At that moment, his eyes swept across the wall of Alex's cell and alighted on the space left by the missing iron bars. I watched as he did a comical double take, then scanned the cell, taking in the bars on the floor and the crumpled blankets, before letting out a yell, unlocking the door and charging across to her bed.

'You... little... Urh! *You* did this,' he yelled at me, as he stretched up and stared through the window at the empty garden before turning back to me.

'I'm a witch, what did you expect? Me to sit pretty and not try and get my friend out? That's what I came to do,' I said.

'But she was just bait, nothing more than a disposable human girl, plenty more of them! But you!

You are a rare gem, and now you are mine. You played right into my hands, Jessica.'

'Maybe, but I always intended to get her out. I intended to get me out too, and I will. I'm not yours and I never will be. If you want me to be any use to you, you will have to release these bonds, otherwise what is the point?' I said.

'There are other ways to break a person Jessica, and I intend to demonstrate one of them right now,' he said, unlocking my cell and stepping through the door. I watched carefully as he pocketed the key. I would need that, and if these magical bonds slipped just a fraction, I had to be ready.

He sauntered across the cell and sat down next to me on the bed. I struggled in my magical bonds but they had no give in them. My legs were stiff and immobile, stretched out ahead of me on the bed, my arms pinned to my sides, paralysed. I watched with increasing horror as he reached out and trailed a hand up my leg. Thank God I was wearing jeans, skinny ones at that, so they didn't give much room for unwanted access and were as difficult to get off as they had been to get on. As his hand reached my thigh I cringed, his fingers rubbed my inner thigh as his eyes sparkled. He leaned over me and pushed his other hand up and under my sweatshirt.

'Is this the only way you get to have sex, Cole? Such a shame no one actually *wants* you. I always wondered why men get off on forcing a woman, but then I guess it comes down to being so pathetically desperate for it, you don't have another choice,' I said, clenching my teeth.

Cole looked up at me and snarled, as his eyes darkened. 'I have plenty of women begging me to make love to them, but after several hundred years it gets boring. I shall enjoy breaking you in.'

'Well, I hope you're feeling confident. You've got a lot to live up to, you know. Luke was my ex-boyfriend, and angels are exceptional, and Wow! Daniel was something else!' I raved, hoping to put him under a pressure that I knew men didn't handle well.

His hand whipped out from under my top and smacked into my face with such force, it pushed the top half of my body off the bed. The lower half of my body was still pinned underneath Cole, otherwise I would have been on the floor. At least his hand was off my breast, for the time being, but my cheek burned and my eye watered. In my head I flailed around, but in reality I was hanging off the bed, paralysed, waiting for him to pull me back on, which he did.

'First lesson, you need to learn how to keep your mouth shut,' he said.

'Oh, I'm sorry, did I touch a nerve? Do we have performance issues in the bedroom?' I stared him in the eye, refusing to back down.

His eyes narrowed and he pulled back slightly. I wondered if he was going to swing at me again, from the other side, but instead his mouth curled up in an imitation of a smile. Seconds later my heart sank as he reached forward and went for my jeans button, opening it and tugging at the material clinging to my hips.

'Let's find out, shall we?' He said, pulling harder at the material.

I tried to wriggle, squirm. I tried to ground and draw in energy. I tried to levitate him off me, and throw him across the cell, like I had done with Aaron all those months ago, but nothing worked. I was frozen. However, after a few minutes I realised that being frozen was actually hindering him in his current mission. The witch, Brittany, had evidently frozen me so well as to allow no movement of my limbs, making it impossible for Cole to remove my tight jeans. He grunted with frustration as he tried to prise my legs apart, but he got as far as I did, nowhere! After a few more minutes, I think even he realised that even if he succeeded in ripping my jeans off, he would never manage to pull my legs apart. Maybe that was exactly what Brittany had intended. I sent her silent thanks and smiled up at Cole.

'Having problems, Cole? It might be easier if you got your little witch friend to break the magical bonds she's tied me up with so well, but then again, maybe she doesn't want to share,' I said.

For a minute he scowled at me, his youthful face the picture of a sulky teenage schoolboy, but then the dangerous, ancient vampire reappeared and he smiled.

'I think you're right Jessica, that's just what I'll do, but this playing has made me hungry and like I said, there are many ways to break a witch.'

Before I even had time to think about what he meant, he had grabbed me and flung me from the bed and across the cell. I landed like a ragdoll, my limbs remained immobile and outstretched like a Barbie doll, my head cracked against the bars. I closed my eyes knowing what was coming next as I saw his body gracefully flying across the space and land on top of me. His fangs protruding fully from his gums, his dark eyes shone red, as he lunged towards my neck.

If I had let him in, if I'd accepted my fate, it wouldn't have hurt so much, but I refused. My mental walls were up, I sealed my eyes and felt every agonising second as he leeched the blood from my body. With my eyes shut, I couldn't help think about

Daniel. Where was he? So much had happened in the last hour that it hadn't occurred to me to try and contact him again. I wasn't sure whether I should now, as he would feel my pain, and I didn't want him to know what I was going through, yet I desperately needed him to know where I was. I needed him to find me, and quick. Even if he was still incarcerated, he could send help… and that's when it hit me. I knew *exactly* who was responsible for the Manchester girls' deaths. I opened my eyes.

'You did it, didn't you? You had those girls killed to keep Daniel and Eva out of the way, didn't you?'

Cole pulled back, my blood creating a horrific clown's mouth around his lips as he smiled and I knew my answer.

'Needs must be met,' he said. 'Your blood, by the way is most enjoyable. I can feel it reviving me in ways I haven't felt for decades. Just a little more and I don't think you'll have the energy to sit up, never mind conjure a spell.' He lowered himself back down and I felt a duller pain this time as his fangs repenetrated the new wounds.

So that was his plan. I needed to contact Daniel before it was too late. I pulled back into my head and closing my eyes, tried to block out the pressure of Cole's body on top of me, to suppress the pain as my body became weaker.

'Daniel?' I said, my mind forming a picture of him, in another room this time, Eva to his side, Sebastian opposite him and others I didn't recognise talking in hushed voices around him.

'Jessie is that you?' he asked I saw the people all turn to stare at him, and Eva's eyes went vacant as she too entered his thoughts, but as his maker she could only converse with him, watch his memories; not speak to me.

'Jessie, what's happening to you?' he asked.

'I can't... I'm sorry Daniel, so sorry, but I don't think we have long. Cole has me in a cellar under a church. Eva, I know you're listening. It was Cole behind the Manchester girl's deaths. He wanted you two out of the way, to get to me. I walked straight into his trap, but I got Alex out. She escaped. You have to find...' I could feel my link with him fading fast even as I sped through my speech. As Cole sucked Daniel's blood out of my body, my bond was being once again destroyed, my hope of escape obliterated. I mentally kicked myself at not thinking to contact him earlier.

As a vampire, my heart only beat every minute or so, under normal circumstances. The witch part of me meant that whenever I got excited or anxious like normal humans my heart beat would increase, but now I could barely feel it. I could feel his weight pressing me into the hard stone floor and as my life force was sucked away, cold began to penetrate my body.

A couple of minutes later, I was drifting in and out of consciousness, when I noticed his weight had disappeared. As I opened my eyes I could just see a dark, blurred shape recede, and hear the dull clang of the door being opened and closed again. He'd gone, but I was still paralysed. I closed my eyes and let myself drift, wondering if Daniel and Luke would be able to work out where I was being kept.

When I awoke I found myself back on the camp bed. There was very little light coming through my window, so I presumed it must be dusk. I instinctively drew the blanket around my freezing shoulders and that's when I realised. I could move again; they'd removed the spell. I rolled onto my side and shivered. I hadn't *ever* felt this cold, even at the beginning, when we realised the banked blood wasn't nourishing me and I had refused all fresh sources... before Daniel. I tried to sit up, but as Cole had planned, I didn't have the energy. I tried to contact Daniel. I closed my eyes and imagined his face. I searched for a way to reach him, but there was nothing. I tried to ground, to draw energy from the dirt beneath the stone slabs and pull it into my frozen body, but I was left panting, dizzy. So I did the only thing I could. I slept.

The next time I awoke there was no light coming through my window, but someone had lit a couple of candles outside my cell. I tried to push myself up into a sitting position and this time I managed it. After a glance around the cells, I reassured myself that I was alone, before taking time to assess my injuries. The spell had definitely been removed, because I had full mobility of all my limbs. My vampire metabolism had obviously been working whilst I had slept as there were no obvious bruises or cuts anywhere on my body. My cheek felt tender where it had been slammed into the wall and punched, but there was no swelling, just dried blood which I could scrape off with my nail.

However, my skin felt dry and cracked, my mouth parched. I knew I was dangerously dehydrated. Without a mirror I couldn't see what my face looked like, but I could feel the dry skin flaking off, cracking around my lips. I could feel my cheeks had sunken into the hollows beneath. I stared at the skin on my hands, they looked like they belonged to a ninety year old woman. My stomach ached persistently, not from the trauma of being thrown across the cell, but from hunger. I could hear my heartbeat pulsing slowly but loudly in my head, drumming incessantly, urging me to find food. I ran my tongue over my fangs, which were evidently staying out whether I liked it or not.

My body had gone into survival mode. I was a starving vampire and I knew that I would literally jump at the chance to consume anything that crossed my path. I knew that if Cole appeared with a pint of blood and a deal to be made, I would jump at any terms he offered. I wanted to stay alive, at any cost. I looked up at the window and frowned. Alex must have escaped, otherwise she would be back in the cell opposite me. So why had no one come for me? It must have been almost ten hours since her escape, so surely Luke had found her. Where was he?

I was now sure that the Council would have released Daniel after hearing about my kidnapping so if Sebastian had forbidden Daniel and Eva to come after me, he obviously didn't think I was worth risking a vampire war over. If Luke hadn't come to find me, he had obviously made peace with his conflicting emotions and decided to stay out of vampire affairs, knowing that Alex was safe. I shrugged. My vampire instinct was taking over and survival was all that mattered. If they had deserted me, I had nothing to lose. All I needed now was a meal, no matter what the cost.

I tried to stand, but my legs gave way underneath me and I fell back onto the bed, my head reeling. I lay back once more and when my body started convulsing with cold, I wrapped the blanket as tightly as I could around myself. I coughed, the membranes in my throat feeling like they were coated in sandpaper. My eyes closed.

'Jess. *Jess*! Wake up.' I dismissed the first whisper, but when the second came I opened my eyes. Brittany, the young witch was standing by my cell, holding a candle and peering through the gloom. She smelled delicious. My vampire senses took over and I could clearly hear her heartbeat thrumming away in her chest, like a butterfly caught in a glass jar. She was nervous, and I was hungry. I sat up with a start, and regretted it immediately as my vision blurred and my head spun.

My eyes zeroed in on her and I could clearly see, in the candlelight, the blush to her cheeks, her veins running beneath the delicate skin over her throat. I wondered if I would be able to launch myself across the cell in one quick movement, something which would be simple to a healthy vampire; just one easy jump. She was standing close enough to the bars that I could reach through and grab her arm; a wrist would do just fine. I would worry about her magic later.

'Jess, don't even try it. It would be a waste of what energy you have left. I have permanently shielded myself against all unwanted vampire contact, so you'll be thrown back across the cell as if electrocuted and you may not have the energy to survive it,' she murmured.

'So why are you here? To taunt me? I need food. Where's Cole?' I asked, my mouth feeling the first moisture since awakening, as her scent made the saliva flood in.

'I'm going to help you. Cole's had to go back to Mayfair. The Council are interviewing him.'

'If you'd wanted to, you could have helped me earlier. Why ward my cell and paralyse me? Why should I trust you?' I asked my voice rising. I still held a grudge towards her for the way she had left me helpless, and that grudge increased my desire to bite her. Oh, how I wanted to bite her!

'I'm sorry. I thought Cole loved me...' she said. I sighed and raised my eyes to Heaven. How old was this girl? How could she be so naïve?

'He said you didn't matter, that he just wanted to speak to you. That I was the only one he wanted to be with. It was all a lie. After he came out of your cell he yelled at me, told me I'd made the spell wrong, that he hadn't been able to... *subdue* you...'

'Rape me, you mean, and thanks for that. If your magic hadn't been so restrictive he probably would have,' I said, remembering. I owed her that much.

'I overheard him, just before he left. He was talking to Ed, his sidekick. I heard something about it all going wrong, that he needed to dispose of the evidence quick. He had too much to lose. He also mentioned something about getting rid of *both* witches, and needing the cells dismantled tomorrow.'

'So why do you want to help me? You could just leave,' I said.

'I'm not going to leave a fellow witch to be disposed of vampire style,' she said. 'Besides, I hate them all, only I thought Cole was different. He said he was,' she said, her eyes sad.

'Believe me, right now I can't feel the witch inside me at all. All I can think of is food... blood. If you want to get me out of here you need to find me some blood packs. That bastard's drained me; I'll need at least three before I can even walk. Ideally more, so I have enough power to support your magic.'

'I'll have a look, but I'm not sure where he keeps them. They don't tend to drink from blood packs, Jess. The nightclub above us is their normal feeding ground.'

'There's a nightclub above us?' I asked.

'Yes, it's his. It's called 'Bite Club! Ironic, huh?' she said, with a small smile.

'Bite Club? And no one's cottoned on?'

'Nope. As he says, fictional vampires are so popular now that a club with such an obvious name is thought to be a human owned club. No supe would dare be so obvious,' she said with a shrug.

Wow! I was so looking forward to kicking this arrogant guy's ass. How had The Council been so wrong about him? I stood up without thinking and, as what little blood I had left rushed to my feet, I sat back down quickly, before I fell down.

'I need food, Brittany.'

'Okay. I'll be back as soon as I can. Here, have this other blanket while I'm gone,' she said, quickly entering Alex's cell and throwing me the blanket through the bars.

'Brittany? Did she get away? They haven't caught her, have they?' I asked, as she began climbing the stone stairs out of the cellar.

'No, she's gone. I believe they searched the area, but nothing has been seen of her.'

I sighed. So why hadn't help come?

CHAPTER SEVENTEEN

Shortly after Brittany left, throbbing music began to penetrate the cellar from above. Bite Club must have opened. I hoped this meant that Cole's cronies would be kept busy, and Cole himself would stay away a while longer. I felt vulnerable whilst Brittany was gone and wished she had opened my cell door first, but then I guess it hadn't crossed our minds at the time. I wouldn't have been able to walk through them anyway. Heck, I could barely sit.

I wrapped myself tighter in the double blankets, laid back and stared at the window. Why hadn't he come for me? I was sure Daniel must have enough information to be able to track me down, and with Alex out, surely she had found them and said where she had come from? Maybe she didn't want to know me any longer? I wondered if too much had passed between us, too much had been stolen from her to be able to look me in the eye.

A noise behind the cellar door alerted me to a

disruption. There was more than one person about to enter. I sat up abruptly, my head again losing the fight for control as the room blurred and whirled in front of my eyes. I needed to lie back down but I refused to show weakness if they had come for me; if I was going to die.

The door opened and I watched as a pair of feet appeared at the top of the stone steps pausing briefly, and I recognised Brittany's voice whispering something to someone else and waited, holding back the door as another pair of shoes joined her on the steps - A *man's* shoes. What was she doing? I had been sure she had been trying to help me. Had she been caught by one of Cole's vampires? But why would she be whispering to him? It didn't make sense. My head had begun to clear and my senses returned to me, telling me what my eyes couldn't work out. She had brought a human with her.

As a witch, her scent was slightly different to the average human, and as all humans smelled different it was hard to distinguish, but I was getting there. The person she had with her was definitely a regular human male. He smelled of the same warm, chocolaty aromas I had grown used to associating with humans. His was a particularly enticing aroma, with dark spicy undercurrents. My stomach began aching again, and the gums behind my fangs, which had failed to retract, were throbbing. Saliva pooled in my mouth as the pair quietly closed the door behind them and walked into sight.

'Brittany, what have you done? I don't feed from humans... I haven't yet anyway. I mean I was going to start but then....' I trailed off, not knowing what to say or do. A part of me deep inside was exceptionally worried about the scene before me, but the vampire struggling to survive was snarling and snapping, waiting to get out.

'Jess, I'm sorry. I looked everywhere I could think of without getting caught, but I couldn't find any blood packs anywhere. I overheard one of Cole's men saying Cole is on his way back. He has talked his way out of whatever the Council were asking him about and he's coming to deal with you. We don't have much time, so that's when I thought of Amir. He's a feeder Jess, he knows what he's doing, he'll help you... and he knows how to stop you if, well you know if you have trouble stopping,' she said, her eyes worried.

'No, I can't risk it. I'm too hungry,' I said, ignoring the snapping vampire and desperately trying to hold onto the tendril of sanity I had left.

'You can, remember I'm here. I can stop you if I need to. I could throw you off him maybe,' she said with a grin.

'It's fine. Jess, is that your name?' Amir asked as he

stepped closer to the cell. Amir was a mixed race, London boy with flawless olive skin and huge brown eyes. His hair was styled fashionably and he wore the all black 'uniform' of the goth code. 'I'd like to help, really I would.'

I couldn't control myself any longer, the pain in my stomach was incessant, my skin felt ancient and crumbly. If I didn't feed, I was going to die, eventually from hunger but more likely within half an hour when Cole reappeared to clear up his mess. I nodded at Brittany and she focused on the cell padlock for a minute before it clicked and fell to the floor. I kicked myself that I hadn't thought of that when I first arrived and frowned.

'Don't kick yourself Jess, if you had tried to open the lock to get to Alex, she wouldn't have escaped. Your entire cell, including the padlock was charmed. The alarm would have triggered, and Alex would probably be dead,' she said.

As Amir walked softly towards me, I could feel the animal inside me waiting to spring, and if I had been left with any energy left inside me, he wouldn't have made it more than a step into my cell. I felt an incredible urge to leap out of my bed and across the cell. My ears hummed with a crashing noise. I felt my nostrils flare as his scent became too strong for me to control my actions. I attempted to launch myself out of the bed, but I was far too weak and fell to my knees on the floor, my eyes flashing as my prey paused mid-step.

'Jess, shhhh! It's all right. It'll be alright,' he said. I'm embarrassed to say, I snarled.

He slowly walked up to me and with every ounce of humanity left inside me I willed myself not to fall upon his leg as he came close. I held on.

'Here, come to me. I need you too,' he said, as he sat on my bed and held his arms out to me.

'I can't,' I stammered, truly scared of what I was going to do, but losing the fragile hold I had on myself.

'Here,' he said, as he reached under my skinny, shrunken arms and hauled me back onto the bed, where he laid down and pulled me down next to him.

His scent assaulted me, my senses blazed and my instincts took over. I needed no further invitation, I could only hope that between them both they'd be able to stop me, before I did what Sebastian did to Alba.

Blood was life, and as his blood nourished me. I finally understood what Sebastian, Daniel and Eva had been trying to tell me. We were vampires, we needed blood to survive and as his blood renewed my strength, I realised how weak I had made myself by refusing to drink the real thing. It was amazing, fiery, like dark hot chocolate with a hint of chilli. Its dark, spicy taste was like nothing I'd tasted before, surpassing Daniel's blood by a mile. With each drop I could feel my skin softening, my cheeks filling out, my muscles hardening and my heart pulsing, growing stronger.

Amir too was enjoying the experience. He moaned underneath me, his eyes slightly glazed and half closed in ecstasy as he ran his hands up and down my side. I could feel him, hard, aroused, pushing against my hip, but he didn't try anything and I kept on drinking.

'Jess, Jess, I think it's time.' I heard Brittany's voice faraway but something didn't connect. It didn't matter. All that mattered to me now, was this amazing experience. This life force being given to me willingly, making me strong. It was instantly addictive. I needed more and more of it, to fill out every last vein in my body. All I could think about was his sweet taste in my mouth, his tantalising aroma filling my nostrils and driving me on.

'Jess, come on... JESS!' Her words irritated me, distracted me, nudging something deep inside. There was something I was supposed to remember, but I couldn't think what. As her words faded out I felt him struggle a little by my side, shift and push gently against me. His voice was quiet, crooning.

'Jess, jess, it's time to stop. You've had enough, come on now... Jess!' His voice rose as he pushed harder against my immobile body.

'Jess, I really don't want to have to do this, but you'll hurt him if you take anymore. JESS! Come...' And then all hell broke loose.

Her words were cut off mid-stream and ended in a yelp of surprise. Noticing the abrupt end to the words buzzing round my head, I moved my position slightly to the side and keeping my teeth still in my meal I glanced up, my vampire vision renewed. Men were pouring into the room, every one of them vampires. Brittany had been grabbed from behind and flung outside the cell. She was now being dragged by her hair towards the stone steps by another smaller vampire I couldn't make out, her feet struggling to gain purchase on the flooring. I knew I should be concerned, but all I could think about was protecting my meal, like a lioness protecting her kill. I snarled and wrapped my arm around Amir's body, holding him tighter, crushing his struggling and flailing limbs.

'What have we here, boys? It seems our little vampire isn't as innocent as everyone thinks. Such a shame we haven't got more time to play...' Cole's voice was low, menacing. I should have let go of Amir and flung a spell at him, but my head was fixed upon my first real meal. I glared at Cole and snarled some more, incapable of letting go.

Not that it made the slightest bit of difference to

Cole and his five colleagues. I was outnumbered. With rough hands grasping my ankles and an arm round my throat, I was pulled back as Amir was dragged out from underneath me, kicking and shouting.

'Hey thanks guys. Things got a bit scary there. Give me a night to recharge and I'll be back up at the club,' Amir said, looking at Cole.

'He knows too much, dispose of him,' Cole said, looking with contempt at the young boy in front of him. Cole then looked across at my frozen face and smiled. With Amir out of my grasp, my belly full and my body restored, sanity finally began to descend upon me and the full meaning of his words fell like icy hailstones, chilling me as I watched helplessly. Within seconds, as I struggled between the three vampires pinning me down, Amir was murdered, his neck broken, his eyes glazed with instant death as they let him fall to the floor.

'Now where's that traitor witch gone, Mary?' Cole asked as a female vampire stalked back into the cell.

'She escaped. By the time I'd dragged her to the steps, she had control of her power and muttered some sort of spell. She disappeared,' Mary said with a shrug.

'Which is why I ordered you to kill first, play later,' Cole said, shaking his head. 'So now there is just you,' he continued, looking back at me.

The fourth vampire who had discarded Amir's body on the floor had now joined the other three who were struggling to hold me. With four pinning me down I needed a new plan. I needed magic, and where the hell was Daniel? I decided magic was more urgent than trying to reach Daniel telepathically, based on the psychotic pleasure Cole seemed to take in killing people.

I stopped struggling and closed my eyes, trying to shut out the situation and concentrate. I grounded instantly. I felt the immediate rush of energy fill my veins, giving an additional power rush to the fresh blood, still humming round my system. I needed a spell to knock out the six vampires… but what? I was stumped; I just didn't have enough experience. If I slammed one into a wall the other three would break my neck. I doubted I could lift all four together… maybe I could electrify myself and zap the across the cell… Nah, too movie-like. I supressed a smile, I needed to know how Susannah had made a vortex, or how Brittany had disappeared.

'Guys, she's grounding. Unless you want to be turned into frogs, I suggest you knock her out… at least until I find a way of restraining her,' Cole said, watching me and taking a quick step back towards the cell door, along with the female vampire, Mary.

As he spoke I looked at the vampire dude on my

left. He was older than Cole, but that wasn't difficult seeing as Cole barely looked about eighteen. He was stocky, with a square jawbone jutting out and pink fleshy lips, which curled back over his sharp fangs. To my right was the vampire who had murdered Amir. He was a middle aged vampire, and would have looked more at home in an Armani suit and a law office. Only his eyes gave away his true nature. Holding my ankles were another two young vampires, who looked like twins, their blonde hair long and tied back in ponytails. I decided they were my least problem, as the other two were next to my head and neck, which posed more threat.

I quickly turned to the murderer on my right, shot my power at him and as his eyes opened in shock, he lifted off the floor and flew across the cell, before slamming into the bars. Seconds later, just as a fist slammed into my cheekbone, I imagined the cell bars the vampire had landed upon widen, just enough to fit his head through. In the seconds before I blacked out, I watched as the surprised vampire slipped down his head falling just where I wanted before I used my magic to pull the bars back together. He was trapped.

Thanks to my vampire metabolism, I was only out for a couple of seconds at most, but three seconds was all a gloved Cole needed, to pounce with vampire speed, binding my wrists and ankles together with some silver chains, that would slowly drain my power. When I came to, the first thing I felt was the silver metal sizzling against my skin. Silver and vampires never mix well. I remembered Eva telling me, when I had wanted to buy a silver necklace we had seen in a shop. She told me how the properties in the pure metal would burn our skin. I had since found out that in addition to this, silver would drain my magic, and could be used effectively to restrain a witch, damn!

I struggled against the burning bonds, knowing I didn't have much time before my magic was lowered to an unusable level. Currently I was still strong, so I quickly sought out the vampire who remained by my head, the one I presumed responsible for my throbbing cheekbone. I stared at him and hate coursed through my system. Cole may be the ringleader, Cole might be to blame for all of this, but I knew from the way they were carrying out his orders without question, that they must be of his blood. He must have turned them, and therefore it stood to reason that it would hurt him, if I took them out first.

The silver chains were doing something to my magic, I could feel it. Control over my magic was fast disappearing, but in its place was something darker, something primitive. The same instinctive magic that had been released in anger, the afternoon I broke Daniel's hand. I looked at the vampire and knew how to eliminate him, and knew Cole would feel every second of it.

Fire! I imagined flames slowly licking at the vampire's feet, climbing up his body, consuming him and destroying him. I glanced down and felt my anger build, forcing all the emotional pain and feeling of my friends deserting me, leaving me here, to fight on my own, into my magic. I summoned the dark witch inside me and cast my spell. With a howl of pure terror the vampire by my side jumped back, stomping his feet on the ground, trying to put out the flames that licked around his ankles.

'Help me, Cole, help me,' the vampire screamed, as he propelled himself backwards away from my bed.

'Get out, get upstairs and start emptying the club,' Cole ordered the remaining three vampires.

'Get me out of here,' the vampire struggling to escape from my prison of bars shouted at the retreating vamps, his eyes fearful as he watched the flaming vampire stumble closer to him.

Cole stood, taking in the scene around him, barely glancing at the imprisoned vampire, who struggled to pull his head out from between the bars, pulling with all his remaining strength to widen them. But he tried in vain, as the iron bars had been made purposefully to be vampire proof.

As the now flaming vampire had stumbled to the

far side of the cell, away from me, Cole stepped forward, his face the calm mask of a psychotic killer.

'I think Miss Jessica, you may have solved my problem for me, for what can be better than fire and silver to eradicate all evidence of a nuisance witch? Even if the Council think I had something to do with this unfortunate episode, after this fire consumes everything in this room, there will be no proof left to back up their suspicions. What a shame.'

I struggled some more with my chains, feeling the metal burn further into my ankles, feeling every second as the skin on my wrists scorched and sizzled. I closed my eyes and concentrated on my remaining magic, drawing it to me and sending it down into my arms, my hands, my fingers. I needed the chains to uncoil. If only I could change them into something else, make them fall off me…

But my magic was disappearing and I was losing my grasp on it. I frowned, scrunching my eyes together, imagining the chains changing density, losing their metal properties, and then suddenly the burning began to recede, the chains felt softer, had a little give in them. It was working!

'Ooph,' the air whooshed out of my chest as Cole suddenly landed on top of me.

'You spoiled my game darling, so before I leave you to burn in the pyre of your own making, I reckon on having a last few minutes of fun.'

With horror, my concentration lapsed and I watched as the vampire on top of my stretched out body slithered down over my hips, his hands running the length of my calves, stopping a cautious distance from my chained ankles. Here, he reared up and sat smiling at me, like some psychotic version of a Justin Bieber doll. After a quick pause for dramatic effect, he popped open the button on my jeans, pulled down the zipper and exposed my naked hips. This was not good!

With a last struggle on my chained wrists I tried to ignore him, as I once again focused on the last dregs of magic. I felt his lips touch my hips and I jerked away, but he held me fast and sank his fangs into my flesh. I screamed as pain and pleasurable tingles simultaneously coursed up my spine. With his hands he pushed my sweatshirt up over my stomach, withdrew and then sank his fangs into my side, just underneath my ribs. I yelled out and screamed some more, bucking and convulsing my body beneath him. It would not end like this. He pulled back and sat up, smirking at me.

'Relax darling, you'll enjoy it more,' he said, before glancing quickly at the vampire who had now stopped screaming and was keening quietly, as the flames had consumed the lower part of his body so that he could no longer move.

'I believe we haven't got much time left, so I shall give you the option dear, as I do like a girl with attitude. Either I leave you here to a fate of your own making, or I can rip out your throat.'

'How about one more bite? I always liked it by my collar bone,' I said, suddenly deciding that if there was no escape, I would take him with me. For a second he paused and stared at me, unsure why I had suddenly given in, but then his ego took over and he smiled and sank down over me once more. With a last mental push I focused on the now softened chains coiled round my wrists and smiled grimly as I felt them dissolve. My ankles were still firmly tied, and I had no strength or magic left to do more than one last thing, and that wouldn't be enough. There would be no escape for me, but I would make sure that whatever pain Cole had put Alex through, he would pay for.

I wrapped my arms round him as he bit into my neck. He jerked back shocked, but I locked my hands together firmly round his back pulling him down on top of me, holding him tight, and then I chanted my spell. The one I had been saying in my head as I torched the previous vampire.

In seconds his whole body was consumed in flames and he was howling. I pushed him off me as fast as I could, but it was too late as I knew it would be. He rolled onto the floor where he stumbled to his feet and ran blindly across the cell, his body burning and blackening before my eyes. As I frantically attempted to pat out the flames which were now slowly snaking their way across my sweatshirt and down onto my blanket, I saw him stumble into the other remaining vampire, who was still struggling to free himself from the bars.

Now there were three vampires burning in my cell, it wouldn't take long before the whole place caught. I had managed to put out the worst of the flames across my chest, but I could feel my skin still smouldering and there were more flames licking the corners of the blanket. The second blanket had fallen on the floor during the earlier struggle and its far corner was now dangerously close to the vampire pyre which burned only a few metres away.

With my hands released, but blistering badly from patting out the flames, I reached forwards and tried untying the silver chains around my ankles, but I didn't have gloves and my hands were already burnt. I screamed as the silver sizzled against my new wounds, and felt myself go faint, as it further drained my energy. The fire was creeping ever nearer to the blanket, so I pulled more frantically, ignoring my poor hands and desperately trying to stay conscious while the thick fumes now swirled around me, and the last of my magic disappeared.

The fire, which had been stumped momentarily by the cold stone flooring, eventually managed to make the leap to the blanket, which it consumed quickly, racing across its fibres, ever closer to my bed. I screamed, hoping someone would hear me from outside. I knew there were no residential houses within sight of this old church, but I was hopeful that someone from the club above would hear my screams. I tried to keep my eyes from the flames licking around the edge of the bed frame, and returned to the task of freeing my ankles.

With a last tug I freed one side and my left foot was out. There were dark burn marks circumventing my ankle, but I could move it. As I turned my attention to my right foot the flames found my mattress and within seconds I was sitting in the middle of a bonfire. I screamed and leaving my last foot chained to the bed I leapt off the bed and half hopped, half dragged the bed, still attached to my burning foot, halfway across the cell, away from the burning vampires, but wherever I went I pulled the burning bed behind me.

My strength was gone, the flames had begun to travel up my leg and my jeans were already smouldering. I'd always known it was unlikely that I would escape, but now my time was up. I let a tear escape and run down my cheek. Pain began attacking me viciously, consuming me and tiring me. I took a last look at the dying Cole and managed a last smile. Weirdly, he was lit up by a strange bright light which was getting brighter, coming through the bars from the direction of the cellar door, but I lost focus and lay down in my corner, taking a moments respite from the cool stone. I drifted off into unconsciousness, thinking only of the coolness against my skin.

CHAPTER EIGHTEEN

I was awakened by someone wrapping something round me, furiously patting out the flames and then scooping me up. The material rubbed against my burnt skin and sizzled where it stuck, and I let out a scream of pain.

'Sorry Jessie, but I've got to get you out of here. It's okay now, you'll be fine.'

As he stood up and jostled my body against him I screamed some more, feeling the fire burning within my body. The flames may have gone, but the fire raged on within my flesh.

'She's not going to make it, Luke,' I heard a female voice say from behind him. I opened my eyes again and glancing over his shoulder and saw another angel. I thought I recognised her, but my vision was hazy. She was dressed in the same plain yoga style pants and tunic, this time black, worn without the robe, which was probably a good thing, as I was sure it would be a fire hazard. She was throwing strange, shimmering grey cloths over the various fires, under which they sizzled and went out. When she reached the remains of a vampire she drew her sword and with one clean swipe beheaded it.

With every step, pain jolted through my body, and each time Luke's arms rubbed against my skin, I felt it begin to flake off, and knew I couldn't take anymore.

'Luke, please end this, I'm dying. Put me down. It hurts too much,' I said, my voice barely more than a whisper.

'Luke, I need to go and secure the building before the nuke. Ten minutes okay?' the girl said, who I now remembered was Caoimhe, the angel who had come to my rescue in Lancashire.

'Sure,' he said, watching as she left the room and ascended the steps to the ground floor.

'Luke please, stop,' I asked once more.

He had carried me out of my original cell and he was now standing with me in the narrow passageway between the two cells. After a quick look down into my face, he seemed to come to a decision and he took a couple of gentle steps into the opposite cell and laid me gently on the bed.

'Are you still burning?' he asked quietly.

'Yes, I don't think it will be long. Stay with me,' I said, and then, 'Where's Daniel?'

'He's coming. They're a couple of hours behind us.

They had to get Sebastian's permission, as there was a whole mess of legalities around threatening their territory. Anyway, I believe they're here now, so you hang on okay? He can help you heal. You can feed from him, and then you'll heal won't you? I've just got to get you out of this building.'

'Luke, there's no time. If you move me now, I'll die. I can feel my insides burning,' I whispered, before a series of nasty coughs spat blood across our shirts. I smiled weakly at him.

'Thanks for coming for me. I didn't think you would,' I said.

'Why? Why wouldn't I come for you?' he asked.

'I got Alex out. She's safe, isn't she? I'm just a vampire and when I die you won't have to feel like you did the wrong thing every time you see me.'

'Yes, it took us hours to find Alex, that's why we were so late, but why would you think I want you to die?' he frowned and looked away.

'Luke, you hate me. I know you can't stand what I am. When I'm dead you won't be reminded of that every day.' Another series of coughs shook my body and left me panting in shallow breaths. I closed my eyes.

'No, Jess you're wrong, and you're not going to die. I saved you once, and yes I may have regretted it, but there's no way I'm letting you die here in this cell…

like this. Here,' he said, and I opened my eyes in shock as a wet, sticky wrist was pressed against my lips.

I pushed it gently away, 'Luke what are you doing? You can't do this,' I said.

'I can, and I will. Just drink, right. Get better.'

I didn't wait another second, but drew his wrist to me and lapped up his blood. My fangs bit through deeper and I felt the immediate relief as the internal fire blazing in my body was dampened.

'Careful Jess, remember I'm an angel, my bloods different, pure,' he said, as a quiet moan left his lips.

I nodded as much as I could to show I had heard, but not willing to remove my mouth from his wrist. His blood had the same deep, chocolaty taste that human blood had, but his carried the same floral notes that I could smell whenever I was around him. It felt like ice slushy, pouring through my veins, healing and revitalising, soothing and refreshing.

'Wow, Jess you're healing. You're skin's going pink again,' he said.

I opened my eyes and stared up at him. I didn't feel the insane, animalistic urge to keep feeding this time, but then I wasn't starving hungry, just burnt to a crisp. Now my body was cool again, the raging fires stilled, my skin regrowing before our eyes. I could stop, pull back and smile at him.

'Why save me, Luke?' I asked.

'I told you, I saved you once before, and there was no way I was going to let you die here in this dump. I couldn't...' He stared down at me, his eyes wet with unshed tears. I reached up, and with a hand on either side of his face, I pulled him down, a little closer to me.

'Luke, thank you. I know...'

I was interrupted by two things, first a weird, low decibel gong resounded quietly around the space, and at the same time two vampires burst down the steps and skidded to a halt outside our cell.

'Oh right, I see! You don't need *me* then. But why does it always take you almost to the point of death, Jess, for him to decide he can't live without you,' Daniel flung at me, his eyes full of hurt as he turned on his heel, Eva scowling at me.

'Daniel, wait! It's not what you think. He saved me, or I'd be dead by now...'

'Of course he saved you, that's what angels do isn't it? But forget it, I'm not interested,' he stormed, walking back towards the steps.

I sat up too fast, struggling to pull myself together, my head still reeling, but not wanting to let Daniel rush off.

'Daniel wait, it's not like that. Listen to me...' I started to follow him, but Luke grabbed me from behind and held me, struggling in his arms.

'Jessie, seriously, that gong means we have about thirty seconds to get out of this building,' he said, half pulling me, half carrying me across the cell to the tiny window.

'What are you talking about? I need to find Daniel,' I said.

'No, Jessie! If you go after him, you are going to die, and this time I won't be able to save you, because I will die too. Anyone still in this building in, what... twenty five seconds time is gone, dust,' he said, pulling his sword from the leather holster slung around his hips and thrusting it towards the old stone around the window.

'Luke you can't cut...' I started to say, but apparently he could, because the sword shone brightly before plunging deep into the solid stone. A few swift thrusts and sweeps and Luke had managed to enlarge the window opening, so the stones tumbled down at our feet, and created a doorway.

'We have to help them... Daniel... Eva,' I shouted desperately, as Luke pulled me into his side, spread his wings and we shot out into the night sky.

The night was black and the cool, fresh air whipped my hair around my face, as we shot like a firework into the sky. When we cleared the treeline I heard another dull boom, a little like thunder, without the storm. Luke stopped, hanging in mid-air as he'd done once before, which he knew I wasn't keen on, and we both peered down.

I could vaguely make out a transparent, flickering, yellow dome covering the entire church and attached building, like the great greenhouse domes of the Eden Project. Around the far side of the church, groups of young clubbers hung around, hoping to see what was happening. I expected to see emergency vehicles screaming towards us, but the streets were silent, the immediate area being semi-industrial or closed down.

'Luke, what's going on?' I asked.

'It's a magical null bomb,' he said. 'They're cleansing the area. When they found out what had happened, and where it happened, it was decided that the best course of action would be to eradicate all evidence of magical activity from the vicinity,' he said with a shrug.

'Magic? So Daniel will be fine then?' I asked.

'Yes, Jess. I'm sure he got out. Eva & Daniel both knew of the Council's plans to cleanse the area. They will have gotten out, I'm sure,' he said, frowning slightly and glancing away.

'But why would they need to? They're not magical,' I said. 'And what about all the innocent humans? You can't cleanse them, they've seen everything.'

'They've seen nothing, there was nothing untoward in the club, they think it's a fire drill, that's all, and if there are any humans left inside the perimeters, it won't affect them... unless they have a magical gene, like you,' he added quietly.

'But what will they see? And vampire's... you said they'll be alright?'

'They'll see everything non-human turned to dust, everything magic touched will be turned to dust, and finally the last twelve hours of their memory will be wiped, and they'll suffer mild amnesia for a couple of days.'

'Everything non-human?' I asked as I comprehended finally what I was being told.

'Yes, everything that is non-human, which is why I couldn't have gone after you, if you had run after Daniel. It would have annihilated us both.'

'But Daniel, Eva, you let them go. We have to find them. Let me down,' I said, panic filling my throat and constricting my chest.

'No, I can't. Not yet. We can't go near for another ten minutes or so,' he said.

'You could still put me down, we could search the area outside the club, find them.'

'No Jess, I can't,'

'Why? You don't want me to find him, do you?'

'Of course I do, don't be silly, but I don't trust you not to go charging in there, as then all this would be for nothing,' he said. 'There's no point in you seeing what you don't need to see, and I don't want to witness the insides of that church turning to dust. We're better up here.'

'You think he's in there, don't you?' I said.

'No, like I said, you vampires can run really fast and they both knew about the warning bell. It's the other vampires that didn't know...'

'What Daniel said was right Luke. Why do you only act like you care when I'm in danger? We don't get on anymore,' I said, as I watched him shrug and look away. 'Why did you save me; I don't understand.'

'I told you, I wasn't going to let you die in that place,' he said, not meeting my eyes.

'Oh, so if it had been somewhere else, it would have been okay?' I said, with a smile.

'No, well maybe. I don't know. I do regret saving you the first time. If I could turn back time, I wouldn't have left you to Daniel. I would have waited while you died and saw you across to the next plane, knowing you were safe and where you should be, but I didn't did I? So now you're here, you're going to be this amazing witch and you've proved to me how you're not just one of them, and that you don't feed from humans like they do. You're different, Jess. So yes, there was no way I could let you die in there.' He paused and I knew I had to tell him the truth.

'Luke, I have fed from humans, well *a* human,' I

said, watching his face fall and then fill with anger.

'But you said you didn't! You said you could eat real food, *and* you drank that tea in the cafe. You don't even have their eyes anymore,' he said, staring at me in disbelief.

'Are they still green then?' I asked, wondering whether my recent meal had changed things.

'Yes, they are, but Jess how could you? Why did you lie to me?'

'I didn't lie… well maybe just a bit about the tea thing. It was disgusting, but you were being such a dick.' I faltered, unwilling to continue, but he just stared at me, waiting for an answer.

'Look, I didn't bite anyone until today. Cole had drained me. I couldn't even sit up, let alone stand, so when Brittany came to rescue me she went to find me a blood pack, but there were none, so she brought a guy she knew from the club. He was willing; he was a feeder Luke.'

'That doesn't make it acceptable,' he said.

'Why? If they want it, and we need it, what is so wrong?' I asked, trying not to think about how Cole's vampire buddy had tossed him to the floor, broken, like trash.

'It's not wrong, it's not unlawful, at least under The Council's rule, but that doesn't make it right either. I suppose though, under those circumstances, there wasn't another option for you. I shall try to understand and forgive you,' he said. 'What matters is that you didn't want to.'

I sighed and wished things could return to how they'd been a year ago. Life had been simple. I believed that Luke was nothing more than a college boy, a boy I'd lived next door to and had a school girl crush on, but now… now I was constantly ending up wanting to shake him, or kick him.

'Luke I don't want your forgiveness, or your understanding. I did what I had to do to survive, and yes it was the first time, but I seriously doubt it will be the last time. I *am* a vampire Luke, and before this whole drama began I had just been telling Eva and Daniel how I had come to realise that I couldn't survive on bagged blood forever. I can't eat real food Luke, it makes me vomit! I need to understand who I am, and then try to be the best that I can be.'

Luke didn't say anything. I expected his eyes to fill with regret and pity, but they didn't. There was a quick flicker of something else, amusement maybe. He looked away.

'You sounded like the old Jess then, the girl who became my best friend and told me I had terrible fashion sense; the girl who had no compunction about telling me my room stank.' He turned back and smiled at me. 'I'm sorry, I need to get over my vampire hatred.'

I shrugged and smiled a little. 'It would help me to avoid wanting to kill you all the time!'

'Hmm, so I guess we can go down and have a look around now, but Jessie you need to stay well away from the humans,' he said.

'Luke, what do you think I am? Just because I've had my first human meal doesn't mean I'm going to turn into a deadly, bloodsucking machine,' I replied, somewhat miffed.

'Duh! I meant to stay away from them because of what you look like, airhead. Have you seen yourself?' he said, grinning like the old Luke I knew.

'Oh!' I looked down and saw that even though my skin was all shiny and new, the same did not apply to my clothes. What remained of my sweatshirt was burnt black, with more singed holes than actual cloth. An occasional blue thread peeped out through the black and greys, and streaks of rust-coloured clotted blood stained the top in a not very charming tie-dye effect, only dampened by the smudges of smoke and dirt.

My jeans were thankfully intact, although the button was still open, so I quickly closed it and frowned, as memories of Cole poured back into my head.

'Did he hurt you Jess?' Luke asked quietly.

'Well, apart from punching me in the face several times, throwing me across the cell into the bars, draining me, and later biting me in various places... No he didn't.'

'You know what I mean, did he...?' He paused and glanced at my jeans button.

'No, he didn't. His witch actually helped me by paralysing me so completely that he actually couldn't get my legs apart or my jeans past my hips.' I let out a short laugh, but it sounded more like a bark.

'Good. I would have killed him, and I still will kill him, when we find him,' he said.

'Luke, I killed him... Well, I nearly killed him, and your friend Caoimhe finished the job,' I said with a smile.

'What? He was one of those burning vampires in your cell?' Luke said, shock showing across his face. I nodded.

'But, Cole is hundreds of years old. He's clever, cunning. He would never risk being found in those cells when we came, and he knew we were coming. He must have.'

'Cole may have been hundreds of years old, but inside he was just a teenage boy, with a very big ego. He thought he was unstoppable, but he was careless. He *did* know you were coming, but he thought he had enough time to play with me one last time, and then he was going to murder me and vanish.'

'So what happened?' he asked. 'You're going to need to testify if we've killed Cole, it will go through the courts. He's vampire royalty.'

'Not anymore,' I said.

'Go on.'

'Look, I want to find Daniel. I'll tell you everything later, but basically he came back with several others. I had enough magic left to turn one into a fireball, and jam another one's head through the bars of the cage. Cole couldn't leave me alone though. The cell was burning around him, and he could have escaped easily, but he wanted me. He jumped on top of me and I torched him... which also torched me. He was still burning when you and your friend came in. I watched her decapitate him.' I shrugged again; there wasn't much else I could say, or wanted to say. I just wanted to find Daniel and Eva.

'But Jess, you are going to need to remember every detail of this night, because there *will* be a trial. We'll all be held accountable,' he said.

'What, for protecting ourselves?' I said.

'It will be fine, I'm sure, but Jess, just make sure you remember everything, okay?'

I nodded. 'What about Alex? She could testify. He hurt her, and he held her here.'

'Alex is a mess. I'll tell you about her later and we

will of course get her story, but as a human she has no part in this,' he said.

'That's bull-shit, and I want to see her, as soon as we've found Daniel and Eva, right?'

'No, it's not bull-shit. The Council will listen to a statement taken from her and a medical report listing what was done to her, but she will not be allowed in court, and her memory will be corrected, if it hasn't been already.'

'You can't do that to her,' I said. 'You can't just take away someone's memory.'

'So you'd rather she remembered what happened to her here? You'd rather she remembered what Cole and his vampires did to her? I don't know exactly what they did, but I bet she didn't cope as well as you did,' he said, staring at me.

I felt so small. I had jumped in thinking I was right, but of course I was wrong, totally wrong. They weren't correcting her memory to protect the supernatural community… well maybe a bit, but they were doing it for her, so she didn't have to live a life filled with nightmares. I nodded and met Luke's eyes.

'You're right. I still want to see her though,' I said.

'We'll see, but I take it you didn't manage to bump off his sister as well did you? That would make things easier.'

'His sister?'

'Yes, both he and his older sister were turned at the same time. His sister, Mary has the same brown hair as him, but usually pulled back into a high ponytail. She likes to wear violet contact lenses. Did you see her?'

'Yes, she came back with Cole that first time, but he sent her off, back into the club to start clearing the humans out, when I started the vampire pyre.'

'Hmm, we didn't see her. I wonder if Daniel found her?'

'Maybe, look I need to explain to Daniel about what he saw. He thinks it was more than what it was…'

'More than saving your life? He should be thanking me,' Luke said, his frown returning.

'Please Luke, don't start. You know we can't be more. We're past that, but maybe we can be friends now?'

'Like old times?' he said with a smile. I nodded.

'Take us down angel-boy,' I said.

CHAPTER NINETEEN

Luke set us down in the tree line, towards the rear entrance of the church. There were a couple of dazed teenagers wandering around with glazed expressions, but the majority appeared to be collected around the front of the building.

'Why do they all look like zombies?' I whispered to Luke.

'They've been corrected. They've obviously seen too much. Maybe they were the ones stuck in the building when the bomb went off, but either way they've had their memories blanked. They'll be herded up and sent home. Tomorrow they won't remember a thing.'

I frowned, I wasn't comfortable with the apparent ease and frequency human's memories were tampered with, and knowing Luke was an angel made me wonder if I too had ever been *corrected.*

'Luke, have you done this to me? I mean when I was human. Did I ever see anything I wasn't supposed too?' He went silent, and glanced down at his feet, before meeting my eyes.

'No, I nearly did, but I didn't. I didn't want to... Again, I was reprimanded for being weak. Story of my life,' he said with a shrug.

'But I don't remember seeing anything. It was a total shock when I found out you were an angel.'

'Was it really? Think back Jess.'

I shook my head, I couldn't remember anything.

'Think back to when your mum was in hospital, that last day. I was sure you'd spotted me then.'

I trawled my memories. My mum, who turned out to be my step-mum and not my genetic mum at all, had died of cancer two years ago. The last couple of days in the hospital had been hard on all of us, but Luke, then seventeen, had been my rock. I still didn't remember anything. I shook my head.

'I was with your mum... as myself, as she died. You had gone to get coffees and she was scared. She was scared of leaving you, scared of what lay ahead. I helped her, I showed her who I was, I told her I would protect you. She died in peace... just as you should have done,' he said, sadness flashing across his features.

'I came in just as she died. I remember now, there was this bright light from behind you...'

'My wings, Jess.'

'Wow, I thought it was the sun from the window.'

'It was a cloudy day,' he said grinning.

'I didn't really think about that. I mean I'm more likely to think, *Oh, it must be the sun*, than *Oh, my boyfriend has wings,* aren't I?!

But sometimes in bed at night, I remembered and imagined it was the light to heaven. Thank you for not taking that away.'

He shrugged, dismissing my thanks. 'I was pretty sure you weren't suspicious. I knew if you started looking at me weirdly, then I'd have to do something about it, but you never did.'

The teenager had wandered away, so we came out of the shadows.

'Is that Caoimhe, over there?' I asked, pointing to a girl dressed in yoga pants, herding a small group of kids towards the front and out of the grounds.

'Yes, we'll wait till she gets back, and ask if she's seen them,' Luke said, 'but you really need to stay in the shadows. You look a state. Don't you know a glamour charm you could use?'

'A what? Like from TV?'

'Yes, pretty much. A spell to change how people perceive you. It doesn't actually physically change the clothes you are wearing, but it casts an illusion so anyone, including yourself, who looks at them will see something different. You really have a lot to learn, don't you?' he teased.

'Yes, I do, and maybe if you had deigned to tell me about being a witch when you first knew me, I could have learned enough to protect myself from the girl gang in the first place, which would have prevented any of this from happening.'

'Jess, you know I couldn't. I was instructed to watch and wait. Your DNA didn't trigger until you died, or was turned. You wouldn't have been able to do any magic before then anyway,' he added.

'Right, well, give me a chance. I've had all of about ten days to practice since I was initiated, and the last four have been pretty full.'

'And yet you learned a pretty difficult conjuring trick, to create fireballs?' he asked.

'I did the fireballs, when I was learning to create energy. It happened by accident, and I learned a transmutation spell the other day to fix the table, but I don't think that would work,' I said.

'Wanting to fit in? How about this?' The voice came from the shadows behind us. I turned quickly and as I did so I felt a blast of energy nearly knock me off my feet, followed by a giggle from behind some bushes.

Luke had pounced forward, drawing his sword from its sheath, scanning the hedges for the perpetrator. Not seeing anyone, he looked back at me and gaped. I followed his gaze. I was dressed head to foot in goth gear. A tight, black boned corset cinched in my waist and doubled my usually tiny cleavage into an embarrassing display. My filthy jeans had disappeared beneath a black lace tutu skirt, my legs were now sheathed in black lace tights, finishing the look with a killer pair of bright pink Doc Martins. I grinned. This was not my normal style, but I could get used to it.

'Brittany, is this you?' I asked, but she stayed silent. 'Luke put your sword away. She's obviously not a danger to us, unless you're worried about getting a wardrobe change too,' I said.

Luke shrugged and stepped back, then replaced his sword and dropped his arms. Brittany appeared from behind a tree right opposite us.

'How did you do that? Were you there the whole time?' I asked, as she smiled.

'Camouflage spell. You can only see me when I want you to see me,' she said, watching Luke warily.

'Is that how you escaped?' I asked.

She nodded, and this,' she said, running her hands over her black satin gothic dress and stripey tights.

'You were responsible for Jess being unable to escape and protect herself. She nearly died because of you. As an accessory to Cole's crimes, I will have to hand you over to the authorities,' Luke said.

'I'm sorry. I tried to help. I...'

'Luke, it's not her fault. She was seduced by him; she thought she was in love with him. She's only young, and she did try to help me in the end,' I said.

'I'm not that young. I'm sixteen,' Brittany interrupted.

'She left you with Cole, to die,' he accused, ignoring the girl.

'She escaped because she had too. That vampire you think was Cole's sister... Mary was it? Well she grabbed her by the hair. Cole had instructed her to kill Brittany. If she hadn't escaped, she'd be dead right now. Let her be.' I held no grudge against this girl, and I selfishly thought of all the spells she could teach me, when we got through this. 'She could testify with me, against Cole... if you don't set her up as his ally,' I finished.

'Fine, I guess she has solved the wardrobe dilemma. Fried vampire is never a good look!' he joked.

'Brittany, have you seen two Manchester vampires, a girl and a boy? Daniel, he's tall, has dark wavy shoulder length hair, looks like a European football player, and Eva is petite with a dark pixie cut. They would have been fighting the other vampires,' I said, but she shook her head.

'No, sorry. I've been pretty much keeping out of the way. The only vampires I've seen were around the front doors, and the angels had rounded up a couple more, but I think a few got caught up inside when the null bomb went off,' she said.

'Right, let's go,' I said.

'Let's wait for Caoimhe to return first,' Luke said.

'No, we've wasted enough time. No one will recognise me like this anyway. Brittany, are you coming?' I asked.

'Sure, I could do with a friend,' she said shyly.

'Me too.'

'You're not going,' Luke said.

'And you're going to stop me how exactly?' I retorted.

'Wow, is he always this controlling?' Brittany asked.

'He tries to be, but mainly he doesn't like associating with bloodsuckers, do you?' I asked aiming a wink at Luke, who scowled in return.

'Are you coming?' I asked him.

'Fine,' he sulked, 'lead the way.'

We started off keeping to the tree line, edging our way past a few more human stragglers, who were being rounded up and sent home with a headache, to wake the following morning thinking they'd had far too much to drink.

Just as we rounded the far corner of the church, which was actually the front, Caoimhe appeared suddenly in front of us.

'Oh! Thank goodness. I was so worried about you Luke. I've been looking everywhere,' she said, her eyes full of concern and happiness.

'Sorry, we saw you a minute ago, but you were taking some human kids back out, so I didn't want to interrupt,' Luke said, moving forward to give the girl a quick hug.

'So Jess, you've healed I see. That's amazing. I really didn't think you'd have the energy left to self-heal. Your wounds were so all encompassing, so deep, I thought you had minutes to live...' she said, trailing off, confused.

'I know, it *was* amazing. Luke h...' I paused, catching a sudden quick frown from Luke, and realised he didn't want her to know... 'helped me so much. He gave me the strength to do it, I guess,' I said with a weak smile.

'Vampires, huh!' she said, with a little sigh, 'but your extra powers must have helped. No ordinary vampire could heal that fast,'

I smiled and looked at my feet. Why didn't Luke want her to know?

'Come on,' Luke said. 'Caoimhe, have you seen Daniel and Eva anywhere? Jess wants to find them. She's worried.'

'Oh, erm, no I haven't, sorry. The last time I saw them was in the church. They came racing back up from the cellar steps, Daniel was in front and Eva looked mad, but he looked so upset. I'm sorry, I figured he got there too late, that he'd found you dead,' she said.

'Did they go outside then?' I asked.

'I'm so sorry Jess, I don't know. At that minute the gong sounded. I rounded up the nearest people I could find and led them out through the front door, away from the dead zone area, and then we had to wait, like you. We've only just reopened the entrance,' she said.

'But you didn't see them come out at the front with you?' I asked, my voice catching in my throat.

She just shook her head, her eyes sad. 'No, but there are other possible exits they could have taken, although they should have stayed around to check in with us,' she added.

It was then that I thought I saw him, across the other side of the churchyard. I set off at a run, trying to curb my natural speed and tone it down to blend in, as I passed a small crowd of teenagers being led away from the church. They were sticking together like startled lambs, the slightest noise spooking them and making a girl dart across my path and huddle against a boy. Their eyes were huge, terrified. Whatever they had witnessed inside the church haunted them, scared them and needed to be erased.

I pushed my way gently through the scrum, keeping my eyes locked on the dark head of wavy hair, so much so, that I didn't see the girl come charging out of the church screaming. I didn't see her until she ran into me, and clamped her arms round me, sobbing and keening, shaking from head to foot.

'Help them, help them… something terrible happened. My friend, my friend… he turned to dust. He's gone. They died, all of them,' she said, haltingly, in between renewed sobbing.

I looked around shocked, not knowing what to do, but absently patting the girl's head. Seconds later, a tall male angel appeared and stared at me for several seconds, looking with wonder at my eyes before speaking.

'Were you with these kids?' he asked.

'No, I was with Luke,' I said, looking behind to see him jogging over, with Brittany just behind.

'Oh right… well, I'll take them now. Don't worry about her. She'll be fine. We're taking them straight to the cleansing area,' he said, gently prising the girl from my side.

As soon as the girl had been led away, with the group behind her, I looked across to where I thought I'd seen Daniel. He was gone.

'Why did you run off?' Luke asked reaching my side.

'I thought I saw him. I was sure it was him, over there,' I said pointing to the area by the trees, where I had seen the man with the wavy hair.

'Are you sure? Did you see his face?' he asked.

'Yes, I mean no, I didn't see his face, but it looked like him, the back of his head.'

'Was Eva with him?' he asked.

'No, I don't know. I didn't really notice. There were several people there, but I didn't look. I'm going to see,' I said, walking over to the edge of the churchyard.

But there was no one there. The small group of people had dispersed and I could see no sign of anyone that resembled Daniel or Eva.

'Jessie, they're not here,' Luke said. 'Maybe they went home.'

'I need to check inside the church,' I said.

'No, Jessie, there's nothing to see in there, there's no point,' he said, holding my arm and gently pulling me back.

'I have to Luke. I need to know. I need to know if they got out.'

'But you won't know, there won't be anything to see,' he said.

'I have to go.'

'Jess, he's right. You don't want to go in there. It's not nice,' Brittany said, coming up behind me.

'I have to,' I said, tears forming in my eyes.

'Why, Jess? I thought you said you saw him? If you

saw him here it just means he's angry with you and has probably gone back to Manchester,' Luke said.

'How did they get here?' I asked, a new idea forming in my head.

'Eva drove I think,' he said. 'Obviously they can't travel ley lines like we can.'

'So her car should be here, if they are... or it should be gone. Do you know where she parked?' I asked.

He nodded his head, 'just round the corner on the next street down. I told them the address and they were to meet me there. That's where I told her to park.'

'Let's go,' I said, heading out of the churchyard through the front gates.

'Stop! Where are you going?' A male angel stepped out from his sentry post as we left the grounds. 'Oh Luke, hi! I thought they were humans,' he said, looking at Luke and then staring at Brittany's and my green eyes.

'It's fine, we're just going to check a friend's car, to see if they've left. Have you seen Daniel around, the vampire from Manchester who was held for the murders of those girls?' Luke asked.

'No, sorry. You'll need to come back and sign out before you leave. We have to get a full register of all magical survivors,' he said.

'No problem Cam, will do.'

It took less than five minutes to walk to the end of the quiet street. By now, dawn was breaking and the sky was lightening. As we turned the corner I stopped. My mouth dried and my tongue felt too big. I swallowed, held back my tears and ran over to the shiny red convertible I knew so well.

'Luke, it's...'

'still here. I'm so sorry Jess,' he said, finishing the sentence that had become lodged in my throat, and wrapping his arm awkwardly around me, contrasting with Daniel's easy embrace that I so yearned for.

'He must be looking for me still. Let's go back,' I said, pulling away from Luke.

Brittany caught my arm and murmured, 'Jess, he would have found you. You were pretty easy to find... for anyone looking.'

'No, we must have just missed each other. I spent forty minutes wandering round Selfridges in the Trafford Centre once, looking for Alex, and she was there the whole time. It's easy to do. Eva's car being here means he isn't mad at me, and they must have stayed behind to look for me,' I said, refusing to allow the other option space in my head, as I headed back towards the church, Luke and Brittany on my heels.

'Did you find them?' Cam asked when we reached the gates, his face saddening when he saw the slight shake of Luke's head. 'Sorry.'

I ignored them and strode back into the grounds, but there were few people left. The final group of teenagers was being herded into a line that led to a gazebo-like structure, with angels stationed at the entrance and exit. Terrified, skittish kids were being led into the screened area, and calm, placid teens were led out a couple of seconds later and seen off to the street, where they were ticked off on a list and sent home.

I scanned the area in front of the church. Two angels stood chatting by the front door, and more lingered around the sides, making final checks of the area. There were no vampires in sight.

'I'm going in,' I said.

'Jessie...' Luke interrupted.

'No, I need to know, because if they died in there, it's because of me. I need to see it for myself,' I said.

'I can't go in there,' Brittany said. 'I've seen the effects of a null before, and I never want to see it again. I'll wait here.

I nodded, taking in her shiny, wet eyes, and wondering what tragedy she had witnessed to be living with Cole, with no family around, at the age of sixteen.

'I'll come with you then,' Luke said, with a sigh of defeat, following me up the stone steps to the ancient oak arched door, guarded by the two angels.

'Luke,' one said with slight surprise. 'There's no one in there now. We are just waiting for the cleaners to finish up.'

'Jess wants to go in,' Luke said, a meaningful look passing between them.

'She doesn't want to go in there. There's nothing to see,' the other declared.

'Try telling her that,' Luke said, with a grim smile.

The angels looked at each other before one shrugged helplessly, and the second stood aside and opened the door.

Even though I'd been told that the null bomb only disintegrated magical things, I still expected a scene of devastation, but as I walked through the door I realised that the angels were right, and there was nothing to see. The electrics were still on and the inside of the church had been transformed into a very trendy nightclub. The old stone walls were draped with huge white sheets which, with clever lighting were turned into bright pinks and purples. The altar area had been lit with dark oranges and yellows, and all the nooks and crannies cast eerie shadows. I walked into the room and a cloud of dust swirled up from round my feet.

'Jess, wait. Careful!' Luke said, from behind me.

'Ugh, why is it so dusty?' I said.

'It's not dust Jess, it's ash,' he said quietly, waiting

for his words to sink in.

'Oh! Urgh...' I said, quickly stepping back up onto the steps. 'How many? How do you know who...'

'We don't know who exactly, until we take the register back to the Council and try and work out which supes have gone missing. Obviously, most of them will be vampires from Cole's clan, but that's why Cam is getting everyone to sign out.'

'But, he said he hadn't seen Daniel... shouldn't they have signed out?' I asked.

'Yes, they should have,' he said, dropping his eyes to the floor.

'But, he wouldn't have stayed here, not after he heard the gong. I mean this room's not huge. Where are the cellar steps?' I asked.

'Over there. You go through that door and into the back room, through another smaller room and then there are the cellar steps, right at the back of the church,' he said.

'But Caoimhe got out, and she saw him. Where are the other exits she mentioned?'

'There is the back door, the one they originally brought you through, that leads onto that back lane.'

'Oh hello, we didn't realise there was anyone still left in here,' an older woman said, as she entered the main room from the other side room.

'It's fine, you carry on,' Luke said to the woman,

who nodded and switched on a large portable vacuum cleaning device and began removing all the ash from the floor, ledges and furniture.

'Is she human?' I asked.

'No, half-breed,' Luke said.

'Half *what*?' I asked, instantly irritated by his derisive manner, to which he gave a quick shrug, and glanced over at the woman.

'Half anything. She's half-angel I think... hard to tell. If you want to go across to the back rooms now, I can get her to clean us a path,' he added.

He clicked his fingers and the woman looked over.

'No Luke, it's fine. You were right. There is nothing left to see,' I said, catching the look of submission in the woman's eyes and feeling uncomfortable. 'Let's go.'

CHAPTER TWENTY

I couldn't believe that they were both gone, I wouldn't believe it, but I had to face facts... they weren't here. I tried to tap into our blood connection, to feel Daniel through our bond, but there was nothing. I told myself that the bond had been broken again as soon as Cole had drained Daniel's blood from my body. I hadn't felt the connection return after I had fed and presumed that due to the magic initiation I could now only be bonded with my mate when I had his blood in my system. I wondered if Sebastian could feel Eva. I knew they remained bonded, as she had told me how she could hear him in her head.

'Luke, we need to go back to Manchester. I need to speak to Sebastian,' I said.

'I'd give him a little time to cool down. I'm sure he won't exactly *blame* you for their d... what's happened, but you did come here without their permission,' he said, as we stood back outside the church with Brittany.

'I'll come with you, watch your back,' she said.

'Jess, we need to find out where she's come from,' Luke said, nodding towards Brittany.

'Don't you have people wondering where you are?' I asked her, a little more gently, frowning at Luke.

The girl looked down and sighed her dark, almost black, curls bobbing round her face as she shook her head.

'Alex thought you were Spanish, but your name...' I said, 'Where are you from?'

'My mother was Hispanic, my father British. When she died, he brought me back to the UK, and when he couldn't explain my *special talents,* he sent me away to this place,' she said, with a frown.

'What place?' I asked.

'It's like a boarding school crossed with a Victorian mental institution. It's secret. The people that run it, they... well, they hate all supernaturals. They think they can cure us. Or they'll kill us trying. I was there for three years, and then a new girl came, she was special, and she helped me to escape,' she said.

'Can you go to her?' I asked.

'She didn't get out with me. I can't explain it. She can change the past and therefore make the future different, but only in small ways. So she can't eradicate the whole place, she can just change one person's past, and future. That night she was helping a boy, an angel,' she said, looking at Luke. 'Everything went wrong and the school caught fire, part of the security system went down. She told me to run, because the staff knew I'd been involved. She stayed behind. I have no idea what happened to her. I ran to London and met Cole the first night I was here.'

'But surely your father will want to know where you are?' Luke said.

'My father didn't visit me once in three years. He left me there, knowing what they do,' she said.

'What about your family in America?' I asked.

'I don't know. I was brought here when I was six, and we never went back. No one ever came to visit us, and my father probably thought they were abominations, like me.'

'Okay, well I have family I never knew about in America too. The coven I'm from is in the north east. So if Sebastian kicks my butt out of Manchester, then we could go there together,' I said.

'Erm, I think you're getting a little ahead of yourselves here, girls,' Luke said. 'Apart from the fact that no one will be allowed to leave the country until the trial is over, I thought you wanted to see Alex, Jess? And even though I never liked Daniel, I feel kind of sorry for him that you're moving on so fast.'

'He's not dead, Luke. I know it. He can't be. There must be another reason they didn't get back to Eva's car. They aren't stupid, and they wouldn't have stayed in the building after hearing the gong,' I said.

'You can't know that Jess. You're not bonded to him anymore. Eva's car's there, so why would they have disappeared and not taken it?'

'I don't know, but there will be a reason,' I said. 'He's not dead.'

'So you want to go to Manchester to see if Sebastian knows where Eva is?' Luke asked catching on to my plan.

'Yes, but maybe they'll go back to the house. I also need to get my Book of Shadows, because it's not safe if the house is empty.'

'*My* book will have been destroyed,' Brittany said, looking glumly back towards the church.

'We can go and look for it,' I said.

'No point! It's magic isn't it? It will be dust now,' she said with a small shrug. 'I can write another one, but it will take ages, that's all.'

'You wrote your own?' I asked.

'Yes, didn't you?' she said.

'No, it's passed down. I...' I faltered, catching Luke's slight frown. He was right, everyone wanted my book and I still didn't know enough about Brittany.

'Oh, you're lucky. I didn't have one, so in school we kept secret ones, making notes of all the spells that worked, what didn't and any new stuff we noticed, even moon charts. Now I'll have to start again,' she said, with a yawn. 'Wow, I'm tired. I need to get back onto a daytime schedule. I've become nocturnal.'

'Right. Here's what we'll do,' I said, smiling at Luke's raised eyebrow. 'Did you say Alex was in the hospital? Here?'

'Yes. When she ran from here she didn't get far, only half a mile or so, where she got lost in a residential area and collapsed. A woman found her and called an ambulance, so she was taken to a nearby hospital, where I believe she caused a lot of confusion, due to her extensive blood loss and her body having no wounds other than bruises. However, the main problem was hysteria, which began when she became conscious, shouting about vampires and witches, and how she had to rescue you. We had to arrange an emergency staff change and edit her notes. I expect by now her memory will have been fixed and the staff will believe they are dealing with an amnesia victim. She won't know you Jess. She won't remember.'

'Fine, but I still want to see her before we go back to Manchester. I want to check that she's going to be alright. Then we'll go back to Manchester; to the house. Hopefully Daniel and Eva will be back, and we can have a nap.'

'Jess… Daniel's not going to be there. You need

to...'

'Look, just shut it, okay! If they aren't there, I'll deal with it then.'

'Drop it Luke,' Brittany said, moving to my side.

Luke shrugged, 'Fine, but she's going to have to accept it soon,' he said. 'I'll tell Cam we're going.'

The hospital breakfast rounds were well underway when we arrived, and after a brief illusion change into jeans and jumper, we barely caused a second glance as we entered the main doors.

'Jess, we can't stay long. I'm tired and can't hold your illusion much longer,' Brittany whispered as we casually walked past the central desk. Brittany had let her gothic dress illusion drop and was now dressed in the same clothes that I had last seen her in when she'd come down to bind me, and later save me, in the cells. Luke looked a little alternative in his baggy yoga pants, but it was me who needed a disguise.

'Don't worry, we'll be five minutes. I just want to check that she's alright,' I said.

'This way. Cam said she's been transferred to the Intensive Care ward on D2,' Luke said, as we walked towards the lifts.

'Are her parents here yet?' I asked.

'I doubt it. We're waiting for her to finish her

course of blood transfusions, then we'll wipe the medic's memories, and her notes of everything connected to the blood loss. Once she is simply an amnesia patient, we'll release her name and her parents will be contacted. Currently, the staff have no idea who she is,' he said.

'So how can we be seen visiting her? It's not even visiting hours. They'll ask us who she is, and who we are,' Brittany interrupted.

'It is a complication, but she's been given a private room, and I'm hoping the few human nurses on the ward will be kept busy. We've placed several supernatural medics on the ward to keep an eye on things.

The lift clanged open and we stepped out into the corridor. All was silent. At the end of the corridor was a wooden door, a security camera and hand cleanser.

'So how do we get past the security buzzer?' I asked.

But before Luke could answer me, the door opened and a middle-aged woman in a nurse's uniform poked her head around the door. Her face was framed with ebony curls, her deep chocolate skin flawless and youthful.

'Hey Luke, so this must be the *Jess* we've heard so much about,' she said, looking directly at me, 'and you, young lady are the new witch, responsible for causing equal amounts of trouble and bravery?'

We both nodded and looked at Luke.

'Come on in, quickly, whilst I've sent the two humans to our most demanding patients. They'll be tied up a good ten minutes with those two,' she said, with a quiet chuckle.

'Who's she?' I whispered to Luke, as we followed him in through the door and down the corridor.

'That is Molly. She's a witch from Jamaica and she loves everyone new at the beginning, but you don't want to cross her. I mean it, just don't go there,' he said with a quick frown.

'Here we are,' Molly said, suddenly stopping by a couple of closed doors, opposite a quiet ward. 'I'll be on the desk here, so just open the door a crack when you're ready to go and wait for my signal and I'll let you straight out,' she said to Luke.

'Okay, thanks Moll,' he said with a wink.

'By the way Jess, your illusion is dropping. I can see your blood stained jeans like a mirage beneath the charmed ones. Take a break in there, where no one will see you, but you'll need it for getting out.'

I looked with horror down at my legs, and sure enough I could see right through the clean, new pair which shimmered above the real ones. I looked over at Brittany who looked pale and tired. Luke quickly opened the door of the darkened room and we slipped inside.

'Let it go Brittany, have a rest,' Luke said and immediately I felt a cool shiver race across my skin, as the charm was dropped and my appearance returned to normal. Well, it was by no means normal, but I was stuck looking like a walking murder victim until I could get a shower and some clean clothes.

'Alex!' I whispered, as my vampire's eyes focused through the gloom and took in the frail girl, asleep and hooked up to several machines. A large machine beeped steadily, monitoring her heartbeat, which thankfully seemed even and strong. A drip trickled clear fluid into a vein in her arm and the third sent a steady stream of dark, burgundy coloured blood into her other arm. The aroma sent me reeling. My fangs exploded through my gums and I could feel my heart thudding faster in my rib cage. I wasn't hungry, but the scent was hard to ignore, and I imagined ripping the tube out of her arm and sucking on it like a straw.

'Jess, it's okay. Stop breathing, you can do that right?' Brittany said quietly, her hand gently pressing down on my shoulder, reminding me where I was... who I was. I nodded and concentrated on the room. This was Alex, my best friend.

Brittany hung back and sat in a chair in the corner, closed her eyes and rested, while Luke and I went to her bedside.

'She's been sedated, so I doubt she'll wake up,' Luke said.

I nodded and tried to pull my eyes away from the tube of blood, which pulsed into her arm, and Luke, noticing my struggle, drew the sheet up and over her. I gave him a sheepish smile, and looked down at her face. It was pale and drawn, she had huge dark rings under her eyes and her lips were pale and cracked.

'It's all my fault,' I said.

'No, it isn't, Jess. You stayed away from her. I have no idea how Cole found out about her being your friend, but it wasn't your fault.'

'I should have come sooner. I knew something was wrong as soon as you said she was missing.'

'I know, I did too, but both of us had orders to follow, and initially what they said made sense. Until Cole whispered in my ear, I didn't believe he'd taken Alex either.'

I nodded and felt a single warm tear roll down my cheek.

'Jess don't worry. She's going to be fine.'

'Luke? What happened? What are you wearing?' Alex's voice was frail and shaky, but we both jumped as her words broke our silence.

'Alex, you're awake. How are you feeling?' I asked, scrubbing my cheek dry.

'Who are you? I don't know you. Luke where am I?'

she asked, 'and who's she?' Alex added, looking over to Brittany who had stood up from her chair in the corner.

'Shhhh, it's okay Alex. You were at a club. We think your drink got spiked. These girls found you. Don't you remember?' Luke asked, reaching down and holding her hand.

'No, it's really strange. I have this weird feeling, like something really bad is hanging over me. I feel shaky, as if I've just narrowly missed being run over by a bus or something, but it's all a complete blank,' she said.

'What's the last thing you remember?' he asked.

'I don't know. It's pretty hazy, but I do remember chatting to you in my new flat in Manchester. I remember giving you Murphy to look after, because he reminded me too much of Jess...' Her eyes flicked over to me briefly, and I stared back into her eyes, uncertain whether I wanted her to remember me or not.

'And after that?' Luke asked.

'I don't know. Like I said, it's pretty hazy. I'm tired. Where's mum?' she asked.

'I'm sure your mum will be here soon. Don't worry Alex, we'll sort it out. Do you remember how you got to London?' Luke asked.

'I'm in London? Oh yeah... I remember, I met this guy after a lecture one day. He was really cute. He said he was scouting for students to model this new club wear, and we were going to get five hundred pounds, plus expenses. He bought my train ticket and everything. We were supposed to meet at this trendy new club in London... ahh! I can't remember what it was called, that's where it's all going fuzzy. I guess that's the club where my drink got spiked. God, I feel so stupid.'

'You're not Alex. It's not your fault, but next time don't go and disappear without telling me... or your friends where you're going, okay?' he said with a smile.

I wanted to hug her, to hold her hand, but I knew I couldn't. She didn't know who I was anymore. I glanced back at Brittany and she gave me a sad smile and held out her hand to me. I smiled at Alex and left her side, joining Brittany in the corner. I needed friends who could protect themselves in my new world. It wasn't safe for Alex to be my friend.

'Time's up guys, you've got two minutes to get off the ward. The consultant is on his way up.' Molly said, her head suddenly appearing around the doorframe. 'I need to disconnect the blood transfusion unit and amend her notes.'

With a swift nod of his head, Luke leaned down and gave Alex a kiss on her forehead.

'I'll come and see you tomorrow, okay?' he said to

her, and then to us, 'Come on,' as he made his way to the door.

'Bye Alex,' I said, taking a last look at my friend, before following Luke and Brittany out of the door.

As we left the room, I felt the silky chill of the illusion charm being thrown over me once more, and looking down I saw the clean jeans and soft pink sweater had returned. I smiled at Brittany and mouthed a silent thanks. The girl looked shattered.

'Luke, we need to get out of here and back to Manchester. Brittany needs to rest and I need to see Daniel, and sort this mess out,' I said.

'Jess, I told you, you need to prepare for the worst. I think...'

'Don't! Let's just get back.'

'Fine.'

CHAPTER TWENTY-ONE

'There's a bit of a problem Jess,' Luke said, once we were outside, standing at the back of the hospital, behind the empty visitor's car park.

'What now?' I asked.

'If you want to get back to Manchester quickly... and I don't think London's commuters are up to seeing you in full zombie costume... there are too many of us. I can manage two people max, but not all three of us, and Brittany is clearly out of energy,' he said, looking at the young girl, who was sitting with her back resting against a tree. My camouflage was gone and I was back to looking like the walking dead.

'Oh! But I've still got enough power, so can't Brittany use mine?' I asked, looking across at Brittany.

'No. Draining another witch's magic uses dark magic. I never use dark magic,' Brittany said, struggling to her feet and walking over to us. 'But what if I showed you how to fly the ley lines? You've got enough power to take us both. That way Luke can travel his own way, and I can instruct you?' she said.

'Ooh, yes please,' I said excitedly.

'No!' Luke said.

'Why not?' I asked, frowning at him. 'I need to learn sometime.'

'It's too dangerous. She's too young, and we still don't know who she is,' he said, eyeing Brittany.

'Luke, she's on our side. She's got the only solution,' I said.

'No. I could take you, and she could follow later, once she's built up her power here,' he said.

'No way! We're not leaving her on her own. Brittany, tell me what to do.'

'Okay, well you know about grounding, don't you?' she asked I nodded.

'Right, well in this case when you ground you'll imagine a container within you, in which you can store the energy and direct it. When the excess energy blast hits you, it will act like a lightning rod, allowing the energy to flow freely without harming you.'

'Okaaay,' I said, suddenly wondering if this was a good idea.

'Once you've done that, it's quite easy. Close your eyes, let your mind drift, up out of your body and into the sky. Let your subconscious float and hover... feel about you until you find a ley line. You'll recognise it by the strong pull of energy. Once you find it, grab hold and make a connection and you'll feel yourself being sucked up into it. Make sure you keep a strong hold on your destination otherwise we could end up anywhere that flashes through your memory,' she said.

'But Susannah, a dark witch who tried to kidnap me a month ago, she chanted a spell... Don't I need to say anything?' I asked.

'Did she create a black, swirling cloud that sucked you both up into the ley lines?' Brittany asked. I nodded.

'Wow, that's pretty strong dark magic. She must come from a powerful coven to create a vortex strong enough to suck you both up. But thankfully, we don't need to do that. White magic is softer, more intuitive.'

'Okay, let me have a go,' I said.

'Jess, be careful, please,' Luke said. 'I won't be able to see you or track you in the ley lines, because you use them in a different way to us,' he said. 'And if anything happens to her en route, I shall hold you responsible and hunt you down, no matter what your age,' he added, looking directly at Brittany, who met his stare head on.

'Fine, and when nothing does happen to her, maybe then you'll believe that I just want to be her friend,' she said.

'Right, I'm going to ground now, so shut up the pair of you,' I said, with a smile, as they obeyed me and went silent.

I closed my eyes, felt the ground steady beneath my feet, and imagined the feel of the individual blades of grass tickling my toes, the soft richness of the earth beneath, humming with energy. I imagined my root going deeper and deeper into the ground, and drawing up the energy, pulling on it, filling all my chakras and washing away any lingering negativity. I created the imaginary box and filled it with the excess energy, the energy I was going to use to fly, and then I reached up and left my body.

I felt myself soaring into the clouds, felt the cool mist swirling against my cheeks. I went higher and paused, letting myself drift, wanting to shout and laugh. I was euphoric.

'Jess, Jess, find the ley line.' Brittany's voice sounded muffled and distant, but I heard her and remembered my task. I felt around me, but there was nothing so I moved higher, instinctively feeling my way through the vapours swirling around me, letting an anonymous energy pull me towards it.

Suddenly I felt it, like a futuristic super-highway with energies flowing past me in a blur. Somewhere below, I felt someone wrap themselves round my waist and seconds later I connected to the slip-stream and felt a huge jolt run through me as my soul was once again reunited with my body. An outpouring of heat and a rush of wind blasted my hair, which swirled around my face, and I looked through my eyes and grinned at Brittany, who grinned back.

'Now think of Manchester, and nothing else,' she said, and we were off.

I tried not to get distracted by the beauty of the lines swirling around us, criss-crossing the English countryside, and focused instead on Daniel's house. I felt us pulled faster and faster, until the lines became a blur around us and I felt Brittany's grip on me tighten.

'Slow down Jess, you're going too fast,' she shouted. But I didn't know how to. My focus was on getting us back to Manchester, back to Daniel. I kept him in my thoughts and felt the world spin past on a fast cycle.

Suddenly I had a vision, a vision of his house, and his garden rose before me, shutting out everything else. I knew we had arrived.

'How do we get out?' I yelled.

'Just disconnect... disconnect from the energy source, but slowly Jess, slowly.'

It turned out landing was much harder than taking off, and disconnecting slowly was pretty hard to do when you're flying through the atmosphere at who knows what speed. But I managed it, I disconnected from the energy source. I imagined us landing in his garden, softly, our toes touching the ground gently. In reality, we fell out of the sky, plummeting into his garden from a hundred feet up and landed in a tangle of limbs in the middle of a rose bush, my arm making a sickening crack as Brittany fell on top of me.

'Ow!' I yelled, but as I gently pushed her off me, worrying about what injuries had befallen her frail human body, she sat back and grinned. She had managed to pull a shield around herself as she fell, and was still encapsulated by a shimmering pale pink bubble.

'You could have extended that round me,' I said, holding my left arm up for her to see, whilst the lower part swung back and forth in a rather stomach turning display.

'Oh sorry! I didn't think you'd get hurt, being a vamp and all,' she said.

'I can still break unfortunately, even if it does heal super quick... but I'm not great at this. Will you just hold it in the right place for me while it heals?'

'Ugh, okay then,' she said, and after hauling ourselves out of the rose bush and onto the grass, she took hold of my floppy arm and held it still, while I felt the bones knit back together.

'That is awesome,' she said, grinning.

'Yeah, but it doesn't feel so awesome, that's for sure,' I said, after a couple of minutes, and then,

'Where's Luke? I thought he'd be here by now.'

'You were fast Jess, I mean *real* fast! You need some serious power to travel that fast, and with a passenger too. It only took us about three and half minutes,' she said, looking down at her watch.

'Oh! Well I guess we'll have to wait about five minutes for Luke then. We might as well get inside the house and see if they're back yet,' I said, knowing in my heart that if Daniel had been in the house, he would have come out to meet us already.

'Jess, you do know he's not going to be there, don't you?' she asked.

I looked down at my feet and we stood up and slowly walked to the same patio door I had left unlocked when I left the house, hoping Daniel and Eva hadn't locked it before they came to find me.

'Yes, I do, but I just can't believe that he is dea... gone. I mean, we had a bond, a connection, and I know that it has been broken, but I'm still sure that I'd feel something... but I don't,' I said. 'And they're so smart, Eva would never let herself get caught out by that null bomb, they would have gotten out. They had to of have.'

Thankfully, the door was unlocked and we let ourselves in. The house was soundless, still, and nothing had changed from when I had left. We walked over to the kitchen table and sat down to wait for

Luke.

'You know what he's going to say,' Brittany said quietly. I nodded slowly.

'That they're gone,' I said, looking at my fingers, which I had tightly intertwined and laid on the table top. 'But they *are* fast enough to get out in time. Eva certainly wouldn't have died for me,' I said.

'Would she have died for Daniel though?' Brittany whispered.

'She was his maker. Once a long time ago, they were more than friends, but not for decades. They are close friends that's all, and she wanted to go to fashion college. I don't understand. They wouldn't have done this.'

'But why was her car still there? They would have taken it,' Brittany reasoned.

'I don't know, but it's just impossible that they would have stayed too long in the building once they heard the alarm,' I said.

'What if they got trapped? Maybe someone stopped them from leaving? You need to face facts Jess. If he were alive, I'm sure he would have come to find you by now,' Brittany said, voicing my own silent fear. I sighed.

'She's right,' said Luke, standing in the doorway.

'So now I need to see Sebastian. He's bonded to Eva, so he will know what has happened. Will I be in trouble? Is it my fault, Luke?'

'No Jess, it's not your fault. You may have left without their permission, but you did *not* force Daniel and Eva to come after you. I will come with you,' Luke said.

'So will I,' Brittany said. 'I can vouch for you.'

'No, you need to sleep. You're exhausted,' I said.

'Brittany, I'm sorry about before, okay, but Jess is right. You need to rest now. I'll make sure Jess gets back,' Luke said.

'Are you two an item? I mean, I'm a little confused... you seem close, but then there's Daniel, and...' she asked suddenly.

'No,' we both said in unison, glancing at each other and laughing.

'Maybe we once were, but not now,' I said.

'We're just friends...now,' Luke said.

'Right, so where shall I sleep? I don't know if I should stay here by myself,' she added.

'Here, I'll show you my room. You'll be fine there,' I said. 'Just give me a minute to tidy it up.'

I left the room quickly and nipped upstairs. It wasn't the clothes on the floor, or the pile of books and dvds that bothered me. It wasn't the unmade bed that concerned me, and I wanted to find my Book of Shadows. I trusted Brittany, I did, but after only knowing her for twenty-four hours I wasn't about to test that trust. From now on I was going to be a girl in control. The book would come with me. I grabbed my favourite messenger bag and stuffed the old book quickly into its folds, along with my purse and the phone that Daniel had given me, then I called Brittany.

By the time we left the house with Brittany sleeping, the sun had sunk on yet another day and darkness was once again creeping in. I was fairly sure I'd find Sebastian in his office at Exodus, so after a short angel-powered journey we touched down some five minutes later in the alley behind the club. With Luke at my side, I stepped up to the bolted door and knocked.

'Hey Jess, you're back,' Johnny said, his eyes flicking nervously to Luke.

'Hi Johnny, can you take us to Sebastian please?' I asked.

'Umm sure, he's been expecting you, but what about him?' he asked, motioning to Luke.

'I'm coming too,' Luke said.

'Right, okay then. This way,' and holding the door open we entered the club and followed him down the now familiar corridor towards Sebastian's office.

'Hello Jess, it's good to see you back safely. I see you've brought your pet along?' Sebastian asked rising from his chair as we entered the room.

'I am a higher being, vampire. Show some respect,' Luke said, his eyes stony.

'That may be so, but you are not quite *normal,* are you fallen one? I can't quite work out whether it is you that *has* the pet or if you *are* the pet.'

'What are you getting at, Sebastian?' I asked, not liking the insinuation.

'Well, first he leaves a dying girl to the mercy of the local vampires, and then it is rumoured that he, not only lets you *feed* from him, but also you have a love affair. Poor Daniel,' he said, 'cast aside for one of God's rejects.'

'How did you hear...' Luke started.

'We are not having a love affair. I fed from him because I was virtually dead and it really was the last option Luke could offer me, and besides, Daniel wasn't there. He was too late. Is he still alive then? Have they contacted you?' I asked.

'Vampires don't die that easily, Jess...' Sebastian began.

'They do when a witch has set fire to them,' I retorted. 'But Daniel, where is he?'

For a moment Sebastian paused, taking everything in, as if he was contemplating several different answers. His eyes gazed across the room, unblinking for several moments and I wondered if he was communicating with Eva, or another vampire. Then he frowned slightly and spoke the words I'd feared.

'I'm sorry Jess, my bond broke with Eva several hours ago, and from the reports I have received since of the Bite Club incident, I can only presume that if you haven't seen either of them, then they must have been caught up in the effects of the null bomb.'

'No! They can't. I mean, you seem so... fine about it all! Surely, I don't know, but surely they would have heard the warning; they *would* have gotten out. How did you know about me and Luke otherwise?' I asked feeling like once again everything was falling in and collapsing around me.

'The last time Eva contacted me was when they had just gotten to the club. They were going down the cellar steps to find you just as I connected with her. I saw what she saw, at the same time she did. I saw Daniel's horror, I saw your guilty face and I saw them turn away from you,' he said coolly.

'Then you too must have heard the warning gong?' I said.

'Yes, I did, and shortly after that they ran into a couple of Cole's vampires in the main hall. I told Eva to get the hell out of there and I pulled out of her head to give her more clarity. Minutes later the bond broke. She disappeared.'

I looked down at the floor. The room seemed to swirl about me. I felt sick. Luke's hand pressed down gently on my shoulder and led me across the room to the soft chairs. I sank into them, not quite able to believe what Sebastian had told me. Had one of Cole's vampires killed them first, or left them unable to flee in time? Once again I was on my own and my new family had been stripped away. My emotions felt raw, but this time the hurt was not as great. The pain was not as intense. Yes, I had grown to care about Daniel very much, Eva too, but I had known them only for three months, and as seemed to be the case with everyone in my life, they had both lied to me. It was time to grow up, time to take care of myself.

'Jess, I saw the same as Daniel and Eva in that cellar, and the sight I saw lasted only a second, but you say you were dying? Am I missing something?' Sebastian asked, in a gentler tone.

'If they'd taken time to look around, or come back when I shouted to them and pleaded with them to listen to me, then they would have understood,' I said feeling bitterness mix with my grief.

'Go on,' he prompted.

'The only way I could fight Cole in the end was fire. I set him ablaze with a magical curse, but unfortunately for me he was on top of me at the time, so I ended up in flames too,' I said.

'Are you mad?' Sebastian asked, his face clearly showing shock.

'It was my only option,' I said.

'And Luke found you... I see,' he said, his eyes flicking up to Luke who sat silently on the opposite chair.

'Luke and Caoimhe arrived as we were all dying. Caoimhe dispatched the remaining vampires and Luke patted out the visible flames, but I was burning inside. I had no energy left. I couldn't self-heal. No one else was there.'

'So he let you feed from him?' Sebastian asked.

I nodded.

'I was going to let you die... again, but I couldn't,' Luke said suddenly.

'I see,' Sebastian said, going quiet again.

'There is nothing going on between us; we are just friends. It was Daniel I kept asking for, but he wasn't there,' I said.

'Will you keep this to yourself? If the angels find out what I did...' Luke said, looking at Sebastian.

Sebastian nodded. 'So without Daniel, you will need a new master... tutor, and without Eva I will need a new employee. We also need to sort out your identity and bank account and draw up your oath.'

I lifted my eyes from the floor and pulled myself together. Did he think it was that easy to move on and sign me up to his clan? I might have been struggling with my emotions but I knew one thing, I wasn't going to be signed up to any vampire clan. I wasn't going to repeat any oath. I was going to follow Brittany and be independent.

'No!'

'I'm sorry? What?' he asked.

'Sorry to be blunt. You're sometimes maddeningly archaic and frustratingly dictatorial, but I think you're one of the good guys...'

'Oh really, well that's nice to know,' he said, his eyes crinkling with amusement.

'After seeing how Cole ran his clan, I guess it doesn't take much to make you look good...'

'Of course, and yet you still said *no*?' he asked.

'Yes, I mean no, well I do mean, *no* I don't want you to be my boss. I'm going to be free Sebastian, independent. I don't fit here, and I don't fit with the witches either.'

'But you need an income, and you need documents Jess,' he said, raising an eyebrow as if humouring a wayward child.

'I want to work for you, if that's okay? But I will not be tied to you with a ridiculous hundred year loan...'

'But that is what it costs to have my protection, use my resources, and be given a whole new identity, along with the documents and bank accounts that go with it.'

'I've been thinking about that, and I reckon the

Council will have to sort that out, seeing as I'm not one hundred percent vampire nor witch. I'm going to tell them that I don't fit in anywhere and I want to be independent. They'll be forced to arrange an identity for me and the legal documents that go with it, and if they don't, I'm sure there are people I can find who can fake a passport for me,' I said, with a small shrug. 'All I need is a salary, and I know you could use a witch...'

'You have changed Jessie, grown up,' he said.

'Not really, I've just found myself again,' I said.

'Well we shall give it a go, on a trial basis, but there are other issues we need to discuss, like your feeding requirements for example.'

'I understand, but I *am* safe, and I *am* in control, so you need have no worries there.'

'We shall see, but I shall feel better if you come to Exodus on the evenings you need to feed and check in with me, at least until we know each other a little better.'

'Deal,' I said, secretly thankful that there would be someone looking out for me, in an activity which remained a frightening prospect.

EPILOGUE

The girl lay frozen in bed, her heartbeat hammering in her chest and tears leaking from her eyes as she awoke with a start and gazed with mixed relief at the hospital ceiling. The nightmare replayed over and over again, every night. She didn't understand it, certainly didn't believe it and desperately waited for it to fade away with the encroaching light of dawn.

Luke had visited her daily, and listened to her frightened ramble of nightmares and dreams, without making her feel like she should be institutionalised. He brought her favourite books and flowers. He sneaked chocolate and cakes into her room and made her laugh again.

For some reason, neither she nor the doctors could fathom out, she was extremely anaemic, but it was put down to an unhealthy college diet, and so she was ordered another week of bed rest. She looked at the sunbeams beginning to sneak in under her blinds and listened out for the noise of the breakfast trolleys, which came just after the shift change. Her clock read five to six, so the day staff had yet to arrive. She settled back and closed her eyes, willing the nightmares not to return.

A quiet knock sounded at her door, which seconds later swung open to reveal a pretty young nurse, her light brown hair swinging in a cute ponytail.

'Hi! I thought I heard you stir. How are you, Alex?' she asked walking over to the bed.

Alex looked at the nurse. There was something familiar about her, and yet she didn't think this was a nurse she had seen at all over the past few days. She was certain she would recognise her if she had been, because she had beautiful, striking violet contact lenses in.

'Yes, it was just another nightmare. I'm okay now, thanks,' Alex said.

'Oh good, because that makes my job all the more fun,' the nurse said, closing the door quietly behind her and suddenly appearing at Alex's side so unbelievably fast, it made her jump.

A memory was beginning to surface, a memory of one of the creatures from her nightmares, a creature with violet eyes. Alex shrank back into her bed and opened her mouth to scream, but a cold hand was clamped down upon it, nails digging into her cheeks.

'Shhhhhhhhh, it will all be over soon,' said the nurse with the violet eyes, as she bent over Alex and bit hard into her neck. Several minutes later the nurse stood up, wiped her mouth, and smiled down at the still, cold girl who would never have another nightmare again, and left the room.

To follow the progress of the third instalment of the Witchblood series or to find out more, stalk me at:

http://www.witchbloodthenovel.com
https://www.facebook.com/Witchbloodthenovel
https://twitter.com/#!/EmmaMwriter

ACKNOWLEDGMENTS

Once again, huge thanks to my mum and my proof reader, Lynne Poulson for managing to make my imaginative ramblings into coherent sentences. Big thanks to my great friends, both new and old who have been great guinea pigs and put up with my incessant facebook updates with enthusiasm and support, along with the great new book blogging friends who have hosted me and praised my debut novel, Witchblood. Finally, and most importantly, I just want to say Thank you and I love you to my husband who has supported me, boosted me and chivvied me along, and who over the past few weeks has worked tirelessly in the office and at home, whilst nursing me through viral meningitis AND looking after the children. Tom Mills, you are a star!

Thanks also to Holland House who did the final edit, although let it be noted that some UK/US discrepancies may not have been altered to US taste! I 'm a UK author with UK characters and the language netimes illustrates that!

Made in the USA
Lexington, KY
27 December 2012